What the critics are saying...

"HARM'S WAY is an edge-of-your-seat romantic suspense...Try Ms. Stewart's newest release if you are a fan of romantic suspense with hot sexual escapades." ~ *Denise Powers Courtesy Sensual Romance Reviews*

"Blazing suspense characterizes this steaming contemporary romance novel...The threat of the stalker, looming in the background and heightening every emotion in the process, is icing on top of an already delicious cake." ~ *Ann Leveille Courtesy Sensual Romance Reviews*

"HARM'S WAY is full of strong characters who are believable both in their actions and their beliefs. The suspense will keep you reading to the end to find out just who the stalker is. Ms. Stewart was able to create a very well-written suspense novel with very hot sexual scenes. Everything in this novel is highly charged...A must for all readers of suspense novels that include hot erotic sex." ~ *Patricia McGrew Courtesy Sensual Romance Reviews*

4 stars "This is an excellent romance with a mystery that'll keep you guessing. Harm is a wonderful alpha hero, matched with a heroine who can— and does— stand up to him...a hero to die for make Harm's Way an entertaining read." ~ *Susan Mobley Romantic Times Book Club*

Elizabeth Stewart

HARM'S WAY

ELLORA'S CAVE
ROMANTICA PUBLISHING

An Ellora's Cave Romantica Publication

www.ellorascave.com

Harm's Way

ISBN #1419950584
ALL RIGHTS RESERVED.
Harm's Way Copyright© 2004 Elizabeth Stewart
Edited by: Martha Punches
Cover art by: Syneca

Electronic book Publication: Novemeber, 2003
Trade paperback Publication: May, 2005

Excerpt from *The Academy* Copyright © Elizabeth Stewart, 2003

Warning:

The following material contains graphic sexual content meant for mature readers. *Harm's Way* has been rated *S-ensuous* by a minimum of three independent reviewers.

Ellora's Cave Publishing offers three levels of Romantica™ reading entertainment: S (S-ensuous), E (E-rotic), and X (X-treme).

S-ensuous love scenes are explicit and leave nothing to the imagination.

E-rotic love scenes are explicit, leave nothing to the imagination, and are high in volume per the overall word count. In addition, some E-rated titles might contain fantasy material that some readers find objectionable, such as bondage, submission, same sex encounters, forced seductions, etc. E-rated titles are the most graphic titles we carry; it is common, for instance, for an author to use words such as "fucking", "cock", "pussy", etc., within their work of literature.

X-treme titles differ from E-rated titles only in plot premise and storyline execution. Unlike E-rated titles, stories designated with the letter X tend to contain controversial subject matter not for the faint of heart.

Also by Elizabeth Stewart:

Stray Thoughts
The Academy
Hearts of Steel

Harm's Way

Chapter One

"The End."

"Well?"

The woman let the final page of the manuscript fall shut and looked across her large, glass-topped desk.

"Beautiful," she whispered. "Just beautiful." She dabbed at her red eyes with the remnants of a wadded tissue, honked once and deposited it in the wastebasket behind her.

"I'm glad you approve, Sheila," the woman on the other side laughed. "I worried about this one."

"I'm sure," Sheila grinned, tapping the pages in front of her with a perfectly manicured crimson fingernail. "You always do, although why is beyond me."

"Because I'm a writer and we're all basically insecure."

"Well having published all six of your previous books, I can say without fear of contradiction that this is the best one yet. You've really outdone yourself, Ellie."

"Thanks."

"I mean it," she insisted. "Not only is Jill a strong heroine and Ted to die for as a hero, but the story itself is so tender...so romantic." The grin got bigger and a malicious gleam appeared in her hazel eyes. "Not to mention it's so hot I thought I'd singe my eyebrows off by the third chapter."

"Well, you keep telling me sex sells."

"Lord, Ellie," Sheila rolled her eyes, "this will fly out of the stores by itself. We'll have to print it on asbestos and slap an 'extremely flammable' warning on the cover. Maybe we should give away a certificate for a free gallon of ice water with every purchase."

"I think you're getting a little carried away," Elgin joked.

"I mean it, El. That part where Jill and Ted are stuck in traffic on the Brooklyn Bridge in that limo and he's giving her oral sex and the cop car pulls up on the passenger side...I thought I'd wet my pants, literally. When they sneak away for a quickie while they're touring that redwood forest with his family and end up in a hollow tree... And don't even get me started about the bearskin rug in front of the fireplace at the ski lodge. Trust me, no one who reads this book will *ever* think of chocolate dipped strawberries and champagne the same way again."

"You know Gillian Shelby's readers always expect something out of the ordinary."

"Well they're going to get it," Sheila agreed emphatically, "in spades. From the first read, I'd say we ought to be able to get this out for the Christmas trade. With *A World of Surprise* out this summer, it'll be a sure double winner.

"Which reminds me. We're launching *World* with all the hype Fantasy Publishing can drum up and then we'll sit back and wait for all those women on summer vacation to trample themselves getting to the bookstores. In fact, I want to arrange a short book signing tour for you to hit some of the vacation resorts."

"Uh-uh." Elgin shook her head. "This summer I've promised myself three full months at the retreat. Rest and recuperate. No television, radio, newspapers, computers or writing. Period."

"You've been saying that since you bought that forest shack," Sheila shot back. "And in the three years you've owned it, as far as I know, you've spent exactly four weekends up there. Let's face it, El. You're a city girl and a writer. Three whole months of fresh air and no e-mail and they'll have to cart you away with a butterfly net."

"Fine," she sniffed. "But when you can't find me from the first of June to Labor Day, don't bother to look 'cause you can't find this place unless I give you directions and that's not going to happen."

"Just make sure you're around for the re-writes on this one. And give me an outline on your next project, ASAP."

"Sheila Forbes," Elgin pretended to grump, "you are nothing but a money-grubbing pimp preying on my fragile artistic nature for your own gain. You treat me like a literary vending machine."

"And you, Elgin Collier, aka Gillian Shelby, are a hack, prostituting your God-given gift for words into piles of money. So if I'm a pimp, I guess we know what that makes you."

Both women laughed. They had this conversation often, in one form or another.

"Well, I've got to be running along," Elgin said, gathering up her purse and rising. "I've got a hundred things to do still and my e-mail's probably backed up to New Jersey by now."

"I wish you wouldn't go online like you do," Sheila told her seriously. "There are an awful lot of weird people running around in cyberspace."

Elgin laughed, reached out and patted her friend's arm. "I have news for you, Sheila, there are an awful lot of weird people running around in the so-called 'real' world too."

"I worry about you."

"You worry about Fantasy Publishing's biggest asset."

"Only asset," Sheila corrected, "but that's not the point. You and I have been friends since way before we both started out in this whacko business. I sometimes wonder who's crazier...you for trying to make a living writing, or me for trying to make a living publishing. I'd hate for anything to happen to you."

"Nothing's going to happen to me," Elgin assured her friend. "My e-mail is under my pen name and I never go online to chat except through the respectable writers' boards and only at designated times. After all, one of the reasons readers buy my books is because I've tried to make Gillian Shelby accessible to them. Made her a friend. Someone they can care about. The Internet has been a big help there. Besides, I'm a big girl and I know how to take care of myself."

"All right. I'm taking your Magnus Opus home with me tonight so I can start hacking away at it with my little blue pencil. I should have the rough cut to you the first of next week."

"Good. Give my poor overworked fingers a chance to cool down."

"Yeah, well, I have no problem with your fingers cooling down. Just make sure nothing else does."

They laughed again and shared a hug.

At the door, the two women paused and Sheila stared into Elgin's face. "Promise me you'll be careful," she said seriously.

"Always. Bye Sheila."

"Bye El."

* * * * *

Elgin hated elevators, especially crowded ones like this, packed with eager souls escaping their cubicles for their mid-day hour's parole. She didn't have any particularly claustrophobic problems as small places had never bothered her. Something, though, about being in such close contact with other people, strangers, made her uneasy although she'd never been able to pinpoint exactly why. Perhaps its very irrationality made it all the more disconcerting.

Stepping in, Elgin instantly found herself crammed backward, finally ending up in the center of the car. Carefully, she raised her briefcase to her chest and pulled her shoulder bag to her front, trying to make room for two burly executive types in matching black power suits. Jostling for position, one of them stepped momentarily on her toe, never glancing at her or offering an apology.

Jerk, she thought disdainfully, I wonder how you'd like a three-inch stiletto heel in your expensive Italian loafers? Accidentally, of course.

As the elevator doors closed and the box continued down, something brushed against her ass. Automatically, she moved her body fractionally forward. There were obviously too many people in too little space. She felt a slight pressure then, like a hand laid lightly on the swell of her cheeks. Again, she shifted her position, but this time, the pressure remained.

A moment of surprise morphed into a flicker of anger. Jeez, Louise, she sighed silently. Some guys were absolutely pathetic. I mean, what kind of a loser is reduced to copping a feel from a total stranger in a public elevator?

But before she could turn around and confront anyone, the elevator shivered to a stop, the doors opened and she found herself pushed out into the lobby by a human tide making for the huge glass front doors and freedom.

Just beyond the elevator doors she paused, turning in all directions looking for...for what, she suddenly wondered. Some stereotypical grinning, leering moron in a raincoat?

The elevator emptied its cargo of perfectly ordinary-looking people, most not even glancing at her. Perhaps she'd been mistaken. Perhaps it hadn't been anything more than a momentary, accidental contact.

With an internal shrug, Elgin joined the lunch crowd pouring out of the building and into the early April sunshine.

Quickly, she crossed the crowded sidewalk toward the cabstand, glancing at her watch as she stopped. If she could catch a cab and the traffic wasn't too horrendous, she could make it home, grab a salad on the terrace and get in a couple of hours at the keyboard. After all, for a writer, one finished book simply meant the start of another.

The start of another book.

Elgin frowned and felt the familiar pang of every author's worst nightmare in the pit of her stomach. That nagging, aching terror that tugged at a writer's very soul. The lurking fear that all the words had been spent, used up. That this time, "The End" had truly been reached.

She knew authors who seemed full and running over with an endless stream of new ideas. Always a work-in-progress (sometimes two or three at a time) and characters literally vying with each other for the writer's time and attention.

But for her, stories only seemed able to come one at a time and then, only after much anxious coaxing. The overwhelming delight she felt at the end of a book was always edged with the stark terror of those words, "So, what's next?"

"Hey!" someone shouted a few feet to her left.

Several heads, including hers, turned at the sound.

"Gimme money!"

A street person, tall and skeletal, stuck a large, grungy, dilapidated plastic soda cup in the face of a well-dressed young man, slightly shorter but stockier than his own six-foot frame.

"I...I don't have any change," he mumbled, turning his head and body a little.

"Don't gimme that shit!" the beggar screamed, his mop of matted, greasy brown hair moving reluctantly with the violent shaking of the thin skull. "A course you got money! Dressed real pretty," he put a grimy, fingerless glove on the young man's lapel. "Gonna eat a big lunch at some fancy place. You got lots a money...way more'n you need. Gimme some!"

Gaunt cheeks flushed red, a spray of spittle flew out from the thin lips, a few droplets landing in the ragged whiskers clinging tenaciously to his pointed chin. Fire blazed out of dark brown, bloodshot eyes.

Quickly, the young man stuck his hand in his right front pocket and emerged with a fist full of coins that he dropped into the cup. With the beggar eagerly examining his prize, the young man made a hasty escape.

Elgin turned back to the street and anxiously scanned the traffic, hoping by sheer force of will to materialize a taxi. She'd lived in the city long enough to know that everyone around the man was evaporating as quickly and inconspicuously as possible and she wanted very much to do likewise.

Her gaze traveled up and down the block but no cab.

A ripple of apprehension fluttered in her stomach, not fear exactly, just a strong desire to avoid confrontation.

With a last hopeless sweep of the traffic, Elgin decided to cross the street to the safety of the cabstand on the opposite corner.

"Hey! You! Bitch!" she heard the angry shout almost in her ear. Instinctively, she gripped her briefcase more tightly, wrapped the fingers of her left hand around the strap of her shoulder bag and took a step.

Instantly, he blocked her way, the stench of body odor, filthy clothes and alcohol-soaked breath creating their own barrier. At five foot nine in her three-inch heels, she could almost look him in the eye, and with her weight of a hundred and thirty pounds, he probably didn't outweigh her by more than about twenty pounds. He might be a street bully but she was not some frail, anorexic fashion model. In her thirty-six years, she'd learned to cover fear in many situations, even while shaking like a leaf inside.

"Please get out of my way," she told him calmly, his smell making breathing, let alone talking, almost impossible.

"Gimme money, bitch!" The cup rattled so close under her nose she could feel the rough edge.

Cold fear warmed a little with a tinge of anger. Elgin stared into his face, her black eyes empty.

"I haven't got any money," she replied flatly. "Now if you'll excuse me…"

Stepping to the side, Elgin intended to go around him but he moved nimbly, blocking her once more. Leaning down, her whole view seemed taken up with him.

"Gimme money, bitch!" he repeated, his rage bellowing out with a force that surprised her, shaking the confident facade.

"I told you, I don't have any money," she continued, still trying to remain calm. "But if you don't let me pass, I will start screaming, and with all the cell phones around here, someone's going to call the police and I'll have you in jail."

Glancing quickly around, he saw several people were slowing to gawk, many of them with phones at their ears, eyeing him suspiciously.

But there was more to his rage than just her refusal to give him money. This was his corner, these were his marks. He knew those who gave freely, from real generosity. And those who gave from a guilt born of too much wealth paid for by others. Most caved in to his dirty, smelly intimidation. If he let this pretty woman, smaller than him, with short, almost boyish black curls and red lips walk away, how much of his power, his livelihood would go with her?

Taking advantage of his momentary hesitation, Elgin took another hurried step and scooted by him. Just as she started to exhale with relief, fingers like a steel vise closed painfully around her left arm between her shoulder and her elbow and spun her backwards.

"Come back here, bitch!" he roared, shaking her like a pit bull with a rag doll. "You give me my money or so help me God, I'm gonna break your skinny little arm!"

Elgin never knew exactly what happened next or even how. Her mind filled with terror, pain and a hysterical urge to run but almost by themselves, she felt her fingers clutch the handle of her briefcase, her arm raise and her whole body swing forward. As if aimed, the sharp corner of the case drove into the crotch of his baggy, filthy pants.

Another roar erupted, this one of surprise and pain. Dropping to his knees and grabbing his injury, a torrent of obscenities mingled with howls of anguish.

For an instant, Elgin stood there, dazed, even the pain in her arm driven temporarily out of her mind by fear and disorientation.

Another figure appeared at her elbow. Flinching, she raised the case again.

"Hey lady," she heard a nervous voice beside her, "it's all right. I'm on your side. I got my hack over here by the curb. I don't think you wanna be here when Junior comes up for air."

* * * * *

"Look at that," Elgin fumed, waving her suit jacket in front of her, "just look at it!" Needlessly, she pointed to the greasy black smudge where her attacker's big hand had grabbed her and the open gash of shoulder seam.

"As filthy and disgusting as he was, I don't even want to think what this might be," she snarled. "God knows, though, whatever it is, it'll probably never come out."

"I can't believe you'd even think about wearing it again," the other woman replied, wrinkling her nose in disgust. "If I were you, I'd just call the Hazardous Materials Disposal Team and have it hauled away."

"Do you know how much I paid for this suit?"

"Probably about ten books, retail."

"Ha, ha," Elgin told her sarcastically.

"I don't understand why you just didn't give the guy what he wanted. I mean, I can't believe you'd risk your life with some crazed junkie street bum over a handful of change. Suppose he'd had a gun or a knife. Did you think of that?"

"I don't like being bullied."

"You mean if he'd been clean shaven, neatly pressed, sober and polite, you wouldn't have been so stupid?"

"I don't consider standing up for myself to be stupid, thank you."

"Yeah, well, just be glad you're explaining that to me and not St. Peter."

"Martha…"

"No, I mean it," she insisted emphatically. "You could have been killed over some pocket change. As it is, your arm looks like a purple tattoo of King Kong's fingerprints. Instead of being so damned concerned about that stupid jacket, you should be in Dr. Mooney's office right now. Or better yet, in a police station picking that vermin out of a line up."

"Oh yeah, there's a great idea," Elgin feigned agreement. "I have him arrested and some shyster lawyer finds out I'm a writer with more than ten bucks in the bank and the first thing you know, I'm being sued by that Bozo for damaging the family jewels. That's five years of being mired down in legal hassles and six hundred-dollar an hour lawyers only to have my insurance company buy him off on the courthouse steps. That, of course, results in my liability insurance premiums being jacked up to roughly the budget of a Third World Country or being canceled altogether."

She shook her head. "Uh-uh. I have enough troubles without that. I took a couple of painkillers and I'll stick to long-sleeve shirts for a few days so as not to offend your delicate sensibilities."

Her tone softened and she smiled. "Look Martha, I appreciate your concern, but you're my secretary, not my mother. So why don't you go and see if there's anything in the 'fridge for lunch while I check my e-mails?"

"All right," Martha agreed with a small sigh of resignation. "There's a pile in your chat folder because of the program tonight but other than that, nothing pressing."

"Okay then. I'll be in my study. Call me when lunch's is ready. Let's eat on the terrace. And hold my calls this afternoon unless it's Sheila."

"Will do."

* * * * *

"Where do you get your inspiration? Do you research everything, including the sex, yourself? Are you married? Have you ever had sex on an airplane? Do you sleep in the nude?"

Elgin scanned through the papers and took another bite of salad.

"I wonder how many times I've answered those same questions?" she giggled.

"Hey, if you wrote cookbooks, people would probably want to know where you buy your eggs or which lemons have the best juice," Martha replied with a little giggle of her own.

"No doubt. It just gets a little repetitive, that's all. I sometimes wonder if anyone ever asked Jane Austin about her favorite position. Or Emily Bronte if she'd ever done it out in the English Moors."

"Well, don't the chat moderators try to weed out the real perverts?"

"Yeah, but there's only so much you can do. This chat is supposed to be a purely fun interview. Let the reader's get up close and personal as it were. Of course, no one wants to know that I work eight and ten hour days just like everyone else and that I wear nighties to bed and I haven't been with a man in so long, I'm writing purely from imagination."

"No, I guess that would sort of blow Gillian's image all to hell."

"So, I'll tell them that I have a whole wardrobe of sexy lingerie, depending on my mood and my company and that it's hot and cold running hunks, twenty-four/seven. I also intend to casually mention that my newest book will be out this summer and that since I'm taking the entire summer off, they better stock up now because it will probably be Christmas before I have anything new."

"Are you still planning on going up to that place in the country?" Disapproval sounded in Martha's tone.

"Yes. I need the rest. And no, as I've said before, you don't have to come with me. I don't want you to come with me. I'm paying you three months' salary so you won't come with me. There aren't going to be any secretarial duties for you and I'm perfectly capable of opening tuna cans and diet soda bottles by myself."

"I can't imagine what you're going to do for three whole months up in that godforsaken wilderness," Martha grumped. "I mean, the couple of weekends we went up there, I couldn't believe how boring the place was. No television. No radio. No neighbors. No nothing. It's positively dead."

"Exactly. I'm going to walk in the woods, swim some, maybe rent a little boat and go out on the lake and I've got two years worth of books I've been wanting to read that I never have any time to start. I'm going to veg out completely."

"Sounds awful."

"Sounds wonderful."

Elgin finished her salad, sat back in the cushioned patio chair and stretched. Immediately, she winced and pulled her arms down.

"You okay, El?" Martha reached out and laid her fingertips lightly on her boss's right arm.

"Yeah, I'm fine," Elgin assured her. "Just a stitch. No doubt my arm's gonna hurt for a few days and it'll probably get worse before it gets better."

"I wish you'd let me call Dr. Mooney. That maniac could have pulled something or strained something. Even a hairline fracture. I've read…"

"I'm fine, Martha, really. I just stretched a little too hard. Now I'm going in and see if I can squeeze out some possible plots for a new book. Sheila says if I'm going to disappear for three months, I have to at least leave her with an outline of my next project."

"Maybe you ought to take a nap. Or better yet, cancel this whole stupid chat thing anyway. I think people will understand when you tell them that some loony tried to break your arm this afternoon."

"You don't know Gillian's fans," Elgin laughed. "They do not take disappointment well, especially from their favorite author. If I'd been murdered, someone would be trying to arrange a séance. Now, I'll help you clear the table and then I'm going to lock myself in my ivory tower and not come out until dinner."

* * * * *

"You okay?"

"Sure."

"You look like hell," Martha observed dryly.

"And a gracious good morning to you, too."

Elgin eased herself carefully onto the sofa and sighed as she leaned back.

"You get any sleep?" Martha asked, handing her a glass of orange juice.

"Enough. It's just that the chat ran long and then even with more painkillers I couldn't seem to find a comfortable position. Not to mention that every time I did manage to close my eyes, that creep was all over me again, stink and all."

"You oughta see Dr. Mooney. Get something heavy duty for the pain. And you oughta call the cops about that bastard. I'd think with everything else that's been going on around here lately, you wouldn't want one more lunatic hanging around."

"Please, Martha," she sighed wearily, "not now. The bruises will heal, the beggar's one of the hazards of modern city living, and you're making a mountain out of a molehill."

"What about the flowers?" she insisted. "And the candy? And the bra and panty set? All anonymous and all delivered right here to your supposedly 'secret' home address."

Elgin heard the concern as well as the annoyance in her secretary's voice. Even though they were virtually the same age, she knew Martha tended to be very protective, almost maternal about her. And while she appreciated the thought behind it, sometimes it did get a little much.

"I've told you. The flowers and the candy and even that outrageous lingerie are a gag, no doubt being played out by one or more of my slightly demented friends. Who else would know about the carnations or the peanut brittle or my taste in underwear? Or my home address? If I make a big production number out of it, they'll just keep it up. Believe me, the best way to make it go away is to ignore it."

"But..." The sound of the intercom buzzer from downstairs interrupted Martha.

The two women looked at each other quizzically.

"You expecting anyone?"

"No," Elgin replied, "but whoever it is, tell them I died and didn't leave a forwarding address. I've really got to try and rough out a new plot before I'm up to my ass in re-writes or I never will get away to the retreat."

The buzzer sounded again and Martha hurried through the living room and foyer to the speaker set in the wall just inside the front door.

"Yes?" She clicked the switch from "talk" to "listen".

"Miss Jackson," came the warm baritone voice of their doorman, "it's Ben."

"Yes, Ben."

"Miss Collier has a couple of visitors down here..." She thought she detected a note of concern in his tone.

"I'm sorry, Ben," she cut in, "but Miss Collier's unavailable today. Please ask whoever it is to call Fantasy Publishing about an appointment."

A heartbeat pause went by before the voice spoke again, this time a nervous strain clear.

"It's the police, Miss Jackson," he told her slowly. "They say they have to speak to Miss Collier right now."

"The police?" A tiny ripple of fear passed through her.

"Yes, ma'am. They showed me their badges and everything. Should I send them up?"

"Yes, certainly." She switched off the speaker and waited tensely for the doorbell. When it chimed, she jumped, even though she'd been expecting it.

Opening the door, Martha found two middle-aged, medium height, average-looking men, one in a gray suit, one in dark blue. Both held up gold badges and picture ID's in small leather cases.

"I'm Detective Sloan," the man on her right announced flatly. "This is Detective Belknap. Miss Collier?"

"Uh...no," she stammered. "I'm Martha Jackson, Miss Collier's secretary. May I ask what this is about?"

"If we could come in," Detective Sloan sidestepped her question, "we'd like to speak to Miss Collier. It will only take a moment." He gazed at her expectantly with clear, calm gray eyes as if there might actually be some doubt as to whether or not she'd admit them.

"Yes. Certainly. Please come in." She stepped back and opened the door wider, closing it carefully behind them when they'd moved inside.

"If you'll come with me gentlemen, Miss Collier's in the living room."

But when they got there, Elgin had disappeared...gone.

Martha felt her heart speed up as she glanced around the room and through the open glass doors to the terrace.

"Uh, please won't you sit down gentlemen?" Martha pointed to the empty sofa. "Let me just go and see if I can find her. I mean...I'm sure she's here somewhere. That is, I'm sure she hasn't left. She was right here a minute ago."

She dashed across the living room, almost tripping over her feet opening the study door and slamming it behind her.

Elgin sat at her computer, scrolling lazily through her e-mail.

"Who was it?" she asked without looking up as Martha came to her side.

"The cops," Martha replied, the words dropping like rocks between them.

"The cops?" Elgin repeated in amazement, her head jerking up, confusion plain on her face.

Her secretary nodded emphatically. "And not just uniformed beat cops either. These are plain clothes. Detectives Sloan and Belknap."

"What...what do they want with me?"

"They wouldn't tell me. Just said they need to talk to you. But from the looks of them, I don't think they're here selling tickets to the Policemen's Ball."

Standing up, Elgin took a deep breath and released it slowly.

"Well then, I guess we better go and see what they want."

As they opened the door, the two men, who'd been seated side by side on the sofa, rose silently and Elgin had the distinct feeling she'd interrupted a serious, private conversation.

Forcing a smile, she extended her hand.

"I'm Elgin Collier," she told them with as much hospitality as she could muster.

"I'm Detective Sloan. This is Detective Belknap." They produced gold badges and picture ID's that Elgin couldn't read without her glasses.

"Detectives. Won't you please sit down? Can I get you something? Coffee perhaps?"

"No thank you, Miss Collier," replied the man closest to her. "We'd like to speak to you if you have a few minutes." His gaze flickered to Martha. "Alone if that's all right?"

"Why...uh...certainly." She turned to her secretary. "Martha, will you please finish going through my e-mail?"

"Sure. Call if you need anything." And with a last quick glance at the detectives, she disappeared back into the study.

The three of them settled back down, the detectives on the sofa, Elgin across the coffee table in a big high-back, chocolate leather wing chair.

"Now, what may I do for you gentlemen?"

Detective Belknap took out a small, ragged green spiral bound notebook and a cheap looking ballpoint pen. His partner waited as he flipped through until he found a blank page. With an almost imperceptible nod, he signaled to the other detective that he was ready to begin.

"Miss Collier, we have a report that yesterday, a few minutes after noon, you had an...encounter with a street beggar in front of the Riverview Plaza building."

Shit!

"Why...yes," she replied carefully. "It was really nothing."

"Could you tell us, in your own words, what happened."

"Well, as I said, there really wasn't anything to it." Out of the corner of her eye, Elgin saw the detective's pen moving rapidly across the paper.

"I'd just come from my publisher's office. Fantasy Publications is in the Riverview Plaza. I came out and while waiting for a cab, a street bum accosted me, demanding money. His intimidating manner naturally frightened me. I told him I didn't have any change and tried to walk away but he grabbed my arm and threatened to break it. I...I guess I just had some kind of self-preservation impulse because the next thing I knew, he was lying on the ground. A cabby hustled me to his taxi and brought me home."

"And you never saw this man before?"

Here it comes. They're probably here to arrest me. And the miserable bastard's lawyer has probably tipped the media so they'll be waiting at the precinct house when I arrive.

"No."

"You're sure?"

"Positive." She took a breath. "May I ask what this is about? I mean, if the man has filed some kind of legal complaint against me, I'd like to know so that I can call my lawyer. And I'd be happy to show you the bruises he left on my arm."

"Why didn't you call the police?"

"Because I really didn't see any point in causing a lot of trouble for a street beggar who, from the smell of his breath, had obviously been drinking. And how would it look to the media for a well-known author to be involved in an altercation with...well, it just didn't seem to me to be worth the trouble. However, if this person is accusing me of something, I'm sure I can find plenty of witnesses to prove that whatever happened, I acted purely in self-defense. Is he accusing me of something?"

"No, Miss Collier," the detective answered slowly, "you're not being accused of anything. And we have several witnesses who've already corroborated your story, including leaving the scene by taxi."

"Then what may I ask, are you doing here?"

"Because the street beggar with whom you had your...altercation...was found murdered yesterday afternoon."

Chapter Two

It wasn't at all what she'd expected.

Perhaps a childhood filled with black and white *film noir* detectives had conditioned her to think in terms of dark waterfront walk-up buildings and tough sounding names in peeling black paint on frosted glass doors. A bleached blonde named "Ethel" or "Vera" behind an antique manual typewriter, filing her nails, great chasms of bored yawns chewing up her hard features. Sam Spade or Phillip Marlowe slouched behind a cluttered desk, his trusty fedora hanging loyally on the ratty wooden coat rack in the corner.

This two-story walk-up was actually a beautiful turn-of-the-twentieth century brick townhouse, saved from the wrecker's ball at the eleventh hour and returned lovingly to its former glory. It stood in a part of town just now emerging from shabby neglect to teeter precariously on the brink of fashionable. All around, upscale professional offices, trendy little stores and cafés with more pretensions than patrons littered the landscape.

Inside the grand marble and oak foyer, a twenty-something brunette sat behind a raised counter, her fingers flying nimbly over a multi-line phone console as she smiled into the tiny microphone of her headset. Red, green and amber lights blinking like miniature traffic signals replaced the sound of ringing phones.

"Good morning," she chirped, "Harm's Way Security. How may I help you?"

She listened a few moments, her face a picture of attentive concentration. In a moment, the smile reappeared.

"If you'll hold just a moment, please, I'll see if he's in." And with the press of a button, the young lady merrily dispatched another poor soul to voicemail hell.

Looking up, she focused her smile and attention on the woman at the counter.

"Good morning," she repeated cheerfully. "May I help you?"

"Yes. I'm Sheila Forbes. I have a ten o'clock appointment with Mr. Harm."

"Certainly, Ms. Forbes. If you'll just have a seat through there," she pointed a slender, magnolia smooth hand to a large archway on her right, "I'll let Mr. Harm's secretary know you're here."

"Thank you."

As she passed through the opening to the other room, she heard the receptionist announce her.

Sheila settled into a comfortable chair and gazed around the room, more front parlor than waiting room. Lace curtains hung at long, narrow windows flanking an enormous bay window that took up virtually the entire front wall, giving a clear view of the front lawn and garden and the sidewalk and street just beyond the short, black wrought iron fence. A gray marble fireplace with painted tiles, a full-length dark wood mantle and ornate brass screen occupied the opposite wall. Enormous closed double doors filled the last wall. An oval coffee table in the same warm oak as the mantle held a diverse array of current magazines and a pair of smaller tables supported little glass dishes of brightly colored wrapped candy.

Another woman appeared, this one middle aged with blonde shoulder length hair and brown eyes behind dark framed glasses, dressed in a tailored black business suit and sensible pumps, her hand extended, a smile on her round face.

"Ms. Forbes, I'm Jessica Weldon, Mr. Harm's secretary. If you'll follow me, please?"

Sheila trailed the other woman a little as they crossed back through the foyer and up a beautiful spiral staircase to the second floor. At the top, a long hall lead straight back, closed doors on either side as they moved along the polished wooden floor, the click of their heels muffled by a thick runner of muted floral and dark blue.

They went through an open door and into a large, bright office. Sheila noted a computer monitor glowing a deep blue on a workstation behind a smallish oak desk, littered with legal size manila folders. A multi-line phone, only slightly smaller than the console at the receptionist's desk took up the right-hand corner. In a few steps, they arrived at another door on the opposite side of the office, this one closed.

Ms. Weldon rapped lightly with one hand as she turned the knob with the other, standing aside to let Sheila enter. The door swung quietly shut behind her.

Even by the standards of the rooms she'd seen, this one was huge and for a moment she had the odd sensation of having stumbled into the library of an elegant, wealthy gentleman from another time. Floor to ceiling bookcases, crammed almost to overflowing stood guard over a fireplace, the little brother of the one downstairs. French windows lined the other wall, thin lace curtains fluttering slightly at an open pair. Beyond them, she glimpsed part of a terrace and a large, padded patio chair.

At her entrance, the man behind the massive dark oak desk stood up and she understood the scale of the room, the building itself.

C.A. Harm, President of Harm's Way Security, stood at least six feet tall, she surmised, probably closer to six three or four. Late thirties, early forties she guessed with wavy, dark blond hair that framed his face in a casual, windblown sort of way and deep, wide set, almost black eyes that studied her intently. She felt for a moment as if he were taking some kind of mental inventory of her.

A swimmer's body she thought with an internal nod of approval. His neatly tailored charcoal suit settled snugly across his well proportioned shoulders, the jacket covering arms she could imagine that were well developed but not muscle bound. Neck like a steel cable but not thick and bulky, solid chest and flat stomach covered beneath his white business shirt and open jacket. Long legs that moved smoothly from behind his desk as he put out his hand.

Automatically she noted his bare left ring finger, not even a "cheater mark". Another point in his rapidly growing list of "pros".

"Ms. Forbes," he greeted her in a warm, mellow tenor that for some strange reason made her think of church bells chiming. The feel of his firm hand against hers and the light in those eyes...

"Mr. Harm," she managed as he guided her to a big saddle leather armchair in front of his desk.

"Can I get you something?" he asked pleasantly as he resumed his seat. Pointing at the large, plain white coffee mug just at his elbow, the smile became an almost boyish grin. "I'm afraid caffeine's one of my more benign vices. I've got just about anything you could think of and a couple you probably never heard of."

"No, thank you," Sheila replied, momentarily captivated by the sound of his voice.

"Tea then? Soda? Water?"

"No, really I'm fine."

He sighed and settled into his chair, the body still relaxed but the smile disappeared, replaced by a look that told her the pleasantries were finished and business had begun. A large hand flipped open the single folder on his desk.

"You told my secretary on the phone that you wanted to hire Harm's Way to investigate a possible stalker and provide personal security until the problem could be resolved."

"That's right." Surprised at the speed with which he'd changed gears but impressed too with his get-right-to-it manner, Sheila braced herself to begin.

Picking up a big gold pen, he poised it over the file.

"Do you have any idea who the stalker might be and why he's made you his target?"

"Oh," she squeaked, thoroughly surprised at the question, "I...I think you've misunderstood."

"Ms. Forbes," he began patiently, "I'm sure that it's very difficult for you to think that someone you might know, someone you may well think of as a friend could do something like this but you'd be amazed at how often that's the case. If you can give us some help...point us in the right direction so to speak, it can save a lot of time, effort and expense on all our parts."

"No," Sheila replied anxiously, "I'm not the one being stalked. It's my friend, Elgin who has the problem."

She thought she saw a flicker of confusion in those deep eyes but it disappeared instantly. "I'm afraid I don't understand," he told her slowly. "If you're not the one with the problem, why are you here and not your friend?"

Sheila sighed, a mixture of resignation and frustration. "To be honest, Elgin's very good at ignoring anything she doesn't want to deal with."

"Well if she doesn't feel there's a problem..."

"Please, Mr. Harm," her voice took on a note of pleading, "at least hear me out. I'll pay for your time, only please, just listen."

"Perhaps you had better explain." His tone was less than a demand but more than a request.

"Well, it actually started a couple of months ago," she began, determined now to match his businesslike demeanor and not be viewed as a hysterical female. "I own Fantasy Publishing. We're a small press, catering to women's fiction."

Instantly, she saw his mouth twitch downward and a look of disapproval like storm clouds gathering in the depths of his eyes.

"Fantasy Publishing," he growled. "I think I've heard of them."

"Perhaps you have," she replied, straightening her shoulders and lifting her chin slightly. "We've been very successful in our little niche the past few years."

"You publish women's porn," he stated coldly.

"Mr. Harm," she told him, her voice as cold as his, "Fantasy Publishing produces women's fiction of every genre including science fiction, paranormal, comedy, horror and contemporary romance. Our authors have won major awards and our readership stretches from New York to New Delhi and is growing by leaps and bounds every month. That growth attests to the fact that many women...indeed, a *great* many women, enjoy reading sex, the steamier the better. And now that I've explained my business to you, I would like to continue with the *relevant* portion of this story."

Sheila took a deep breath and picked up her thread as he eyed her silently.

"Elgin Collier is our most popular author. She writes under the pen name Gillian Shelby. She's written six books with another one due out this summer."

She watched as he scribbled on the paper in front of him, barely taking his eyes off her as he wrote.

"Anyway, one morning about two months ago, we were sitting in her living room discussing her latest novel."

"Where does Ms. Collier live?" he interrupted.

"The Whittier Towers," Sheila replied. "She has a large condo overlooking the park."

He paused and waited for her to continue.

"The doorbell rang and Martha...Martha Jackson her secretary/companion answered it. Turned out to be a box of three-dozen long stemmed carnations. What they call 'variegated'. Red and white like the old milk cans. They're Elgin's favorite flowers. As a child, her father used to grow them in their garden. These are special though, because they're field grown, not raised in hot houses so they have this wonderful cinnamony smell. There's only one florist in the state who stocks them."

"Was there a card?"

Nodding, Sheila reached into her bag and produced a small white envelope, which she handed to him.

"To my Gillian," he read. "That's Ms. Collier's pen name?"

"Uh-huh. Gillian Shelby."

"Doesn't sound particularly ominous. More like a fan."

"Elgin keeps Gillian completely separate from her 'real' life."

"So?"

"So how did this 'fan' know that red and white carnations were Elgin's favorite flowers? Or her home address to have them delivered?" That pesky note of panic reappeared and Sheila had to fight it back.

"Maybe one of her friends played a prank," he offered vaguely.

"About six weeks ago, she began getting candy. Now Elgin has a metabolic disorder, her body doesn't handle carbohydrates in the normal way and she has to be pretty careful about what she eats, especially candy, which she happens to love. She searched high and low and finally found some places that sell low-carb candy. Chocolates from a place in California, jelly beans from Texas, peanut brittle from Kentucky, and salt water taffy from New Jersey."

"All of which were delivered to Ms. Collier?"

"Every day for a week."

"Did you check with the stores?"

"Of course we did. They all said the same thing. A postal money order and the name and delivery address came in the mail. With no return address, they threw out the envelopes. Since they're all small outfits, they recognized her name and address and didn't think anything about it."

"Any cards?"

Sheila shook her head. "No. Just the candy. Elgin tried to pretend it was all some kind of joke but I know it spooked her because she had Martha put all of it...every single bit...down the garbage disposal."

"Go on."

"Well, time went by and nothing else happened and Elgin got wrapped up in finishing the book and we all kind of forgot about the whole thing."

"Until?"

"Two weeks ago she got a package delivered at home from one of those...those online adult toy stores. Their 'honeymoon special'. You know, a little leather whip, handcuffs, edible lotion. That kind of thing."

Harm nodded and his pen moved quickly across the paper.

"There was also this skimpy little bra and panty thing. Black. Sort of a string thong and pasties. It really shook Elgin up."

"Completely understandable," he agreed without enthusiasm. "Even as a joke of some kind, it wasn't in very good taste."

"The toys themselves were bad enough," Sheila continued, "but worse still, the bra and panty were her size, exactly."

"No card?"

"No."

"What did the store say?"

"That their customer records were confidential and that if the lady didn't like gift, she could return it and the original purchaser would get a credit but that they couldn't and wouldn't give out any customer information. I got so mad I threatened to sic my pit bull lawyer on them. Miserable twerp just laughed, told me to go ahead because they had a barracuda lawyer who ate pit bulls for lunch and hung up."

"Ms. Forbes, I really don't see anything here to be particularly alarmed about. There've been no threats, no overt actions of any kind that would suggest anything but ardent, if misplaced affection."

"You haven't heard the whole story," Sheila told him acidly. "Since I'm paying for this time, I'd at least appreciate the courtesy of your attention before you pat me reassuringly on the head and send me on my way."

Anger prickled lightly down his spine. He wasn't used to being talked to like this, especially in his own office. Especially, not by a client. And, most especially, by a woman. But she was indeed paying (and handsomely he consoled himself) for his time so he could afford to tolerate her a little longer.

"I'm sorry," he mumbled, "please continue."

"Thank you. As I said, we'd sort of let the whole thing drop. Two days ago, Elgin came to my office in the Riverview Plaza to bring me the finished manuscript of her book and just generally chew over the state of the world. She stayed...oh, maybe forty-five minutes to an hour and left about noon. Later, she told me the elevator was packed when she got on and she got crammed to the center of the car. Just after the car started down again, she said she felt something brush her ass. Chalking it up to just too many people in too small a space, she tried readjusting her body a bit. The next thing she knew, she felt a hand definitely resting on her ass."

"Could have been purely accidental."

"Mr. Harm, I assure you that grown women can tell the difference between an innocent accident and a grope."

She took another deep breath to calm herself and went on.

"Elgin was just about to turn around and clock this pervert when the elevator reached the lobby, the doors opened and people poured out, pushing her with them. Outside the elevator she looked around but didn't see anyone suspicious-looking so she shrugged it off and went on outside.

"At the stand, a street beggar came up to her and demanded money. Elgin told me he was big, filthy, smelled like someone had poured cheap whiskey in an open sewer and verbally abusive. She didn't have any change and when she started to walk away, he grabbed her, started shaking her like a shark with its prey and threatening to break her arm."

Sheila paused as Harm's pen flew across the folder. It took several seconds before he looked up, ready for her to continue.

"Terrified of course, Elgin said something just sort of clicked in her mind and the next thing she knew, she'd swung her briefcase as hard as she could and put the corner of it right in the...old family jewels."

In spite of herself, a nervous little snicker escaped her as the man across the desk squirmed slightly in universal male empathy.

"A cabby who'd just pulled up and seen the tail end of what happened, hustled her to his taxi, calmed her down enough to get her address and took her home. Her jacket had a huge, greasy stain where he'd grabbed her arm and torn the shoulder seam wide open. And you can still see the ring of purple bruises on her arm where he grabbed her."

She shuddered a little and closed her eyes.

"Did Ms. Collier file a police report?"

"No, although Martha and I both told her she should. But she said that if she did, someone would find out who she was and then a shyster lawyer would convince this creep to sue her. Maybe even have her arrested with all the attendant media frenzy. Unfortunately, that happens an awful lot to famous people."

"Did someone at the scene call the police?"

"Uh-huh. A couple of gawkers with cell phones called 9-1-1 but it happened so quickly, by the time they got there, Elgin had already left and apparently, when he realized the police were on the way, the bum managed to get up and stagger away too."

"And that was the end of it?"

"Not quite," she answered gravely, reaching into her bag again. Slowly, she placed a small piece of paper face down on the desk and pushed it toward him.

Turning it over, Harm saw a three-paragraph newspaper "filler" item.

Homeless Man Killed, read the small headline. The short article stated simply that the body of John Richards, a forty-eight year old transient, had been found in an alley by a busboy emptying garbage from a nearby restaurant at about three p.m. Police believed he'd been stabbed about two hours before he'd been found. There were no witnesses and no suspects.

"The man who assaulted Ms. Collier?"

Sheila nodded. "If the police are right about the time he was killed, it couldn't have been more than an hour after he attacked Elgin." Concern now mingled with real fear in her voice.

"And you think the two incidents are related?"

"Yes, I do."

"I'm sure you're aware, Ms. Forbes, that a street person's life is precarious at best," Harm told her, keeping his tone serious. "You said he was panhandling. He could have been murdered for his money. In that world, even pocket change can be worth killing for. And if he was as aggressive and abusive as you describe, he could have gotten into another altercation that escalated into violence. Or perhaps he just ran into someone who was meaner or crazier than he was. Whatever happened, the chances of it having anything to do with your friend are extremely remote."

"That's pretty much what the police told me," she retorted sharply. "They came by yesterday to talk to Elgin. Of course they don't think she had anything to do with this bum's death, but they were trying to track his movements before he died and they found out about the incident, and the cabby told them where he'd taken her so they wanted to get her story. 'Purely routine,' they called it. But I'm absolutely convinced this murder is tied to what's been happening to Elgin.

"I believe whoever is stalking her has been following her around. That's how he discovered where she lives. How he found out what kind of flowers and candy she has delivered. He even got close enough to her to fondle her ass in a crowded elevator. That, combined with the stalking itself, shows how unstable he is.

"When that animal attacked Elgin, the stalker probably went berserk, followed him and stabbed him. Having killed the beast who'd sullied his lady's honor, he's no doubt feeling very good about it, too."

"And what does Ms. Collier say about all this?" Harm asked quietly. "I'd think if she was concerned about her security, she'd be here in person."

"Elgin is a writer," Sheila explained tartly. "Like most writers, she lives in a universe of her own creation where everything runs to her whim."

"So she doesn't think there's a problem, either?"

Sheila rummaged in her bag once more, this time pulling out a check, which she placed squarely in front of him. The number of zeros surprised even him.

"Your secretary quoted me your rate when I made the appointment." She nodded toward the check. "You'll see that's your rate times twenty-four hours, times seven days, times two weeks. Plus what I deem a generous allowance for expenses. I want you to investigate this matter, quietly but thoroughly. I also want you to provide discreet but constant security for Elgin Collier.

"If, as you seem to think, there is no problem, then you should be able to wrap things up quickly although you may keep the entire retainer. My peace of mind will be well worth the money. But if there is a problem, I want it resolved. Permanently."

A smile touched the corners of her mouth. "And don't worry, Mr. Harm. Not only is the check good, but there's lots more where that came from."

"All right, Ms. Forbes, we'll take the case. We'll deposit your check and draw our daily rate plus expenses against it. Any amount remaining after the case is closed will be refunded to you."

"No, Mr. Harm," she corrected, "*you* will take the case. Personally. I've checked around carefully and you're the best there is at what you do. Ex-police, ex-FBI, ex-Secret Service. I'm paying for the best and that's what I expect for my money."

"I can assure you that all my detectives..."

"Are no doubt top-notch," she cut in, "and I expect you'll assign the watching and digging to them. A brain surgeon doesn't boil his own instruments. But you will be in charge."

"If you insist, Ms. Forbes," he smiled and leaned forward. "But my time is very valuable. For me to handle this case myself, it will cost you double the agency rate."

Without blinking, Sheila produced an eight by ten-inch photo, her checkbook and a slender jade green pen. Quickly, she filled out another check and set it and the photo next to the first check.

"I'll expect you to begin immediately. You seem an honest sort, so for the time being, we'll seal the bargain with a handshake."

They stood up and she extended her hand. "Messenger the contract to me at my office, I'll sign it and messenger it right back. Goodbye, Mr. Harm."

Slightly dazed, he shook her hand.

"Goodbye, Ms. Forbes."

The door had just barely closed behind her when his secretary came in, steno pad at the ready. Leaning across his desk, he handed her the checks.

"Open a new case file," he told her as she began taking notes. "Our client is Ms. Sheila Forbes. Her information's in the file from the intake when she made the appointment. We'll be investigating a possible stalker and providing personal security to the victim until we can get it sorted out. I'll be overseeing this myself."

Jessica's hand stopped in mid-flight and a quizzical eyebrow shot up.

"She handed me the first check," he replied to her unspoken question, "and told me she wanted me to handle the case personally. I told her it would cost her twice the office rate and without so much as batting an eyelash, she wrote out the second check."

Unexpectedly, he chuckled. "Never let it be said that C.A. Harm ever prevented some willing woman from showering him with money."

His secretary shrugged slightly and flipped the page in her notebook. "How do you want to proceed?"

Harm rubbed his chin thoughtfully. "Get a hold of Charlie Simons and have him get everything he can on the stabbing of a transient named John Richards. There's a clipping in the file to point him in the right direction. Tell him I want not only copies of the written stuff but for him to talk to everyone involved in this death, from the busboy who found the body and the beat cops who responded all the way up to the investigating detectives and the ME. And find out who we've got for surveillance duty, twenty-four/seven. We'll be shadowing the victim at a discreet distance primarily to see if she's being followed and if so, by whom. I'd like to get someone in the field as quickly as possible. According to our client, she lives at The Whittier Towers and works at home. There's a photo in the file."

"Will do," she told him crisply, closing her notebook and taking the file from her boss.

As she headed for the door, she began to scan the notes he'd taken. About midway across she stopped, staring at the words.

"Anything wrong?" he asked. His professional, efficient secretary didn't pull up short with a file in her hand.

Looking up, he could see bewilderment in her eyes. "Sheila Forbes," she began, pointing at the slightly open file in her hand. "She...she's Fantasy Publishing?"

"Yeah. Why?"

"And this Elgin Collier? She's Gillian Shelby?" Amazement drenched her words.

"If that's what I wrote, yeah. Why?" In three and a half years, he'd never seen her act this way.

"Oh my God," she breathed. "Gillian Shelby. I...I can't believe it. I love her! She's on my auto-buy list." She took a step back toward him, her voice filled with awe. "You wouldn't believe how hot she writes. Her *Blue Monday*? Got five alarms and a fire extinguisher from *Ecstasy Romance* and was voted "The Book Most Likely to Be Banned in Boston" by readers of *Heartbeat*, which is the biggest romance magazine in the country. Maybe the world. I know when I read it I had to change my panties. Twice."

The shocked look on her boss's face snapped her instantly back to reality. Gathering herself, she swallowed hard and began backing toward the door.

"I'll...uh...get started on this file right away." And with that, she scurried out of the room.

Chapter Three

Silently, he slouched in the shadows, watching her intently as her slender body, bathed in the moonlight and the aquamarine glow of the pool, knifed through the water like some pale, exotic sea creature. From his hiding place in the heavy foliage just at the edge of the clearing, he could make out every detail of her as she swam slowly back and forth from one end of the pool to the other.

Long, beautiful legs propelled her with hardly a ripple as her perfect arms pulled through the warm water. The crest of her lovely ass just visible. Abruptly, she turned on her back and floated near the deep end, her breasts like soft, tantalizing mounds of cream with cherries at their centers, her dark hair ringing her head like the rays of some Renaissance painter's halo.

Inside his jeans, his cock stirred, taken by the sight of this magical being, at once pure and seductive. Sexual and simple. Heat and desire flashed through him. He wanted her, needed her. Everything that had gone before had built up to this.

Slowly, carefully, he moved himself around the clearing, keeping to the jungle's fringe, fearful that the snap of a twig, the sudden rise of a startled bird, might alert her to his presence.

At last, the foliage made an inward sweep and he found himself almost at the pool's edge. By sticking to the shadows between the torches, he managed to get within striking distance of his quarry.

Rolling onto her stomach, she stroked lazily back to the shallow end, emerging up the stone steps like a sea nymph, her sleek, wet body covered in tiny diamond sparkles. Dripping wet, she paused at the pool's lip and stretched, a long, contented, almost feline movement. Lacing her fingers together, she raised her arms to their full length, pointing her round, pale breasts to the moon and pushing her dark pubic curls forward a little.

He swallowed hard and ran the tip of his tongue over his dry lips. As swiftly as he could without taking his eyes off her, he began stripping off his pants and shirt. A hot tropical breeze caressed his naked body as he stepped out of his jeans, his cock already hard and full of need and desire.

Leisurely, she picked up a large, multi-colored beach towel and walked the couple of steps to the grass just beyond the cement walkway hugging the pool. Spreading it out, she lay down on her back, arms at her sides, legs slightly apart and closed her eyes to let the warm night air and the moonlight dry her.

His dry mouth suddenly filled with the imagined taste of her lips, her breasts, her sweet pussy. A ripple of fire swept through his body as in his mind he took her in his arms, the feel of her warm, wet flesh melting to him, surrendering. The ripple became a tidal wave as he felt himself slipping inside her willing, waiting body.

Leaving his clothes where they lay, he crept the last few yards until only a thin curtain of lush green foliage separated them. For a few more precious moments he let himself feast on her nakedness, her ethereal, almost dream-like beauty. He'd waited and hoped and fantasized about this moment for so long, he could scarcely believe the time had actually come.

Stealthy as a jungle cat, he moved out of the covering vegetation and inched toward her, his throbbing cock straining with every step. Just as he reached her, he kneeled down and in one fluid motion, pressed his shin across her chest to keep her from moving and covered her mouth with his huge hand to keep her from crying out.

Instantly, her eyes flew open, stark terror showing in their dark depths. Her whole body flinched and went rigid under him. He moved his face to within an inch of hers and they stared at each other in silence.

And then he felt her relax, the muscles of her cheek under his hand changing their shape. Slowly, he moved it and she smiled. Breaking into his own smile, he bent down and kissed her, feeling her mouth open wide to receive him.

"You bastard," she breathed between passionate kisses. "You damned near scared me to death leaping out of the bushes like that. How...how long have you been hiding out there?"

"Long enough to watch you skinny-dipping. By the way, you're very beautiful, especially when you're wet and have nothing on but moonlight."

"Pervert," she teased as he moved his leg and settled on his side next to her.

"Why? Because I like watching the woman I love?" He rubbed his aching cock along her thigh as he took a nipple between his fingers.

"I thought you said you had to work tonight," she murmured, closing her eyes again and sinking into a cloud of pleasure.

"Deal closed over drinks instead of dinner." His mouth replaced his fingers and she shivered with delight. "So I explained that I had a very hot deal on the verge of climaxing, apologized profusely, told him to have dinner on me and shot over here as fast as I could. The thought of you made me so horny I almost slammed my cock in the car door."

"Then why didn't you just come to the front door like any other respectable gentleman caller?"

"Because I figured on a night like tonight, with the moon and the stars and a private beach cabana, you'd be out here instead of inside. I wanted to surprise you. Finding you naked's just an unexpected bonus."

"I couldn't sleep," she whispered hoarsely, turning on her side so that his cock rubbed tightly between their bodies. "I kept thinking about how much I wanted to fuck and you were off making another gazillion dollars or buying an aircraft carrier or some other dumb macho thing and you left me all alone. I finally came out here hoping to...cool off a little."

"Did it help?" he asked.

Easing herself onto his naked body, she took his face in her hands and forced her tongue deep into his mouth, dancing a furious tango with his.

"Not...a...bit."

"Good," he murmured as he pressed her to him, feeling her cool, damp flesh on his hot body as his hands ranged over the ridges and valleys of her shoulders, back and ass.

She rubbed her wet pussy over the length of his pulsing cock, pressing it between his flat stomach and her own engorged clit. A sound between a growl and a moan escaped him as they closed their eyes and let their bodies explore each other, seemingly on their own.

Without opening his eyes, his hand reached down to reposition her so that his aching cock could slide inside but she resisted.

"Not so fast," she grinned, opening her eyes to enjoy the surprise in his face.

"What's that supposed to mean?"

"Just that since you made me wait, you're going to have to have a little patience yourself."

His cock rubbed against her and he could feel her wetness and not just from her swim.

"Come on," he kidded weakly, "you're as hot as I am."

"Uh-huh," she agreed readily. "And you're going to do something about that right now."

He grinned, his dark eyes shining in the moonlight. "Now you're talking."

But instead of sliding down, she pulled herself up until her breasts hung over his mouth, like ripe inviting fruit. Lightly, she brushed her right one against his cheek, dragging it slowly to his waiting mouth. Immediately, he attacked it like a hungry baby.

She purred as he turned his attention to her left breast, feeling her growing heat as she moved her lower body against his smooth flesh.

His cock pulsed, sending fire through him with every heartbeat. Pushing down on her ass he forced her wet pussy against his stomach, the tip of his cock just barely touching her wetness.

"Oh God," he mumbled into her cleavage. "I need you so much."

"I needed you too," she whispered, "but you didn't care."

"Business," he answered hoarsely, "just business. But now I'm here and I want you. And you want me."

He grabbed her and tried to slide her backwards to his waiting cock but she slipped away again, pulling herself up until her pussy replaced her breasts.

"Me first," she told him haughtily, "and then, depending on how well you do, you. Maybe."

Lowering herself, she felt his lips brush her swollen clit.

So that's how she wanted to play it. All right, he'd show her that two could play that game.

"Bitch," he snarled just before his tongue found her. The first long, slow flat sweep made her jump as if she'd gotten an electrical shock and he felt her whole body quiver.

The feel...the taste of her warm, willing body made his blood burn and his cock scream but he was determined to make her pay dearly for putting him off. Before he released her, she'd be begging for mercy.

Broad strokes alternated with swift licks and sucking that created a vacuum on her full clit. He grasped her trembling ass and listened with wicked delight to the growing moans and her short, ragged breathing.

"Oh God," she cried softly, "oh...oh..."

He slowed his movements almost to a stop, leaving only the tip of his tongue to tickle her.

"Please..."

The tickle stopped, leaving nothing but his lips covering her, sucking softly.

Her body jerked over him.

"God!" the cry became a poorly stifled shriek. "Don't...oh please..."

His own body was past endurance. With two more quick, hard passes, he felt the tremble become a shudder as she released herself to him, her sweet juices gushing into his mouth and down his cheeks, her screams of ecstasy ringing through the still night.

Sagging, he pulled her down to him, settling her back so that she slid effortlessly onto his cock.

"Is it my turn yet?" he grinned.

In reply, she smiled and began working herself gently up and down his rock-hard shaft, the smoothness of it like a piston moving inside her.

She was everything he'd imagined. Soft and giving yet holding and gently squeezing every inch of him as she moved, easily and unhurried. In his present condition though, he knew he wouldn't last long, glad now that he'd made sure of her satisfaction. Of course, he knew that the night would not end here and that once they'd taken the furious, crazed need off their passion, they could take their time and linger over the exploration of their sexuality.

He wanted to savor this, enjoy it and make it last but his body, in control now, overrode everything but the need to come in this beautiful woman. The woman he'd yearned for and hoped for and fantasized about in his lonely bed.

Pulling her to him, she laid out flat against him as he cupped her ass in his hands and pressed harder, deeper into her. Parting her lips, she bent her face down and their tongues met, moving as frantically as their bodies now.

His climax began with little ripples that became, in another heartbeat, a roaring tidal wave of physical pleasure like nothing he'd ever known before. His body rocked to a series of internal explosions, fountains of streaming ecstasy washing over and around and through him like liquid fire. Only the beautiful, magical creature above him kept him from shattering like multi-colored crystal.

In the moonlight, not a breath of air stirred as they held each other and felt their heartbeats returning to normal. Together, they lay in a sated tangle of arms and legs, the physical and emotional intensity of their joining wrapped around them like a cocoon that shut out everyone and everything else in the world...

A knock sounded on the door even as it opened.

Elgin spun around and sighed in frustration. "How many fucking times have I told you *not* to disturb me when I'm having sex?" she growled. "Jesus! You're worse than my mother."

"How the hell am I supposed to know what you're doing in here behind closed doors?" Martha replied dryly "Besides, you're always having sex. God knows maybe if you actually *had* sex as often as you have sex, you wouldn't be such a damn pain in the ass all the time."

"Yes, well, don't forget it's my sex life that keeps you dawdling in the lap of luxury instead of out having to hold down a real job like everyone else." Elgin grinned evilly. "And besides, if I actually had sex as often as I have sex, I'd be too tired to write and we'd both be out on the street."

"Maybe we could work out a signal."

"Like what?"

"Well," Martha ventured, "in college, I roomed with two other girls. If one of us was 'entertaining,' we'd tie a red bandana around the front doorknob so the others would know to steer clear." She paused and sighed dreamily. "We finally had to stop doing it though."

"Run out of guys?"

"No. The bandana fell apart from being knotted around the doorknob so much."

Elgin rolled her eyes.

"Did you want something?"

"Just to let you know it's almost eleven. You're gonna have to beat feet and hope there's no traffic."

"Damn!" Elgin yelped, glancing at her watch as she jumped up. "Why the hell didn't you tell me it was so late?"

"Because this morning at breakfast you told me not to disturb you. I figured that since you've been getting your hair and nails done every Wednesday at eleven-thirty at The Beauty Spot since before you could afford it, you'd remember on your own. Should have known better."

"When I said I didn't want to be disturbed, I meant for silly crap like the President or World War III. This is important. I keep Wanda waiting and I'm liable to end up with a real poodle cut and green fingernails."

She pushed past her secretary, out into the living room and started for her bedroom.

A shrill whistle brought her up short and she turned just in time to see two of Martha's fingers leaving the corners of her mouth.

"Your sweater and bag are on the sofa," she smiled. "Ben'll get you a cab downstairs."

Grabbing her things from the sofa, Elgin hurried over to her friend.

"What did I ever do without you?" she asked, grinning sheepishly.

"Damned if I know."

They embraced warmly as Martha patted her lovingly on the back.

"Now get going."

Catching an elevator, Elgin had just reached the lobby doors when the bulk of her doorman, Ben, appeared and pulled open the heavy glass door for her.

"Mornin' Miz Collier," he smiled, touching two fingertips to the brim of his cap. Elgin loved his soft, New Orleans drawl that seemed to flow out like molasses.

"Good morning, Ben," she replied with a smile of her own.

Rumor around the building said that Ben, at six feet, six inches tall and at least three hundred pounds, had been hired as a large, scary deterrent for the front doors of this high security building.

But in his dove-gray uniform, matching hat and gold buttons, he always seemed to Elgin more teddy bear than grizzly. His ready smile and unfailingly sunny disposition seemed to brighten even the dreariest day.

They moved to the curb as Ben blew a single shrill blast on his ref's whistle and raised a long arm above his head, waving once into the on-coming traffic. Almost instantly, a taxi appeared about half a block away.

"Ben," came a female voice behind them.

Turning, they recognized Mrs. North, a sweet elderly little tenant trying with one hand to hang onto a small, two-wheeled metal cart filled with packages and open the huge door with the other.

He glanced quickly up at the nearing cab, to Mrs. North and down at Elgin.

"That's all right, Ben," she assured him with a pat on the sleeve. "I can get the cab. You help Mrs. North to the elevator."

That grin flashed again.

"I'll be just a sec," he promised and hurried back to the door.

The cab slid to a stop and Elgin took a step toward it, reaching for the rear door handle. As she did, a huge hand reached out and covered hers, trapping it on the door handle.

Startled and frightened, she looked up.

"Oh, pardon me." A long heartbeat and the hand released hers. "I didn't know you were waiting for this taxi. My apologies."

Tall, dressed in a lightweight black trench coat, thick black hair, dark eyes behind dark rimmed glasses and a neatly trimmed mustache and goatee.

"I'm sorry," she stammered, "I didn't see you. If you were waiting for this cab, please, take it. I can always get another one."

"A gentleman would never think of taking a taxi and leaving a woman standing," he smiled down at her as he opened the door for her. "Especially a lady as lovely and charming as yourself. Please. I insist."

"Well, thank you sir," she smiled back, feeling a little sheepish. "That's very gallant of you."

His head lowered to her a bit. "I'm pleased that I could show you that while chivalry may be on life support, it isn't completely dead. At least not yet."

Taking her hand, he helped her into the taxi.

"Thank you again," she told him through the partially open window.

"My pleasure, I assure you."

As the cab pulled away, Elgin looked through the rear window for a last look at the stranger, but he'd already turned his back and disappeared into the crowd.

* * * * *

"Charlie," Harm grinned, stretching out his hand to his friend. "Good to see you."

"Good to see you, too, Camp," the other man replied as they shook hands.

"How's it going?"

"Eh," he shrugged. "Sometimes I'm not even sure it's a different day."

Harm threw back his head and laughed. Charlie Simons had been his friend and mentor since his FBI days. The best natural detective in the business in Harm's opinion, a sniper's bullet in the back had creased the older man's spine and ended his active career. When he'd decided to open Harm's Way, Charlie'd been his first call.

At fifty-seven, lean, tan, salt and pepper hair and sea blue eyes, Charlie hardly looked the part of the grizzled old detective. In fact, he prided himself on being able to blend in virtually anywhere, sometimes a life and death skill in their business.

When they'd settled in with their coffee and exchanged a few minutes of personal chat, Charlie got down to business. Opening his briefcase, he laid a thick file on Harm's desk.

"Here's all the official stuff," he nodded to the file. "Interviews, forensics, the ME's report, the whole nine yards. You can curl up tonight with a warm fire and a bottle of Scotch and wade through it, so I'll just give you the highlights."

"I'm all ears."

Charlie took out a leather bound notebook from his breast pocket and adjusted his reading glasses.

"Late lamented was John Roy Richards, born forty-eight years ago in a little place upstate named Winslow. Parents are dead, one younger sister, married, two kids, still lives there. From what I could dig up, he had a pretty uneventful life until, at nineteen, he went away to college where he became acquainted with John Barleycorn."

He grinned at Harm. "Apparently, it was love at first sight. Went almost overnight from virtual teetotaler to the life of every beer bust. From there, a quick slide to the hard stuff. By his sophomore year, his grades were in the toilet. Got expelled at the start of his junior year when he blew his tuition and living money on booze."

"At thirty grand a year that must have been some thirst," Harm commented.

"In those days, more like fifteen, but yeah, it musta been a snootful. Anyway, that was the beginning of the gutter, jail, rehab, gutter, jail, rehab, gutter cycle of his life for the past twenty-five years."

"What about the sister?"

Charlie shook his head. "According to the cops and my interview, she hadn't seen him in about six years. Last time she took him in to dry out, he repaid her by stealing a portable television, a VCR, some jewelry and the contents of her children's piggy banks."

"Charming fellow."

"Pretty much his MO. Petty theft, a little car and home burglary, penny ante stuff mostly. Lately though he's been panhandling in the Riverview Plaza area. Police have had some complaints but no one wanted to press charges for fear of retaliation. Looks like the first person to ever actually do something about him was your client."

"Not my client," Harm corrected acidly. "My client would have ripped off his balls and gulped 'em down right there. Probably carries mustard and catsup in her purse just in case."

The other man laughed. "Thanks for the tip. I'll remember to start wearing my cast iron jock when I come in here."

They both laughed and sipped their coffee.

"Where was I?" Charlie scanned down his notes.

"Oh. Anyway, by the time the cops got there, it was all over but the shouting. The combatants were gone as was most of the crowd. But the couple of people who'd called 9-1-1 both said the lady got into a cab and the guy staggered off down the street, his ego and various other parts dented but definitely alive."

"Anybody get a look at where he went when he left?"

"Downtown. Towards the river. But no one actually saw him after he melted into the crowd. Pretty heavy at that time of day as people had just let out for lunch."

"How far from Riverview was he murdered?"

"Eight blocks. In the alley behind a deli on the corner of Thorn and Fitzgerald. Real zoo at lunch. Things slack off about two o'clock so they start cleaning up. About three, a busboy named Jose Sanchez took some garbage bags out to the dumpster. Well, he comes running right back in, white as a sheet and starts screaming in Spanish. One of the waiters tried to calm him down but he just keeps screaming, '¡Muerta! ¡Muerta!' Finally drags the guy out into the alley and there's what's left of Mr. Richards."

"What'd the cops find?"

"Not much, but fairly interesting what they did find."

"Such as?" Harm leaned forward, listening intently.

"For one thing, he had almost seven bucks in change rolled up in an old handkerchief and tied around his ankle, under his sock and pant leg. Sort of a street bum's idea of financial security I guess. His panhandling cup was on the ground, squashed flat."

"Like someone had stepped on it?"

"More like someone had stomped on it."

"They also found the remains of a smashed whiskey pint. From the amount spilled on the ground, probably still full. The police checked with every place he might have bought it between Riverview and the alley but no luck. And I'd think that someone would have remembered Mr. Richards."

"Maybe he bought the bottle before he went to Riverview."

"Trust me," Charlie snorted, "if this guy'd had a pint for more than five minutes, it wouldn't have been full."

"Somebody gave it to him?"

"Be a good way to get close to him. Put him off his guard."

"Any defensive wounds? Blood or skin under his nails?"

"Uh-uh. Whoever did this jumped him from behind."

Charlie took another gulp of coffee before he continued. "Medical Examiner told me that calling this a stabbing was the understatement of the year."

"How's that?"

"Well, for starters, there were nine stab wounds."

"Nine?" Harm repeated incredulously.

His friend nodded emphatically. "ME says the weapon was probably an ordinary kitchen knife, maybe a carving knife or a butcher knife. Eight inch blade. First blow caught him in the right side of the neck. May have started to turn around or even run. Or whoever did it may have moved around to his front. At any rate, he got another thrust in the throat and a slash in his left arm, maybe trying to protect himself. Then a straight jab in the belly. ME says any one but the arm could have been fatal and that five of the of the wounds were made *after* Richards was on the ground and helpless."

"Sounds more personal than a mugging."

"A lot more personal," Charlie agreed.

Harm frowned thoughtfully. "Anybody see or hear anything?"

"No. Back door of the deli opens right on to the alley but it's fifty feet from where it happened. I took a stroll back there at lunchtime. With the racket in that place, you could shoot off a cannon in that alley and no one would hear."

"What do the police think?"

Charlie shrugged again and snorted. "Mugging. Maybe a fight over the booze or just two bad asses mixing it up. At any rate, filed under, 'To Be Solved After the Next Ice Age'."

"What do you think?"

The older man rubbed his chin and gazed at the desktop for a few moments.

"Right now, I don't have enough facts to 'think' anything. The evidence, what there is of it, could point to nothing more sinister than what it looks like. Random street violence."

"But?"

"But my cop's gut tells me there's more to it than that. Lots more. We're talking rage...a literal killing fury. And knives are up close and personal, especially nine times. Whoever did this didn't care about money or booze. He wanted John Richards *dead*."

"My client seems to think this may be connected to the panhandling incident at noon. That whoever's stalking her friend, Elgin Collier, saw Richards grab her, went nuts and stabbed him to avenge her honor."

"Would explain the ferocity of the attack if nothing else." He paused, drained the last of his coffee and considered his next words carefully. "Of course, if this guy's willing to kill a total stranger for putting his hands on the object of his obsession, she could be tap dancing with a cobra. Especially if it's someone who's already close to her."

Harm nodded. "That's why I've made arrangements with my client for Billy and I to go over to Miss Collier's apartment and check out her computer. If that's how he got in, we may be able to pick up his trail."

"Good idea," the older man agreed thoughtfully. "God knows we've both seen enough of this kind of thing to know that it's a razor's edge between undying adoration and murderous hatred. One day it's roses, the next it's bullets."

"Well, thanks for all the information. I'll go over everything tonight with a fine tooth comb and if I've got any questions, I'll be in touch."

"Good luck, Camp. I have a feeling you're going to need it."

Chapter Four

"Oh Sheila," Elgin snapped, "how could you?"

"Because something needed to be done and obviously you weren't going to do it," Sheila replied calmly.

"But a private eye?" Elgin countered, still incredulous at her publisher's announcement.

"A security professional," the other woman corrected.

"Well I don't care what you call it. I will not have some big, dumb rent-a-cop rifling through my life and trailing after me in a Groucho nose and glasses."

"Surprise," her friend smiled wickedly, "he's been investigating this since we found out from the police that panhandler'd been murdered. His company's also been providing round-the-clock surveillance and security on you and not a Groucho nose anywhere."

Elgin blinked in disbelief. "Surveillance? Of me?"

"Uh-huh."

"I don't believe you. You're just saying that." She didn't sound the least bit convinced.

"Would you like to see the video tapes? I get one every twenty-four hours. And by the way, that guy who gave up the cab for you was a hunk. You should have at least invited him to share."

Stunned, Elgin dropped into her high back burgundy desk chair. Sheila came to her side and bent over her.

"I didn't mean to upset you, El," she soothed, "really, I didn't. It's just that you could be in real danger here. Even Mr. Harm thinks there might be a problem. At least something that should be investigated."

"Mr. Harm?"

"Oh, I forgot. C.A. Harm. He owns Harm's Way Security. He's handling this. I checked him out thoroughly and he's the best there is."

"But..."

"No 'buts,' El," Sheila cut her off firmly. "I know how you feel about your privacy and I respect that. But face it. Someone's already invaded that privacy. All Mr. Harm and I are trying to do is find out who and why. And the sooner you start cooperating, the sooner this will all be over and forgotten."

Elgin exhaled a long, resigned sigh. "Do I have any choice?"

Sheila grinned again. "None. Now get yourself together 'cause he's in the living room."

"I hate this," Elgin pouted. "And I hate him. And you."

"I know you do," Sheila agreed lightly, "and I certainly don't expect you to be bosom buddies. In fact, I'd settle for you just not clawing his eyes out at this first meeting."

"No promises," she sulked, rising from the chair and starting across the room.

* * * * *

They looked, she thought sourly, like Mutt and Jeff as she and Sheila came through the office door and the two men rose from the sofa.

Well, perhaps not two men exactly, she corrected herself silently. More like one tall, fairly nice looking man and a gawky, be-speckled young boy who looked to be about twelve. The only thing missing from his total geek look was a pocket protector.

"Mr. Harm," Sheila began by way of introduction, "this is Elgin Collier. Ellie, this is C.A. Harm of Harm's Way Security."

"Miss Collier," he said noncommittally, giving her hand a perfunctory shake.

"Mr. Harm," she replied with an equal lack of emotion.

Oh, Jeez, she grumbled to herself, an alpha male. Strong, assertive type. Like I don't have enough problems already.

"This is Billy Wendell," he announced, turning slightly to the young man beside him. "He's our in-house electronics and technical wizard. He'll be checking your computer."

Elgin noted it wasn't a request, just a statement of fact.

"Checking for what?"

Harm's mouth turned down ever so slightly, obviously not used to having his word questioned.

But instead of answering, he glanced down at Billy, apparently giving him approval to speak.

Grinning, Billy pushed his thick black glasses back up to the bridge of his nose.

"If you've got a stalker," he explained cheerfully, "he probably came in through your computer. Hacker with…"

"Mr. Harm, Mr. Wendell," Elgin sliced in sharply, "I'm not a complete technical moron. I'm very familiar with computer bugs and hackers. As a writer, I'm acutely aware of the vulnerability of the Internet and the need to keep prying eyes out of my affairs. I have a very complete security program including anti-virus and firewalls. If there is someone…well, I'm sure he didn't break into my life through my computer."

The boyish grin remained unfazed. "I'm sure you've probably got good programs," he agreed, "but hackers are always one step ahead. Not to mention that new worms and trojans are coming out on the net all the time. A program can't detect what it doesn't recognize as harmful. If nothing else, it won't take very long for me to check you out and if there's no problem, it'll be good to know that too."

"I have a lot of very confidential information on my computer," Elgin insisted.

"That's all right," Billy practically giggled. "I've been everywhere. Even the Pentagon computers. Hell, I could tell you what color the Joint Chiefs' shorts are."

"What he means," Harm finished flatly, "is that despite his youthful appearance, Mr. Wendell has a security clearance of the highest level. You can be assured that your confidentiality won't be breached."

There was no way around it. She would just have to stand aside and let this techno-geek teen run amok in her personal life.

Bending down, he retrieved a black laptop computer bag.

"If you could show me where your system is?"

Reluctantly, Elgin turned and the four of them moved to her office, Billy plopping down in her chair and critically examining her CPU as he pulled his own laptop from its case and set it on the desk next to her monitor.

"Nice setup," he commented. "Cable's way better than DSL." He plugged a connector wire between his machine and hers and began typing rapidly on his keyboard.

"You'll need my password," Elgin told him.

"No I won't," he responded gleefully. A few more keystrokes and his computer screen suddenly filled with her e-mail.

"Hey," she shrieked, "how did you do that?"

"Not hard," he answered, his eyes never leaving the screen or his fingers on the keyboard.

"I demand to know…" she began but stopped when a flashing red highlight suddenly appeared over one of her e-mails.

"There it is," Billy crowed triumphantly.

"What is that?" Sheila asked, leaning over the boy's shoulder a little.

"The Trojan Horse," he told her. "This is my own program. It's designed to ferret out unwanted e-mail hitchhikers. Blue is a virus, yellow a worm and red is a trojan. Once it activated, whoever planted it had open access to your system."

"But...but that's impossible," Elgin cried even as the screen blinked red. "Look, it's in the 'delete' file. I never even opened it."

"Didn't need to," the young man continued. "Once it was here, it launched by itself."

"Nine weeks ago," Harm said almost to himself as he read the e-mail's date.

"Yep. Just about when you figured. Want me to see how bad it is?"

Harm nodded once and the kid's fingers flew over the keys again. For several minutes, they watched silently as Billy went methodically through Elgin's computer. Finally, he looked up.

"Total breach," he told Harm, his voice now serious. "E-mail, incoming and outgoing, schedule, To-do list, shopping, surfing the net, everything. Even the writing. He's been sitting right here, keystroke by keystroke."

Elgin felt suddenly lightheaded and nauseous. As if her home had been broken into. As if she'd been personally violated. Sheila grabbed her arm and got her to a chair just as her knees gave out.

But the two men seem oblivious to everything but the computer monitor.

"Here's where he got the flower and candy," Billy remarked as they went through her list of favorite websites.

"And there's the bra and panty sizes," Harm noted as a mail order lingerie shop rolled by.

"All her schedules and appointments. He knew everything about her practically before she did."

"Can you track him?"

Billy frowned. "I can put a trace on the computer but we'll have to wait until he logs on again."

"Okay, get everything set up."

Harm turned, surprised to see Elgin so pale and shaken.

"Billy's going to be running a few more tests," he said quietly. "Perhaps we should go back in the living room."

"I think that's a good idea," Sheila agreed quickly. "I'll have Martha get us some fresh coffee. You all right, El?"

Elgin nodded and stood up. Instantly, the room listed to port and she put out her hand to steady herself. Without thinking, Harm's hand flew out and caught her, feeling her limp weight against him for a moment, a ripple of mini-firecrackers exploding through his body. She shifted herself slightly and leaned on Sheila, sliding out of his grasp but leaving a distinct tingle on his skin.

"So Mr. Harm," Sheila asked quietly, "what now?"

He took another sip of coffee. Good, he thought idly. Unless his taste buds deceived him, a rich, hearty Colombian served in a mug big enough for a man to get his hand around. He despised weak, watery, flavored coffees served in tiny, fragile china cups.

After they'd settled on the sofa and coffee had been served, there'd been a few minutes to let the shock wear off and the reality set in. Now they had to pick up the pieces.

"Well," he answered slowly, "Billy's putting a tap on the computer as we speak. It'll alert us the next time our friend logs on. With any luck, we should be able to follow the electronic breadcrumbs right back to his lair. Once we've pinpointed him, you can swear out a complaint and wherever he is, the local police can handle it.

"We'll also install a new security program on the computer that will continuously update, looking for viruses, worms and Trojans and automatically send a signal to our central monitoring location if someone tries to break in again. It's not perfect by any means but it's definitely an improvement over what's there right now."

"How...how long do you think it will be before he...he comes back?" The uncertainty and fear in her voice seemed far removed from the tough, strong image she'd given him at first.

"Hard telling," he replied carefully, "but probably not long. My guess is that he probably checks in at least once a day to keep tabs on you."

She flinched a little and shut her eyes tightly. For some inexplicable reason, Harm felt a twinge in his chest.

"Until we catch whoever is doing this," he continued, "you'll have to make some adjustments."

"Adjustments?" Elgin repeated, opening her eyes. "What sort of adjustments?"

"Well, for one thing, you're going to have to change your schedule. One thing I've seen since surveillance started is that you're very much a creature of habit."

Something flashed in those dark eyes.

"I lead an ordered life if that's what you mean," she shot back coldly. "It's one of the ways I maintain the discipline I need to write. My busy life makes scheduling imperative."

"Yes, well, I understand that, Miss Collier," Harm replied, feeling a little tense himself, "but predictability in this situation makes you vulnerable. Makes it possible for someone to make plans of his own. Plans that may not be as pleasant as yours."

"I like my life the way it is," she answered flatly.

"And hopefully, we can track this person, have the police apprehend him and you can have your ordered life back. But until that happens, your personal security is our primary objective. Right now, he knows a great deal about you and we know nothing about him. That gives him a tremendous and potentially catastrophic advantage. By denying him that advantage, we level the playing field."

"I would think that any change in my routine would alert this person that he's been discovered and send him into hiding. I'd think it would be far better for me to just keep going as if nothing's wrong."

"By now he knows that you've received his gifts and that you're aware, however dimly, of his presence. The fact that he's spooked you into altering your routine will probably delight him no end. Make him feel powerful and closer to you by exercising his control. It may even make him bolder and bring him out into the open. But he doesn't know that we're on to him so he won't be looking over his shoulder."

"But I thought you said you could track him from Elgin's computer," Sheila commented nervously.

"I said we could *try*. A lot's going to depend on how computer savvy this guy is. Picking up a trojan from the net doesn't take a lot of technical genius. Hiding your tracks in cyberspace does."

"You still didn't tell me what kind of 'adjustments' you meant."

"First of all, you're going off-line. Completely. Billy's re-routing your computer to our main monitoring system now."

"What?" Elgin shrieked, practically dumping her coffee in her lap. "I won't have that! I mean it. The Internet is one of my most valuable marketing tools and e-mail is a vital link to my readership. I won't do it. Absolutely not."

"You don't have any choice," he responded coldly. "We've got to close the door on him and bolt it from the inside. Until we catch this guy, anyone who tries to contact you or log onto the system is going to get an error message telling them the system's down. In reality, they'll be coming right into our central monitoring system where they'll be identified and if necessary, traced."

"Now see here…" Elgin began but Harm shook his head.

"And you'll have to change your schedule. Stop doing the same thing at the same time on the same days. Change the stores and the restaurants you frequent. Be more careful about who knows where you're going to be and what you're going to be doing. Except, of course, for Harm's Way. We'll have to have a daily schedule of your comings and goings. We'll have people providing you security, but we'll also want to be able to check out places where you're going to be before you get there as well."

"Well I won't do it," Elgin shot back, her voice tense and raised with anger. "I will not be bullied or intimidated by some stalker who may be more imaginary than anything else and I will most certainly not be bullied by you."

"The stalker isn't imaginary," he replied, his own voice requiring an effort to keep under control, "he's very real and he's here, whether you like it or not. We were hired to find this guy, stop him and protect you and that's what we're going to do."

"You're fired, Mr. Harm. You and your geeky little technocrat and your rent-a-cops who've been following me are officially off the case. I want you out of my computer, my home and my life. Now."

He glanced at Sheila and back to Elgin. "You're not my client, Miss Collier, Miss Forbes is. I'm not fired until she says I am."

"Well then tell him to go away, Sheila."

"No Elgin, I won't," she replied quietly.

Elgin's jaw dropped in surprise. "What do you mean, 'you won't'?" She could barely get the words out.

"Because he's right and you're just being pigheaded and stubborn. There is a stalker out there El, and God only knows what he's got on his warped mind. You saw where he's broken into your computer. He knows where you live, where you shop, where you get your hair done. He could be anywhere, anyone. Until this is over, you do what Mr. Harm tells you to."

"I won't," Elgin told her defiantly.

"Oh yes you will."

"And who's going to make me?"

"If it comes to it, I will."

"And how the hell do you propose to do that?" Elgin asked coldly.

"Well, as your oldest and dearest friend, I'd hoped to try and reason some sense into that thick Irish skull of yours. Since that didn't work, I'll put on my boss's hat instead."

"What's that supposed to mean?"

"It means that if you'll check the fine print in your contract, you'll find there's a clause that prohibits you from doing anything that would be harmful or detrimental to your health, well-being and your capacity to produce books for Fantasy Publishing. That includes such things as swimming nude with piranhas, drinking battery acid or playing chicken with a stalker."

"Sheila..."

"Any of which constitutes a material breach of your contract. If you don't behave yourself, I'll have you tied up in court so long, your grandchildren will be testifying. And I'll make sure that not only do you not publish again with Fantasy, but that no one else will touch you with a ten-foot lawyer either."

"You can't be serious."

"You, of all people, El, should know I don't kid about money and you're screwing with my biggest business asset."

"But..."

"No 'buts' Ellie."

"Miss Collier," Harm broke in again, "my motto is, when you're in harm's way, you do it Harm's Way."

* * * * *

"Did you hear *that*?" Elgin shrieked in Sheila's face. "The nerve of that...that..."

Sheila sipped her coffee in patient silence. As soon as the door had swung shut behind Harm and the Boy Genius, Elgin had gone into her seething rant. From long experience, she knew the futility of talk until her friend had exhausted her rage.

"When you're in harm's way, you do it Harm's Way," she mocked acidly. "My God, he made it sound like one of the commandments."

"He was just voicing a sentiment," Sheila offered.

"*His* sentiment," Elgin shot back. "He sounded as if he expected me to sit down then and there and cross stitch him a sampler of the damn thing! Well you know what? Fuck Mr. C. A. Harm and his pithy little saying and his pissy little geek toad and the horse he rode in on!" For emphasis, a small sofa pillow sailed past Sheila's head.

"Are you through?"

"No, God damn it! Not by a long shot! If that arrogant, know-it-all gorilla thinks for an instant that I'm going to turn my life inside out for him, not only is he stupider than he looks...a neat trick in itself...but he's going to be bitterly disappointed in the bargain! I will go where I choose, when I choose. I will not allow some phantom to hang over my life like a childish boogeyman and I will most *definitely* not roll over and play dead for some chest thumping, self-delusional alpha male, who by the way should check his calendar to see what millennium this is."

"You might as well stop this tantrum," Sheila told her quietly. "I meant what I said about your contract. And Mr. Harm isn't suggesting you crawl under your bed and hide. He only said you have to change your schedule a little and let them know where you're going to be.

"This stalker is absolutely real. You saw the whatchamacallit on your e-mail. He knows your whole life. There's every reason to think he's been close enough to grab your ass and he may very well have killed a total stranger for you. God only knows what he might be capable of."

"Sheila..."

"No, I mean it." She shook her head firmly, put down her cup and came to where her friend stood.

"If nothing else, think about me," she cajoled. "How the hell do you think I'd feel if you disappeared and they found your body raped and mutilated? Or it was never found at all? How do you think I'd live with myself if I knew that I could have done something and didn't because of your mule-headed, obstinate Irish temper?"

Elgin's faced screwed into a defiant pout.

"You'd collect on that fat insurance policy you have on me, go to the south of France with some good-looking nineteen-year-old stud for a month and then come back and re-issue all my books in special limited edition collectable volumes for which you'd charge twice the price and for which you wouldn't have to fork out any royalties."

"*Ooooh,*" Sheila pretended to agree. "Special limited edition collectable volumes. I hadn't thought of that. Maybe even hardback if I could get a good deal on the printing."

"You would, too," Elgin commented sourly.

"Damn straight." She grinned wickedly. "God knows just because you'd be dead doesn't mean I should suffer too."

"If I did die, I'd come back and haunt you except you'd probably want me to keep 'ghost writing' Gillian Shelby."

Knowing that the storm had passed, Sheila put her arms around her friend and they hugged.

"It's only for ten more days. I hired Harm's Way for two weeks and with the tap on your computer, I'm sure they'll be able to catch this nut in that time. Probably sooner and then we can all get back to normal. Surely you can put up with Campbell Harm that long."

"I suppose," Elgin conceded grudgingly. "But I'm serious too. In ten more days, he's outta here. By then, I should be pretty much finished with the re-writes and then three months in the country. Promise?"

"Pinky swear."

* * * * *

"You're sure?"

Billy nodded glumly. "I triple checked."

Harm exhaled a deep, frustrated sigh and threw the stapled pages on his desk. The young man standing in front of his desk shifted his weight nervously.

"And you're positive this is our boy?"

"Yes sir," he replied apologetically. "He's the only one of Ms. Collier's computer 'visitors' who can't be accounted for legitimately. He's tried to log on at various times, mostly between two and five a.m. and has been very persistent in his attempts."

"You think he knows we're on to him?"

"Hard to say, sir," he shrugged slightly, "but I'd guess not, just from the fact that he kept trying. Building a 'blind' isn't all that hard. Wouldn't take a whole lot of smarts or technology. And if I was stalking someone from cyberspace, I sure as heck'd have someplace to hide, just in case."

"All right, Billy. Thanks for the report. As always, it's complete and thorough."

"I just wish I could have been more help."

"I know you did everything humanly possibly. Did you give your time sheet for this project to Jessica?"

The young man nodded.

"Okay then. You better get on back to the monitoring station. I know this isn't your only case."

Alone again, Harm reread the report carefully, frowning as he did so. At last, he set the papers down again and reached for his phone.

"Jessica, please get me Ms. Forbes at Fantasy Publishing. Tell her it's important."

* * * * *

"I'm sorry, Mr. Harm, I still don't think I understand." Elgin looked at him, those huge dark eyes filled with questions and, he thought, a tinge of alarm.

"I know it's a little complicated," he explained patiently, "but the gist is that everyone who tried to log on to your computer, either by e-mail or alternate method, has been identified and tracked. All of them could be accounted for as friends, fans, business, etc. Except one. We believe he's the stalker. He tried several methods of entry and his times were always between midnight and five a.m."

"But if you know all this, why weren't you able to locate him?"

"Because he has what is known as a 'blind'. You know, the little camouflage huts that duck hunters use so the ducks won't see them. He managed to route through another ISP address."

"Well," Elgin pressed nervously, "how do you know it's a 'blind'? Maybe it really is his address. Did you check?"

"Yes, Ms. Collier," Harm replied, slightly annoyed that she thought him stupid or incompetent, "we checked. The ISP account belongs to a convent of nuns in Belgium. They make pottery and candy and have recently moved to the Internet to increase their sales. Apparently our stalker hacked into their system so that he could hide his own address."

"But can't you tap into their computer?"

"He's gone. More than likely, he's got several of these 'blinds' scattered around and probably knows how to build more."

"So...so he knows you're on to him?" The tiniest tremor appeared at the edge of her voice.

"We just don't know. Building a 'blind' or even several isn't that hard. Ours is the most sophisticated, cutting-edge technology available. It's designed to track without being tracked. I find it difficult to believe that our stalker has either the technology or the expertise to evade it."

"But he did evade it."

"He didn't evade it, Ms. Collier." She made him hot under the collar again.

"He just covered his tracks. My personal opinion is that he's either lost interest in the game or been scared off. At any rate, Harm's Way will continue to monitor the situation and provide personal security for the rest of the agreed upon period. At the end of that time, I'd say that you can call it a day and consider the problem solved."

Unexpectedly, he smiled. A warm, genuine, very nice smile. Elgin felt her anxiety disappear like vanilla ice cream under a summer sun.

"I really don't think there's anything to worry about."

Relieved both at the thought that the stalker had gone and that she would soon have her life back, Elgin smiled too. At least, that's what she told herself, hastily trying to squash the unexpected tingle his smile produced.

"Well that's good," she murmured. "I'm looking forward to it."

* * * * *

"I really think I ought to call Mr. Harm," he repeated anxiously.

"Good heavens, why?" Elgin badgered. "I've rearranged my whole life for this foolishness. This is your last day. Tomorrow I have to go back to living the way I did before I ever knew Harm's Way existed. What difference does it make if I get started a little early?"

"Ms. Collier, I understand that you're anxious to get back to normal after all that's happened. But I'm assigned to protect you until my shift ends. And Mr. Harm gave very specific instructions about you not keeping this beauty appointment. At least not today."

Elgin glared at him. Pete Fowler had been her day escort for the entire two weeks that she'd been under Harm's Way's vigilant eye. Nice enough, medium height, medium build, short brown hair, kind brown eyes. Until they'd been formally introduced, she hadn't even noticed him trailing her.

"Look Pete," she declared, "I'm going to keep my hair appointment. I have been going to this woman for longer than I care to admit and long after you are gone and Harm's Way is mercifully forgotten, I will still be going there. If there's a stalker lurking out there somewhere, he'll know where to find me next Wednesday at eleven-thirty a.m. so what's the difference?"

"The difference is, next Wednesday at eleven-thirty a.m., I won't be responsible for you."

"Goodbye Pete," she grumbled and pushed past him and started for the cab waiting at the curb. In two long strides he'd caught up with her.

"All right, Ms. Collier," he grinned, "have it your way. But I still have to call and let Mr. Harm know."

"Anything you want, Pete, only let's get going while I still have a hair appointment to keep."

* * * * *

The Beauty Spot, a small salon in the less impressive side of town, wedged itself between a neighborhood grocery and a dry cleaning shop. Wanda Jacobs, the shop's owner and principle employee, was a large, motherly woman with perfectly coifed silver hair and friendly blue eyes that seemed to disappear in the laugh lines around her eyes.

She and Elgin had met many years before when the recently widowed Wanda had agreed to do the struggling author's hair in return for newspaper ads and flyers. Copies of all of them hung on the shop's walls along with autographed covers of all of Gillian Shelby's books. Wanda never missed an opportunity to let people know that she'd "discovered" Gillian Shelby.

"You don't actually have to go in," Elgin teased, seeing the look of discomfort on Fowler's face. "There's a wonderful little coffee shop down on the corner. Breakfast all day long. The homemade waffles with blueberry syrup are to die for. Read the paper and have a second cup of coffee and I should be finished about one."

"Thanks," he grinned, obviously relieved that he wouldn't have to venture into no-man's land. "I'll be back at one."

Inside, Wanda listened on the telephone at the front counter. Seeing Elgin, she immediately smiled, nodded and pointed to an empty chair as she listened intently.

"Uh-uh, hon," she replied into the receiver. "Just can't squeeze you in Friday. Prom season."

She listened a few moments longer, running her finger down the pages. "Not a chance. I'm booked solid. Why don't you try Missy's…"

More silence as the other party spoke. Wanda turned toward Elgin and shrugged helplessly.

"Look," she cut in firmly, "I can't do it. You know I would if I could, but I just don't have any time. You call over to Missy's and talk to Joan. Tell her I sent you and that it's an emergency. She'll do right by you and Olivia. And I promise I'll call you first thing if I get a cancellation. I've got to go now. I've got a client under the dryer who's going to cook if I don't get her out. Yes. I promise. Okay. Goodbye."

Wanda put down the phone and sighed as she reached the back of Elgin's chair.

"Connie Armstrong," she explained, taking a large pink cape and settling it over Elgin. "Daughter Olivia's got a date for the prom Saturday night and her mother's desperate for me to 'give 'er the works'." A hearty chuckle rumbled through her big body. "Child doesn't need a beautician, she needs a magician.

"Me? I'm tickled pink for her although I can't imagine any boy being that hard up for a date. Don't get me wrong. She's sweet as homemade apple pie and bless her heart, with parents who look like Ed and Connie, the girl can't help being homely as a mud fence. But Lord, she doesn't have to make things worse by eating like food's going out of style. Poor thing looks like a hippopotamus after a three-day bender."

"You're terrible," Elgin laughed.

"No, just honest. I guess, though, sometimes it's a gnat's whisker between the two. By the way, speaking of truth as we were, who's that good-looking man I saw you getting out of the cab with? Any good gossip I can spread?"

"Put away your trowel, Wanda dear. Strictly business."

"That's how Pat and I started out," Wanda nodded knowingly. "He delivered genuine Egyptian Henna to that fancy salon I worked at right out of school. We ended up with five kids and twenty-six too short years."

"Well, for one thing, he's already got a wife and kids so could we please change the subject?"

"Oh, all right," Wanda agreed, reaching for a comb and her spritz bottle. "How's the new book coming? Lots of hot sex I hope."

At one straight up, Pete appeared on the sidewalk outside The Beauty Spot. He seemed relieved once more after Elgin had paid the bill and came out a moment later.

"I don't see much of a difference," he remarked, examining her hair from several angles.

"Good. You're not supposed to. That's the whole point of spending all this money to have it done once a week. People are supposed to think I'm naturally gorgeous." Elgin put a hand to head and pretended to strike a pose.

"I can definitely vouch for the gorgeous part. Inside and out."

Elgin blushed bright red and glanced down at her feet. She and Pete had spent the last ten days together and they'd grown very friendly, discovering a mutual love of horse racing and Italian food.

"Well, thank you," she smiled shyly. "It's nice of you to say, even it isn't true. But don't let your boss catch you saying something like that or he may fire you for poor eyesight."

Pete grinned. "Okay, it'll be just our secret. You want me to hail a cab?"

"No, I called from the salon. I told the dispatcher we'd meet the cab across the street. That way, he won't have to go 'round the block to get back to Grant."

"Speaking of which, that must be him now." He nodded to his left and Elgin turned to look. A cab pulled around a corner two blocks up.

"We better get over there."

Gently, he took her elbow and they stepped off the curb.

They'd just reached the yellow line in the middle of the asphalt when she heard it.

The roar of a powerful engine being gunned caught their attention. Following the sound, she turned her head to the right in time to see a huge dark blur careen out of the alley just on the other side of the salon.

Later, in her nightmares, Elgin saw headlights glowing like pale eyes and a wide evil chrome smirk of bumper. But in that split second as it happened, sound and sensation collided and ran together, the pieces knotted in a smashed jumble.

Pete's frantic cry, "Look out!" Something pushing fiercely in her back and the asphalt biting her hands and knees and head as she fell. A loud "thump" and wind rushing past her. A door slamming and a woman screaming.

Somewhere, the engine faded and with it, the warm spring sunshine, disappearing above her as she tumbled down a dark well. For a moment, her mind tried to rouse her and slow her descent but her body rebelled, suddenly too tired to resist the onrushing night. Closing her eyes and feeling her muscles go limp, Elgin gave up the struggle and surrendered to the blackness.

Chapter Five

"Wake up dear." Elgin heard her mother's muffled voice. "You've slept enough. It's time to wake up."

But she hadn't slept enough. Not nearly. Her head still seemed fuzzy and her body exhausted. A few more minutes.

"Wake up," the voice called again and while it sounded female, she now recognized that it didn't belong to her mother. Or Martha. Kind but firm, it kept insisting.

So finally, Elgin opened her eyes. Or at least she tried to. But the overhead light flashed unexpectedly bright and she shut them immediately. Too late. It shot past her eyes and exploded in her brain, setting off a chain reaction of pain that filled her skull with a mushroom cloud.

"Doctor," the voice called, "she's coming around."

Footsteps and movement and a large hand picked up her wrist. Cautiously, she opened her eyes a fraction.

"Hello," boomed an entirely too loud, too cheerful male voice. "Glad you decided to rejoin us. We were beginning to worry."

Her eyes, growing accustomed to the light, opened a little more. The voice came from a kindly looking old man in a white coat. He seemed very tall, looming over her like an NBA center. It took several seconds for her to realize she was lying down and he was standing up.

"What's your name?"

"Elgin Collier."

"Do you know what day it is?"

"Wednesday the last time I checked."

The room started to materialize out of the muddle in her mind. Propped up a little on a narrow bed with a thin sheet and cream colored blanket laid loosely over her, her shirt and jeans gone, replaced with a shapeless cotton bag with armholes and covered in tiny blue dots. Metal rails stood at attention on either side of her.

"Do you know where you are?"

"A hospital, I think," Elgin mumbled. Thinking made the nuclear holocaust in her head worse.

"How many fingers?"

"Three."

"Tell me the last thing you remember."

Elgin squeezed her eyes tightly shut again, the light and the pain becoming unbearable. Thought lay beyond her, mired somewhere in the wreckage of what had been her brain.

"Come on," he coaxed gently, "the last thing."

"I...I was standing on the... No, I was crossing the street...I think."

Fragments of thought and recollection flitted through her mind like shredded videotape, spliced and jumbled together but making no sense. And full-scale nuclear Armageddon raged between her temples.

"Please," she whimpered," my head...pain...please..." She felt tears stinging.

"We'll give you something for the pain," he promised. "Head, neck and spine X-rays were negative but we had to make sure you didn't have a concussion and we had to wait until you were awake to check. You're plenty banged-up and you're going to be awfully sore for a while, but considering what happened, I'd say you got off pretty lucky.

"I'm going to admit you overnight just to make sure we haven't missed anything, but you should be right as rain in a couple of weeks."

She felt a small needle prick in her arm, almost lost in the pain now engulfing her entire body.

"What…what happened?" she croaked.

"There was an accident," the voice replied but it was getting muffled and far away again. So was the pain.

Elgin wanted desperately to ask about the accident but she could feel herself stepping on to a cloud and drifting away. In her head, the mushroom cloud fizzled to a firecracker. One thought though emerged from the chaos just at the edge of consciousness.

"Pete," she mumbled, "Pete…"

* * * * *

"I'm sorry," the young uniformed police officer apologized, "but only authorized personnel allowed beyond the tape."

Harm snorted. "I'm looking for Duff Gustafson. Where is he?"

"He's busy right now with the investigation, sir. If you'd like…"

Spotting his friend, Harm waved a long arm and shouted.

"Yo, Duff."

A plainclothes detective looked up from the group of uniformed officers semi-circled around him. Seeing Harm, he nodded and raised his hand. Nimbly, Harm ducked under the tape and in a few quick strides, joined the other man.

"Fan out for ten blocks in all directions," he told the officers gruffly. "Check streets, alleys, parking lots. Anywhere someone might have stashed a car. Ring doorbells and get permission to check private garages. Buttonhole anyone you meet. Anybody gives you grief, run 'em in for obstruction. I want that car."

Roarke "Duff" Gustafson was the grand old man of the local detective squad. At least sixty with graying hair and dark eyes, he came across as a barrel-chested bull, seeming much larger than his five-foot-nine stature. Combined with a hard

New York accent he could wield like a billy club, he epitomized the quintessential old-line cop. Only people like Harm who'd breached that crusty armor plated exterior knew of the warm, gentle soul inside. He'd also been one of Pete's Academy instructors and later, a personal friend.

The officers scattered and the detective turned to Harm.

"What kept you?" he inquired, mock cynicism drenching his words. "When I got here and found out about Pete, I figured you'd be leapin' tall buildings to get here."

"I left my cape in my other suit," Harm shot back, picking up the game but knowing the seriousness of the matter. "The central monitoring system picked up the call on the scanner. Soon as they heard the address, they knew we had trouble and called me. I sent Jessica to pick up Sarah and take her to the hospital then came right over."

"How is he?"

Harm glanced quickly away and then back. "Don't know yet. Jessica says he's still in surgery. Right now, that's all she knows. I told her to call me every half hour...more if...if anything..."

They avoided each other's eyes for several seconds.

"So what happened?" Harm asked, taking a deep breath and squaring his shoulders.

"Hit and run. Pete and the lady..." he consulted his small notepad, "Elgin Collier, were crossing the street, apparently to catch a cab she'd called from the beauty shop over there." He gestured in the general direction behind him.

"Cabby said he'd just turned the corner up at Franklin heading this way when a car suddenly came tearing out of that alley." Again he gestured. "Pete managed to push the lady out of the way but didn't have time to jump clear himself. EMT's say the only reason he didn't die on the spot was because he somehow managed to move just enough the car sideswiped him instead of hitting full on."

"I suppose it would be too much to hope the cabby got a license plate number? A look at the driver?"

"No such luck," the detective confirmed. "Paying attention to the pedestrians and the traffic and the car just came outta nowhere, hit 'em and screeched around the next corner at Pullman. He sped up but by the time he got there, all he saw were tail lights disappearing onto Broadway."

"What about the car?"

"Big and black. His exact words."

"Any other witnesses?"

"Beauty shop owner said she didn't see anything. Heard tires squealing and a 'thump'. Went to the window, saw the bodies in the street and ran out. I guess this Collier woman is a friend of hers. Pretty shook up. Saw a car speeding around the corner but beyond thinking it might've been black, she couldn't tell us anything. With lunch over, most people had gone back inside the buildings."

"Is there any possibility this could have been accident?" Harm pressed. "Drunk driver? Speeder who couldn't stop?"

"Over here," Duff ordered, turning and walking a few feet to the middle of the street, Harm following after him. A large pool of blood and a smaller one about two feet away were drying on the sun-baked afternoon asphalt.

"You used to be a cop," the old detective commented. "You tell me."

Harm surveyed the scene, tracing the path of the car in his mind, watching it speed out of the alley, engine roaring, striking Pete as he pushed Elgin Collier to relative safety and then continuing around the corner and away. His gaze swept the entire street.

"No skid marks," he observed quietly.

"Nice to see being a private eye hasn't ruined your cop sense completely."

"Pretty obvious."

"Which brings us to the sixty-four thousand dollar question. Why? I mean, I assume this had something to do with your client, this Collier woman."

"I can't breach client confidentiality, Duff, and you know it."

"Why was Pete with her?"

"Harm's Way was hired to investigate a problem Ms. Collier has and to provide her with personal security." He frowned and looked into the middle distance. "Today was supposed to be the last day of the assignment. Pete and Sarah were going away for a few days."

"What kind of problem?"

"Look, Duff, Ms. Collier isn't exactly my client. I mean, I was hired for her but not *by* her. It's sort of complicated. I understand she's been admitted to St. Luke's overnight for observation, but her doctor seems to think that aside from some cuts and bruises, she'll be fine. You can talk to her and she can tell you whatever she feels comfortable with. No doubt my client will want to talk to you as well. I can't say for sure, of course, but if you want my opinion, both personal and professional, yeah, I'd say it was meant for her."

"Any idea who might have been behind the wheel?"

"Not a clue. Yet."

"Okay Harm," the other man agreed, "I'll leave it at that until I talk to the lady. But this is a police investigation now. Anything you know or find out, you give to us. I know how you feel about Pete. I feel the same way. But I won't have you pulling some lone wolf, avenging angel crap on me. You're not a cop anymore. You get sideways of this investigation, I'll throw your ass in the can. Remember that."

* * * * *

"Harm," he growled into the tiny cell phone, almost lost in his huge hand.

"It's Jessica."

The sound of her voice made his stomach tighten and he gripped the steering wheel harder.

"Pete's out of surgery," she continued solemnly. "Doctor says he came through okay and he's probably gonna make it. There's a lot of damage though, internal organs, broken bones. He's in Recovery right now. As soon as they take him up to ICU and get him settled, they'll let Sarah see him. Right now, only family's allowed. Twenty-four hours at least."

Her voice faded and Harm could almost see her gathering strength to drop the other shoe.

"His right leg is shattered," she whispered, "both bones almost crushed below the knee. Probably got run over by the wheels. They did what they could but...but with the nerve and muscle damage, they're not even sure they'll be able to save it. If they do, he'll probably never be able to use it again." Tears overwhelmed her.

At least she had her tears, he thought bitterly. All he had were rage, frustration and a horrible sense of helplessness. A red haze of violence engulfed him, something primitive and elemental. Plainly and simply, he wanted to kill this bastard with his bare hands. Or better yet, with his car. Feel the impact of steel on bone and flesh, the thump of his bumper and wheels squashing him like a bug.

"All right," he murmured, "stay with Sarah. As long as she needs you. Don't worry about the office. I don't want her going through this by herself. You're on the clock and the company credit cards are yours to the max. Whatever she needs or wants. Make sure the doctors know anything Pete needs...specialists, medicines, therapy...anything, is covered. Tell them not to bother Sarah with the details. Just do it."

"You're a nice man, Campbell Harm," she sniffled.

"Yeah, well don't go spreading that around," he told her gruffly. "It's lousy for the image."

"If you say so."

"I do. And thanks for calling. I appreciate it. Keep me posted."

"Will do."

Flipping the phone closed, Harm's mind had already focused on the problem of finding the driver. Chances were slim to none that the police would be able to catch him. If the car had been stolen, it would have been abandoned, probably within the ten-block police search area and would, no doubt, be found wiped clean and devoid of forensic evidence.

A bulletin would have gone out almost immediately to mechanics and body shops to be on the lookout for any suspicious body damage to the front of big, black cars. That meant, the car was probably at the bottom of the river or more likely, hidden safely in a garage, no doubt far from the crime scene and would remain so for several days or weeks or months even until the furor died down and it could be taken somewhere and safely repaired.

As much as Duff might be personally involved, a hit and run, especially that cost no lives, would very quickly get moved down the priority list by the other myriad, never-ending crimes of a big city.

No, it fell to him to nail this sonofabitch. It would require a cunning, foolproof trap. He didn't know just yet how or where he'd spring that trap but he did know one thing, he already had the perfect bait.

* * * * *

Irresistible.

He'd known it from the first moment. Something…mystical and magical about her that excited his heart and his mind as well as his cock. She'd captured his soul, his body had simply followed her Siren song.

What had begun as furtive glances, stolen caresses, secret longing from afar, smoldering under its cover of anonymity had suddenly blazed forth into uncontrollable passion. A fiery heat sweeping away everything and everyone standing between them.

All the careful planning, thoughtful work was about to pay off. In a little while, he would possess her at last.

Closing his eyes, the thought of her stirred his cock. Warm, full, inviting lips. Eyes, dark and lit with desire. Ivory velvet skin, hot with longing, under his fingertips. Her body, naked, waiting only for him.

His cock strained inside his silk briefs and bulged like an angry fist against his zipper.

You have to put it out of your mind, he told himself, at least for a little while. Until you're safely away and she's yours alone.

But the picture of her refused to leave him. In his mind, her nipples hardened under his fingers, his tongue raising them taut and erect as his cock. Soft moans and purrs of pleasure and need escaped her.

Her scent overpowered him...a hint of wildflower perfume, hot, ragged, peppermint breath and aroused female musk surrounding and tying him to her like silk cords. He had become a willing prisoner.

No use, he knew. She called him and his body, mind and soul screamed to go to her.

Quickly, he moved to the other room, locked the door and removed his trousers and briefs, releasing his strangling cock. Reaching to the vanity, he grabbed a tiny bottle of hotel lotion and shook a large dollop into his hand, sitting there creamy and white as she would be soon.

Closing his eyes, he smoothed the thick, cool cream over the length of his cock, the shaft like hot steel, the head tender and engorged. He felt her kneeling in front of him, taking him gently into her mouth. Her tongue made slow, soft circles around his swollen tip and her sucking sent shock waves of molten lava through his blood.

"How handsome you are," he heard her murmur, taking her mouth from his cock and running her lips lightly down the underside of his cock to his balls. "So big and hot and just for me." Her teeth nipped playfully at the tender skin of his sacs for a moment before she retraced her path.

The tip of his cock slid into her waiting, anxious mouth but didn't stop, instead, slowly taking him up, almost to his full length, easing up and down in a rhythm that made his blood pound white-hot in his ears and his body quiver.

He felt her hands on his ass, grabbing and kneading as her tempo increased. The pleasure of her wrapped itself around him like a velvet cloud. She knew exactly how to fill him to bursting with need and desire and exquisite torture. Soon, he'd have a lifetime of her. Completely, willingly, totally, his.

With that last thought, he erupted, physically and spiritually, his seed spurting out over his fist, his soul shattered by the sheer power of her over him.

Spent, he sagged against the vanity, still keeping his eyes shut, letting himself drift slowly back to earth. Soon, she would be his but for the moment, the fantasy would have to suffice. But even as this climax faded, the thought of her still stirred in him.

Slowly, he opened his eyes and grinned into the mirror, his hand still holding his cock. This had been the fantasy...the reality would be a thousand times more.

"That scene turned out really well," Sheila told her. "I didn't know how the hero jacking off while fantasizing about the heroine right before the wedding would work, but it does. Romantic and hot. I can't imagine a guy being so horny for me he couldn't even get through the wedding ceremony without...relieving the pressure as it were."

"All through this book," Elgin told her quietly, "they've had great sex, but there's always been that 'open door'. The knowledge that either one or both could just walk away. Now, they've resolved their problems and are ready for the big 'C,' commitment. Far from looking at it as closing off his options, he sees it as the beginning of a lifetime of love. And great sex."

"Well, it's an ingenious little twist…seeing it from the guy's point of view on his wedding day…and I loved it. I'm sure Gillian's readers will too."

"Hopefully," Elgin agreed with a sigh. "All I know is that I'm glad it's put to bed. After writing and re-writing, I'm frankly tired of looking at it. I just want to go somewhere and read someone else's words for awhile."

"You shouldn't have pushed yourself with these edits. They could have waited until you'd recovered."

"I'm not sure I'll ever recover," Elgin answered quietly. "Oh, the pain relievers take care of the bruises and aches but every time I close my eyes, I hear squealing tires and that sickening thump. Sometimes, I'll be working or walking or…or just sitting and suddenly, I'm back there on that street again. Flashbacks, the doctor called them. Says they're very common after a trauma."

She trembled and Sheila put her arms around her friend.

"After everything that's happened," Sheila ventured, "I don't see why you still want to go away. Especially to that godforsaken place. If you want a change, why don't you and I go down to the Islands for a while? In the daytime, we'll sip tall, cool, exotic things with rum and little umbrellas, and at night, we'll chase good-looking native cabana boys. With any luck, we may even catch a couple."

"It's precisely because of what's happened that I do want to get away, particularly to the retreat. I don't want to be around anyone, even you. I just want to be far away from here, from the stalker, from Pete. Which reminds me, have we heard from Dr. Criner yet?"

"Not yet. Being one of the top orthopedic men in the country…maybe the world, he's a busy guy, even for an old college chum like me. But I did get through to him. He's giving a paper at some kind of symposium in Toronto and then he'll fly down and consult on the case."

"You made sure to tell him that no one, especially Pete or Mr. Harm, is to know that I'm paying for this?"

"Yes, El, I told him and he understands that you don't want your name mentioned although he doesn't understand why. He's going to tell them that he read about the case in the paper and he thought it sounded interesting and decided to come down and see if he could get a look. They won't turn him down. Frankly, I don't understand why you don't want Pete to know you're helping him. I know he doesn't hold you responsible for what happened."

"Perhaps not," the other woman answered, "but I do. If it weren't for me, he wouldn't have been out on that street. He tried to tell me I shouldn't go to the appointment because the stalker would know about it. But would I listen? No. Like always, I knew more than anyone else. I feel guilty enough as it is. Letting Pete or Harm know I hired Dr. Criner would be admitting I was wrong. I couldn't stand that."

"That is *the* stupidest thing I ever heard," Sheila snorted. "Even from you."

"Well, it doesn't matter now. I've finished the re-writes and as soon as I can get packed, I'm gone."

"And what about the stalker? Have you considered that he may just be sitting downstairs waiting for you to leave so he can follow you? Get you alone?"

"Already taken care of," Elgin smiled. "The day I decide to leave, Martha's going to put on my clothes and a pair of dark glasses, have Ben hail her a taxi and with suitcases in hand, is going to the airport where she's going to fly first-class to San Juan and then a lovely cruise through the Panama Canal and a nice visit with her family in California. All at my expense. After she leaves, I'm going down to the parking garage, get the totally inconspicuous blue sedan I've rented and leave by the side entrance. And when I'm gone, even mega-P.I. C. A. Harm won't be able to find me."

* * * * *

"The reason Elgin's been pushing herself about the re-writes is so she can get away from here...the city, her condo and especially the accident. Martha says she hardly sleeps and when she does...well, she seems to think a change of scenery is what she needs."

Harm felt a quickening of his blood, his mind racing ahead of the woman's conversation. Could it be...a second chance?

"I'm no doctor," he replied carefully, "but after all that's happened, maybe a good long rest away from everything is just what she needs."

Suspicion flashed in those hazel eyes and for a moment, he feared he'd overplayed his hand, squandered his opportunity.

But the look flickered and disappeared.

"Perhaps," she agreed cautiously, "but what about the stalker?"

Anxious excitement pulsed through him and it took an effort on his part to continue appearing calm.

"Has there been anything else since the accident? Deliveries? Contact of any kind?"

"Not that I know of and Martha would tell me even if Elgin wouldn't. Why? Is that significant?" Sheila leaned forward a little.

"Hard to tell," he replied, shrugging slightly. "Obviously he wanted to get Ms. Collier's attention, convey his feelings with the increasingly personal gifts..."

"And grabbing her ass in the elevator and killing that homeless man," she added coldly.

Harm stifled a grunt of exasperation. Why couldn't this silly bitch shut up so he could make his point and get to the heart of the matter?

"Well, since we don't have any proof those incidents are connected, we'll leave them out of the equation. For now, let's just say his frustration mounted as she ignored him and that frustration only increased with his inability to get into her computer and track her movements and her change in habit. No doubt he felt rejected and angry.

"Catching her going to the beauty parlor for her regular appointment, especially on the arm of another man, may have pushed him over the edge. In a moment of rage, he ran his car at them, probably intending nothing more than to scare them. But something went wrong and now he's guilty of hit and run, being hunted by the police. For all we know, he could be in another state, another country, by now."

Sheila eyed him for a moment, weighing his words.

"But you don't believe that for an instant, do you?"

Bingo! He had her. Leaning forward, he folded his hands on the desktop.

"No, Ms. Forbes, I don't," he told her solemnly. "The car was parked in that alley, waiting for them. It sped up as it came down the street toward them, and there were no skid marks that would have indicated the driver tried to slow down or swerve to avoid them. In combination with everything else, including the possibility that this person did indeed kill that homeless beggar, I think Ms. Collier could still be in serious danger."

"Then perhaps going away to her retreat for the summer might be a good idea."

"Depends." He had to be careful now. Lead her to the right conclusion but not seem overly anxious. "Where is this retreat? Is it secluded? Does she have a telephone to call for help? How far away would that help be? How long would it take to get to her? Are there close neighbors? Would she be alone?"

"I've never been there myself, but from what Elgin and Martha tell me, it's in the middle of nowhere someplace upstate. No phone, no neighbors. Says that's why she bought it, although she's spent practically no time up there. But she's truly frightened now and predictably, she's running. It's her pattern when she doesn't want to face something."

"What about her secretary? Is she going?"

"Unfortunately, no," Sheila sighed. "Elgin's cooked up this hare-brained scheme for throwing the stalker off the scent and getting away. Says when she's gone, even you won't be able to find her."

Sounded just like that wise-ass bitch, he thought, but he had to keep his head.

"Beyond advising strongly against it, I don't know what else to suggest."

"What about surveillance?" Sheila offered. "Shadow her as you did in the beginning. She wouldn't even have to know."

Smart question but he had all the answers now.

"Tailing someone in a large, crowded city," he began slowly, "is one thing. Tailing them in the country is another. For one thing, it's hard to remain anonymous, blend into a small, isolated place where everyone knows each other and a stranger sticks out like a sore thumb." He paused a heartbeat and shook his head.

"No, I don't think having someone tailing her, especially the multiple people needed for twenty-four/seven duty for three months would work." Pausing again, he looked into the other woman's eyes for some sign his clues were being picked up.

"Maybe if we could plant someone at her cabin...a handyman say... Of course, in that case, she'd probably choose someone local."

Sheila sat quietly again and Harm forced himself to wait as well. The suspense was killing him.

"Suppose," she said finally, "she brought someone with her?"

"Brought someone with her?" he repeated, sure now of her direction and almost breathless with excitement.

"Yes. A secretary or a companion. You must have female detectives who could pretend to be her secretary but would really be her bodyguard."

Another sharp question. Smarter than he'd given her credit for. But he'd always been good at thinking on his feet and he recovered quickly.

"Of course we have female agents," Harm answered, "any one of whom would be excellent. But…"

"But what?"

"I just had a thought. Something almost guaranteed to provide Ms. Collier with optimum personal protection and privacy."

"And that would be…?"

"A male agent."

"What?" Sheila barked, amazed at the suggestion.

"Certainly. Not only would she have protection from the stalker should he actually find her, but from the local wolves as well. Nothing would insure Ms. Collier's privacy like a man around the place."

"That makes a certain amount of sense," she agreed. "In fact, I like the idea very much. Provided, of course, that you handle this personally."

He wanted to jump for joy! Leap across the desk and kiss her. But the scene had to be finished.

"I don't know, Ms. Forbes," he feigned concern. "I mean, aside from the personal animosity that Ms. Collier seems to have for me, which might make close, daily contact unpleasant for both of us, I have a business to run. I can't just go off and leave it for three months. I have several very good men…"

"Peter Fowler is a good man," she cut in, "and he ended up in the street, half dead. 'Good' is no longer acceptable, Mr. Harm, I want the best and that's you. I'll give you a retainer today of whatever amount you say. The arrangements in our last contract were agreeable. Have a copy sent over at your convenience. I'll call Ellie and tell her you'll be by tomorrow to discuss the details of the trip. Say three-ish. I'll call you if there's a change."

They got to their feet and shook hands.

"Thank you, Mr. Harm. I hope this whole thing is resolved by the time you get back."

"I hope so, too, Ms. Forbes."

"Goodbye then."

"Goodbye."

For a long time after she left, Harm slouched lazily in his chair and considered his good luck. He'd gotten a second chance to catch the guy who'd almost killed his friend. So far he'd eluded the police, but he wouldn't get away from C. A. Harm.

As soon as he got the location of this retreat, he'd send his people in to scout the place. Check out the terrain, the locals, the cabin's physical layout. A GPS tracking device on the car. Infrared scanners and night vision scopes for stealthy, round-the-clock surveillance.

Of course, using Elgin Collier without her knowledge as bait for a lunatic didn't sit completely well with him, but he had no choice if he wanted to catch this guy. And he did want that. Very much.

Besides, she wouldn't be in real danger as he'd see to her safety personally. That's what he got paid to do. And a man hanging around her, living in her cabin with her, only increased the pressure, upped the chances that his quarry would be forced into making a move.

Pete hadn't been expecting him. But Harm would be waiting. With both barrels.

Chapter Six

"Let's get one thing straight, from the beginning, Mr. Harm. I'm submitting to Sheila's blackmail only because I have no choice. Personally, I'd rather eat ground glass than spend one day, much less three months with you."

"Fine. Then you won't be offended when I tell you I'm getting hazardous duty pay for this job." The corners of his mouth turned up ever so slightly.

Baboon!

"If the job's so distasteful," she goaded, "you certainly didn't have to take it. Yourself, I mean. Surely you must have minions you could have foisted me off on."

"Not after what happened to Pete Fowler," he shot back without thinking.

Elgin blanched as if the words had struck her physically. A look of real pain appeared in her dark eyes and unaccountably, he felt an instant pang of sorry. An apology formed in his throat and he had a momentary urge to reach out and touch...no, comfort her.

A look of cold fury replaced the pain. Taking a step closer, she pulled herself straight and glared up into his face.

"How dare you speak to me like that you knuckle-dragging Neanderthal," she growled. "I didn't shove Pete in front of that car. You put him in that street. You and Sheila and some maniac. Difficult as it may be for your macho, pea brain to accept, Pete's my friend too."

Her voice caught and she had to stop a second to regroup.

"I'm not going to have you or anyone else laying this off on me. It's not my fault."

"Then who the hell's fault do you think it is?" Harm felt his own temper rising.

"I don't know. Some lunatic who's developed a sick crush on me. It's nothing I've done. And anyway, I thought you were supposed to catch this creep." The snarl's volume escalated.

"Crush?" he repeated, a short, derisive snort punctuating the word, his own voice raised. "The guy's a nut and a pervert. But considering the porn trash you crank out, what did you expect to attract? A minister?"

Flash point!

He saw it erupt, not just in those fiery eyes but in the crimson flush spreading up her face and her balled fists.

"Don't you say that," she screamed. "It's not trash and it's not porn! I'm a good writer and don't you *dare* come into my home and attack me or my writing."

Another snort and he waved his hand dismissively.

"News flash! Ayn Rand was a writer. Agatha Christie was a writer. You? You're no writer...you're the madam of a literary whorehouse."

For a long moment she stood there, trembling with silent rage, her fists clenching and opening at her sides in tempo with her rapid breathing. Harm thought she might even try to hit him and he felt his own hands close tightly.

But worse yet, he could see in the blazing fire of those deep eyes he'd blown his chance. Even if her publisher made good on her threat, he could feel that Elgin Collier had made up her mind that he wouldn't get anywhere near her or her retreat. Ever.

"I'm..." he started.

"Get out," she growled.

"I'm sorry."

"Get out of my house, this *instant*." The flat, cold tone of her voice more chilling than the screams.

"Ms. Collier, can't we discuss..."

Abruptly, she turned on her heel and went to the phone. Holding it up so he could see the keypad, she placed an index finger almost touching the nine.

"You see this? That's my emergency speed dial. Push it and in thirty seconds it will bring security. Three more minutes and this place will be full of police. I don't think the head of Harm's Way Security wants to be arrested and charged with attempted rape. You look like you're in shape so I'll give you fifteen seconds to get out of here, starting now."

The look in her eyes told him further talk was useless and would only bring security and the police. In her present emotional state, any accusation might have a ring of truth.

"God damn it!" he cursed to the empty elevator as it took him swiftly back to the lobby. He'd been this close to setting his snare. Why did she have to be such an irritating, short-fused, crazy bitch? And why did just being around her seem to make him crazy too?

Perhaps, he thought forlornly, he could give her a couple of days to cool off. Be reasonable. After all, both the stalker and the danger were very real. He could press Sheila Forbes a little more too.

Harm slid behind the wheel and stuck his key in the ignition.

A peace offering maybe. Flowers. Women liked flowers.

The engine rumbled to life. As he pulled away from the curb, he wondered idly if Jessica still had the name of that carnation florist.

* * * * *

"Excuse me?"

"I said, I've changed my mind."

Sheila shook her head in disbelief at her friend sitting calmly across the desk from her.

"Let me see if I understand this. The last time you and I spoke about Campbell Alexander Harm, you were screaming incoherently about castration, dull straight razors and boiling oil. Now, fast forward three days and suddenly the idea of going into the woods with him for three months is the best thing since sliced bread?"

Elgin smiled broadly. "You got it."

"Okay El," her publisher asked suspiciously, "what gives?"

"Why Sheila darling, whatever do you mean?" Elgin batted her eyelashes innocently.

"Don't give me that shit. I've known you long enough to know your life's motto is, 'Don't get mad, get even.' I also know what an evil, black Irish soul and devious mind you've got. You're cooking something up and it doesn't smell like Grandma's gingerbread. Give."

"Actually, I'm just doing my oldest and dearest friend a favor."

"Such as?"

"Well, didn't you ask me to work on an outline for my next book at the cabin?"

"Uh-huh." The more her friend talked, the less easy Sheila became.

"Well, suppose I bring you back a whole, finished book? Would that make your greedy, grasping little banker's heart go pitter-pat?"

"I don't know. Is it a romance or a murder mystery?"

Elgin got up, settled on the corner of her friend's desk and grinned.

"I've been thinking and if I'm the madam of this literary whorehouse, C. A. Harm is about to become the piano player. My next book is going to be about two lovers in an idyllic, secluded paradise."

She leaned down and her voice dropped to a conspiratorial whisper. "It's going to be *non...stop...sex*. Morning, noon and night. In the cabin. In the woods. In the lake. In a hammock, even, if I can choreograph it right. I've got things planned for these two that will have the Chinese acrobats scratching their heads."

Rising up again, şhe laughed and her voice returned to normal. "What do you think of Kemp Harmon for the hero? Sound macho and studly and alpha enough? And just to make sure no one misses the point, I'm even going to dedicate it 'to my dear friend Campbell Alexander Harm for being...*invaluable* to my research.' What do you think?"

"I think when you play dirty pool, you run the table." Sheila frowned. "Are you really sure you want to do this?"

"Absolutely," Elgin assured her emphatically. "When I'm finished with the great C. A. Harm, he's gonna think he tangled with a buzz saw."

"I don't know, El."

"Oh come on, don't be such a Fudd. He's a mean, heartless sonofabitch and a bully in the bargain. It's time somebody took him down a peg and Yours Truly is just the girl to do it."

"But he's only doing this to protect you."

"Bullshit! He's doing it for the money and I'll wager, to salve his guilty conscience for not catching this homicidal maniac *before* he almost killed Pete."

"Still, you could damage his reputation, his business. His life even."

"Don't dramatize," Elgin snapped. "Oh sure, there'll be a huge flurry of excitement when the book comes out and he'll be embarrassed. But he'll get tons of free publicity and far from damaging his reputation, it will probably put a whole new luster on it. Besides, three months later, the whole thing will be forgotten."

Her eyes twinkled. "Not to mention this book is going to be your biggest seller yet. You won't have to worry about it being banned in Boston, either. It's going to be so hot, you'll have to worry about the environmentalists picketing the place for contributing to global warming."

"Well, maybe I could look at the draft."

Elgin laughed again and patted Sheila's arm.

"That's the spirit. I get to kick that brute in his furry little balls and we both make a ton of money to boot. Who says there's no justice? Now, call our friend Kemp...I mean Camp and break the good news to him."

"Suppose he's changed his mind?"

"Add more zeroes to the check. I'm sure he's got one of those big, honking, macho SUV's so we can go in that. Tell him to pack his silk boxers, bikini swim trunks, leave his cell phone and other assorted James Bond toys at home and be at the Roxbury Street entrance to my parking garage at six-thirty Monday morning. We're shoving off at seven sharp."

She stood up. "Well, I've got to be running along. I have about a jillion things to do before I leave. I probably won't see you before I leave but I'll call Sunday night."

"Which e-mail will you be at if I need to get in touch with you?"

"I told you, Sheila, no e-mail."

"Well if you're going work while you're up there, you'll have your laptop."

"I'm only taking the little one and some CD's for storage."

"What if there's a crisis? Yours or mine?"

"Don't know about you," Elgin giggled, "but I'm not going to worry because I'm going to be with the world's biggest Boy Scout." She stopped and wrinkled her brow in thought for a moment.

"That's great," she announced with a snap of her fingers.

"What is?"

"The Scout thing," Elgin replied, her eyes gleaming as the scene began unfolding in her head. "Camp...I mean, Kemp and the heroine are out backpacking or something way to hell and gone. They stop to look at the view and fuck and she gets concerned about protection and presto, he whips out a condom, smiles and says, 'I was a Scout. I'm always prepared.' Then they go at it like rabbits, being sure to dispose of their used rubbers in an environmentally responsible fashion."

"You are a sick and depraved human being," Sheila told her seriously. "You know that don't you?"

"Good thing for you, too," Elgin agreed cheerfully. "Otherwise, you couldn't afford to indulge your weakness for cheap guys in expensive leather."

"Bitch."

"I love you too, Sheila. See you after Labor Day."

When Elgin left, Sheila picked up the phone and pressed the intercom for her secretary.

"Lynn, get me Harm's Way Security, Mr. Harm please. Tell him it's important."

* * * * *

"Well," Sheila chirped, "I guess that takes care of everything." She put down her pen and smiled at the woman across her desk. "I'm glad we could get everything taken care of so promptly, but Mr. Harm really didn't need to send you personally."

Jessica smiled. "It's all right, really. I'm actually delighted to be here at Fantasy Publishing and to meet you." Her cheeks colored a bit and she looked down at her lap for a moment. "I'm...well I'm a big fan of Gillian Shelby's. I was totally blown away when I discovered that not only is Ms. Collier really Gillian...I mean, the other way around, but that she...rather you, were going to be a client. I kind of hoped I might even get to meet her."

"Well, maybe that can be arranged," Sheila replied. "After all, she and your boss are going to spend three months together. At the very least, I'm sure I could get you an autographed copy of her latest book."

"Oh that would be wonderful," the other woman exclaimed. "I mean, I'd love to meet her in person but an autographed book would be terrific too."

"Consider it done."

"Thank you. And thank Gillian...I mean, Ms. Collier too."

"When I tell her what a fan you are, she'll be delighted."

"I'm actually kind of surprised that Mr. Harm took this case," the secretary remarked. "I mean, he's got a pretty low opinion of what he calls 'women's porn' to begin with and I got the distinct feeling that he and Ms. Collier didn't exactly hit it off. Then, after what happened to Pete...well, it just surprised me, that's all."

"How is Pete?" she asked, trying to sound casual.

"Doctor's say he's coming along fine although it's still too early to say absolutely about his leg. But Dr. Criner...you've probably heard of him. World famous orthopedic surgeon?"

"I think I've heard the name."

"Dr. Criner read about the case in the papers and called to see if he could consult. It's practically a miracle. Anyway, he seems to think that with a series of operations, maybe as many as six or seven, Pete could get enough use of his leg back so that he'll at least be able to walk. Probably won't be able to be a field agent anymore, but Mr. Harm's already offered him a desk job when he can come back to work. Regular hours, an office and a raise."

"I'm glad to hear things are going so well. Remember me to Pete the next time you see him."

"I will, thanks. Can I...can I ask you a question, Ms. Forbes?"

"Sheila, please."

"Okay, Sheila. I'm Jessica. It's about Gillian...Ms. Collier."

"Ask away. If it's not too personal, I'll try to answer."

"Why did she agree to go away with Mr. Harm for three months? I mean, I know they don't get along and he said they got in a terrible fight in less than five minutes at their last meeting. How can they possibly think they can go that long without killing each other?"

Sheila smiled. "When El and I were in college, we had a Western History class in our sophomore year. First day, she got into it with this great looking guy named Jeremy Hodge. Spent half her time telling me what a moron and a gorilla he was and the other what a great ass he had.

"Every time they saw each other, they ended up in a fight. Then, one Thursday afternoon before midterms, he up and calls her out of a clear blue sky and asks if she wants to come over to his place and study. Amazingly, she said yes."

"What happened?" Jessica asked anxiously.

"I didn't see her again until Sunday night. Her neck and other portions of her anatomy were covered in hickey bruises and teeth marks, she had her blouse on inside out, one sock missing and she could barely walk. In class the next day, you could see the scratches on Jeremy's back through his T-shirt, his neck practically purple and he not walking any better than Elgin."

"You mean...?" Her eyes were big with amazement.

Sheila grinned and nodded once.

"But...but I don't understand. I mean...if they didn't like each other how...?"

"When's your boss's birthday?"

"Uhm...July twenty-eighth. Why?"

The publisher nodded again. "I thought so. A Leo. Elgin's August sixteenth. She hates wimpy men almost as much as she hates giving up control."

"I still don't understand."

"Have you ever seen those nature films? The ones about the big cats mating?"

Jessica nodded her head, the amazement in her eyes now replaced with bewilderment.

"And you've seen their foreplay usually consists of a lot of growling, snarling, snapping and biting?"

"Uh-huh."

"Well," Sheila finished, the grin growing larger, "I have a feeling that when these two Leos finally get it on, the jungle will *never* be the same."

* * * * *

Harm checked his rearview mirror again but the road behind them remained empty. Glancing at his watch, he saw that they'd been on the road for almost three hours and he still had no idea where they were going.

Expecting her to be "fashionably late," Harm had been surprised when, pulling up to the garage entrance at six-thirty, he'd found her waiting for him, two large leather duffel bags and a computer carrying case sitting at her feet, an oversized maroon fanny pack around her slim waist. He also saw that her well-fitting blue jeans and simple long sleeved white turtleneck revealed nice curves of breast and hip he hadn't noticed before.

After exchanging perfunctory greetings, he'd loaded her gear in the back of the SUV.

"Take the Barksdale Parkway to Thirty-six north," she'd told him and that had been their last conversation. Tipping back her seat slightly, she'd buckled up and concentrated on the scenery sliding by outside her window.

The city had rapidly melted into the suburbs that had gradually given way to flat, open farmland, the interstate reduced to two lanes in each direction. In the last half an hour though, they'd begun a gentle climb into rolling hills covered with pine forests and small meadows. He didn't know much about this part of the state and the knowledge two of his best agents were tracking them with the GPS did little to quiet his vague sense of unease.

Up ahead, a road sign appeared to let them know the next town lay three miles further on.

"If it's all right with you," she said, turning to look at him, "I'd like to stop at French Creek. I always like to top off the tank, check the car and get a bite to eat before I head into the mountains. Cabin's still about three hours away and it makes a nice stopping place."

"Well, since you're the only one who knows where we are or where we're going, I guess we'd better do it your way."

Inside, Elgin grinned. She'd deliberately given him only sketchy directions. He liked doing things "Harm's Way," and she knew it must gall him not to be in control.

Get used to it, she thought maliciously. This is only the beginning.

The off-ramp curved to the right and became the main street of French Creek. A smallish, old-fashioned coffee shop called The Maple Grove and an adjoining gas station, a small market across the two-lane blacktop street, a few shops and a little post office completed the town.

At her direction, he pulled into the gravel parking lot of the restaurant and alighted. She stretched, raising the hem of her shirt and showing a couple of inches of pale, bare skin.

Soft, I'll bet. The rogue thought vanished almost as soon as it appeared, but it surprised him even so.

Inside, the almost deserted shop consisted of large picture windows on either side of the glass entrance, a few scattered tables, three booths and a row of red stools in front of the white laminated counter. The walls were covered in knotty pine paneling, sharing their space with large framed photographs of what he supposed were the surrounding mountains and forests and advertising signs of all kinds, some modern, some not so modern. Cooking aromas hung in the air, completing the homey, Grandma's kitchen sense of the place.

They slid into opposite sides of a high backed, knotty pine booth and almost instantly, a chubby, matronly woman appeared, a large floral apron covering her T-shirt and jeans.

"Mornin' folks," she remarked cheerfully. "Getcha somethin' to drink?"

"Coffee, please," Elgin answered.

"Make that two."

"Okay then. Be right back."

The menus were small, tucked neatly behind the stainless steel napkin holder.

"What's good?" he asked scanning the page.

"If I were you, I'd definitely have the Country Breakfast. It's the one at the top."

"Juice, three eggs, any style, choice of ham, link or patty sausage, or bacon," he read. "Cottage fries, hash browns, biscuits and gravy, grits or seasonal fruit, toast, English Muffins, short stack of pancakes or homemade biscuits and fresh preserves."

"That sounds pretty good," he said. "I'm hungry too."

The woman arrived with their coffee. "Now, what ken I getcha?" She poised her pencil stub over her order pad and looked expectantly at Elgin.

"I'll have the Good Morning platter, please. Scrambled eggs, bacon, fruit cup and biscuit."

"And you?"

"I'll have your Country Breakfast, please. Orange juice, eggs over easy, link sausage, cottage fries and fruit please and a double order of biscuits and preserves."

"You must be hungry," the waitress commented as she finished scribbling.

In a moment, she returned with a water glass of orange juice.

Harm, expecting a juice glass half the size, looked at it quizzically and then at Elgin.

"I guess you looked like you needed extra vitamin C," she responded, trying not to giggle.

Shrugging, he drained the glass in a few gulps and replaced the glass.

"So, you say your place is about another three hours?"

"Uh-huh."

The door opened and a man and woman came in, dressed in jeans and T-shirts. They took a table on the other side of the room. The waitress went to their table.

"Howdy folks," she greeted them brightly. He ordered coffee and she ordered tea and the waitress retreated again.

After bringing the newcomers their drinks and taking their orders, she reappeared at their table, burdened with platters and smaller dishes.

"Okay, here ya go," she grunted, retrieving plates and placing them on the table. "One Good Mornin' and one Country." She set a regular sized dinner plate in front of Elgin and a serving platter in front of Harm and a soup bowl of mixed fruit off to the side. A covered basket, two tubs of butter and a rack of small glass jelly jars, red, orange and purple.

"Getcha anything else?" she inquired. "Catsup er hot sauce fer yer eggs? More coffee?"

"No, I think we're fine."

"Well, you holler if you need somethin'. Enjoy."

Harm stared at the mountain of food facing him.

"Christ," he exclaimed in a hushed whisper, "look at this. These must be ostrich eggs. And there's gotta be half a pound of sausage here. I didn't realize when they said 'Country' they meant enough food to feed one."

"Well, I'm sure you can handle it."

He could almost feel the sharp point of her jab. She was making fun of him, convinced he couldn't get it all down. Well he'd show her.

They ate in silence but he could almost hear her counting the bites, waiting for him to throw in the towel and admit defeat. *Fuck you, bitch.*

She sipped her second cup of coffee when he finally forced down the last bite of potato and dropped his fork.

"Whew," he breathed, "that's quite a feed."

"I'm surprised you finished it," she purred. "Takes quite a man to handle the big jobs."

"Yeah, well if you'll excuse me, I've got to see a man about a horse."

He stood and looked around the room.

"In the back," she helped. "Down the hall, all the way to the end. Can't miss it. Got a picture of *'John'* Wayne on the door."

Stuffed, he could barely move and the men's room seemed to be on the other side of the moon. Inside, he checked the single stall and went to the urinal. A few moments later, the door opened and the other male patron took his place beside Harm.

"Anything?" the stranger asked.

"Just that we're still about three hours from wherever we're going. We stopped here to eat and top off the tank before we start into the mountains."

"Jan's keeping an eye on her. When our friend hits the powder room, she'll try and strike up a conversation. See if anything drops."

"Wave her off," Harm replied. "She's a smart cookie and despite the façade, she's nervous as a cat. Caught her watching our back practically as often as me. If she sees you coming in here and then Jan starts asking questions, she's bound to add it up. I don't want to take any chances on blowing this. Again."

"Okay. We'll peel off here then. GPS is tracking you from about two miles back. We'll keep in touch."

"Thanks."

Finished, Harm washed his hands and left, still weighed down with the enormous breakfast. It had been a stupid, childish thing, he realized now, taking her up on what had amounted to a dare. Something Jeanne might have…

Stop it, he told himself, angry that she'd surfaced so unexpectedly, especially in the same thought as this woman.

Returning to the main dining room, Harm saw that the booth and the table were empty. Oh well, it couldn't be helped.

Women used the restroom in places like this and perhaps Jan could glean something useful in passing.

Raising his hand, he signaled to the waitress.

"Can I have our check please?"

"Lady already paid it," she answered uncertainly. "Right after you went to the men's room, she asked for the check, got up and went down the hall. Expect she's in the ladies."

"Thanks."

A couple more minutes went by and Harm checked his watch again. Why the hell did women always take so long in the bathroom?

Jan appeared at the other table but didn't sit down. Instead, she threw Harm a panicked glance and tilted her head ever so slightly toward the restrooms. Picking up her jacket, she moved back down the hall. After waiting a few seconds, he stood, stretched and followed her, trying to appear casual and unhurried.

He found her just around the corner, pretending to use the pay phone.

"She's gone," Jan blurted out, anxiety and fear making her voice a harsh whisper.

Chapter Seven

Harm felt his heart miss a beat and his blood go cold.

"What do you mean, 'She's gone'?" he growled, leaning down into the smaller agent's face.

The young woman flinched and went pale.

"She…she called the waitress over," the woman managed to stammer, "paid the check, got up and came down here. I thought she'd gone to the ladies' room so I waited a few seconds and then followed her. I didn't want to make her suspicious. When I got there, the door to one of the two stalls was closed so I went in the other one and pretended to use the toilet. When I came out, it was some other woman.

"I got back out here as quickly as I could and then realized there's an exit up there, just before the ladies' room door. It leads to the side of the building. Nate's out checking the parking lot and the woods now. The trees come up to within about fifty feet of the door."

"Okay," Harm breathed, trying to think, "she can't have gone far. Go on out the front and scout the street. Make like you're window-shopping or something.

"I'll go out and help Nate. We'll meet back at my car in five minutes. My radio and cell phone are packed in my bags. She didn't want me to bring them and I couldn't take a chance of her spotting them. If you see anything, contact Nate on his radio. Now get going."

Jan scurried away and Harm almost ran down the narrow hall to the door, opening about midway down the side of the building. On his left, down near the rear corner, sat two big, green dumpsters, one open, one closed. To his right, part of the gravel parking lot and the road beyond. Directly in front of him and curving as far as he could see, a stand of tall pines against a pale blue sky.

It would be so easy he thought. Pretend to be coming or going to the men's room, hanging by the side door. A gun jammed in her back, a hand clamped over her mouth, "make a sound and I'll kill you," a car parked just outside the door. Gone in a matter of seconds.

But how could this have happened? He'd watched the road and had seen nothing, there hadn't been a car parked here when they'd pulled up. He was sure of that. No one could have known where they were going, where they'd stop.

A figure emerging out of the trees riveted his attention, bringing his hand instinctively to his shoulder holster before his brain remembered that too sat in the SUV, packed in his bags. But it didn't matter because he recognized Nate, jogging quickly toward him.

"Nothing," he said simply, panting to catch his breath.

"It wouldn't make any sense, anyway. He's not going to drag her into the woods to do whatever he's got in mind. He'd want his own place, his own sweet time." Harm wiped his hand across his dry mouth and tried to reason rationally but all that came to his mind were terrified eyes and a cruel, victorious smirk.

"You want me to call for reinforcements?" Nate asked cautiously.

"No, not yet. Let's see what we can find out first. Jan's gone to check out the street. Go back to your car, get on the radio and notify everyone we've got on the road, behind and ahead, to keep an eye out for her. He's probably got her in the front passenger seat so he can gloat. Tell her all the romantic things he's got planned for her. He won't be expecting us to have people posted so we might get lucky. I'll meet you and Jan at my car in about three minutes."

Nate nodded and hurried toward the street.

Acid and adrenaline pumped into Harm's already overcrowded stomach and churned with his breakfast, knotting his insides. He felt a stab of pain but he pushed it out of his mind. There couldn't be anything in his brain except Elgin. Especially not the pictures trying to seep around his mental barricades...images of what this maniac would no doubt do should he slip through their fingers once more.

Pushing everything away but the search, he waited a few more seconds and then followed Nate, rounding the corner and striding toward the sidewalk.

Jan strolled casually down the street about a block up to his right, a slightly bored tourist lady killing some time but actually scanning cars, license plates, people and store interiors. After a half-hour walk through this sleepy little burg, Harm knew she would be able to draw a detailed map of the place including the location and description of every car and person she saw.

On the other side of the parking lot from his car, Nate sat in a blue minivan, the back crammed with what looked like camping gear, speaking on a cell phone. The windows were up and the casual observer would think, from the calm expression on his face the call nothing more than checking road conditions or conversing with a friend. After all, even in a small place like this, a cell phone would not bring any undue attention.

The only other activity he could see centered at the gas station to his left, a national brand, big and modern for such a small town but where two men were filling up their vehicles, a big new pickup and an older, dark green sedan. He couldn't see anyone else in the vehicles.

Keeping his pace normal and even, Harm walked toward the station. The pickup, on the far side of the island, faced the direction they'd come from. It didn't seem reasonable that a man would throw his kidnap victim in the back of an open truck but he couldn't take the chance.

Coming up to the island, he pulled a couple of paper towels from the dispenser, leaning over slightly so he could peer into the truck bed, empty except for a spare tire. The driver glanced questioningly at him and Harm smiled a little, bringing the towels to his shirt and pretending to rub.

"Breakfast," he explained sheepishly. "Nice truck."

"Thanks," the man replied and turned back to the pump.

From where he stood, Harm could also see into the sedan, empty too. But he had no way of knowing what...or who...might be in the trunk. The driver stood in the station paying for his gas and Harm couldn't get a good look at him through the glare of the sun shining through the window.

Tossing the towels in the trashcan, he circled behind the car, noting make, model and license plate. He bent down, as if to look at something on the ground and listened carefully for any noise coming from the trunk, but he heard nothing.

Inside, the man signed his credit card slip. *Good*, Harm thought, *it will give us a name and address should we need it.* He also had two bottles of soda and six assorted candy bars.

Harm moved to a rack of maps and guidebooks just inside the door and began scanning them as if looking for something. Out of the corner of his eye, he watched the man as the clerk put his purchases in a brown paper bag. Medium height, broad shoulders, Butch-cut brown hair, light blue, short-sleeved tee shirt, faded light blue jeans.

As he reached the door, Harm moved slightly, bumping his back into the other man's chest. Immediately, he turned to the other man's face, just inches from his own. Long, horse face, dull eyes the color of his jeans, no more than twenty-five he guessed.

"Sorry," Harm told him.

"Okay," the young man mumbled and pushed out.

"Getcha something?" the clerk asked.

"No. Just looking, thanks," And he too stepped out in time to see the green sedan pull away and down the street going away from the city.

He'd make sure his people up ahead were alerted to the car and driver but Harm's cop gut told him that baby face and vacant stare didn't belong to a kidnapper and murderer.

His gut wrenched again and he turned back toward the parking lot, already plotting the strategy of the hunt.

Out of the corner of his eye, a shop door opening across the two-lane street caught his attention. Turning his head, he stopped short and literally did a double take.

She'd paused just outside the door, zipping her fanny pack closed with one hand and juggling her sunglasses and a brown paper sack in the other.

Heart pumping, he dashed across the pavement, earning an angry honk and the traditional gesture as he narrowly avoided a car coming from the other direction.

By the time he reached her, Elgin had slid her dark glasses over those deep eyes, her face a calm mask.

As he grabbed her by the shoulders, perhaps a bit more roughly than he'd intended, relief and anger welled up inside him. Harm literally didn't know whether to kiss her or turn her over his knee and spank her.

"Where the hell have you been?" he demanded.

With a quick shake, Elgin slipped from his grasp.

"Don't touch me," she shot back.

"I asked you a question."

"In the grocery store, if you must know." She jerked her head behind her. "I needed a few things."

He could tell from her voice they were headed for another screaming match but right then, he didn't care.

"Why the hell didn't you tell me you were leaving...where you were going?"

"Stop treating me like a child," she fumed, her voice rising in anger and frustration. "I'm perfectly capable of crossing the street by myself and counting my change."

"Then stop acting like a child. A spoiled, stupid child at that. And why didn't you go out the front? The waitress told me she thought you'd gone to the powder room."

Instantly, the anger disappeared, her body sagging slightly. She sighed deeply and looked down at the sidewalk between them.

"Because," she answered in a quiet little voice, "I was afraid...afraid someone might be watching, waiting. I knew that if anyone was there, they'd think I'd gone to the ladies' room and I could slip out the side door and then sneak back and check out the parking lot and street without being seen. It was silly, I know, but...well..."

It had been silly and potentially very dangerous for her to risk running around, even for a moment, by herself. But it had also been very clever to think of using the side door for her escape.

"Well," he relented a little but still trying to sound stern, "please just don't do it again. When I realized you were gone, I..." the words died in his throat but not before she seized on them.

"You were what?" Her head tilted quizzically to one side and her whole body moved toward him a little.

"Nothing," he growled, now not wanting to own up to any personal feelings he might have had. "Let's just get out of here."

Turning, he felt her hand on his wrist, her skin warm and soft but the muscles tense underneath.

"You were *what*?" she repeated, and he imagined those beautiful eyes narrowed to thoughtful, inquisitive slits. And he knew also he wouldn't get away with anything but the truth.

"I was worried," he practically spit. "Okay?"

The muscles in her hand relaxed and she stared up at him for several long seconds.

"You...were worried?" Surprise dripped off her words, not an acid, cynical tone but one of almost childlike wonder. It both excited and annoyed him.

"Of course," he tried to wiggle out. "Your boss is paying me a lot of money to keep you in one piece for three months. Wouldn't look very good to lose you the first day."

"Oh," she answered simply, her hand dropping back to her side. Without another word, she moved away, stopping at the curb only long enough to check the road in both directions and then heading directly back to the SUV.

Damn it!

He should be roaring mad at her. Stuck in a godforsaken, dinky-ass, wide spot in the road to nowhere, not a clue where they were headed, with this foul tempered, bubble-headed nut job...for three months no less...who'd just scared the shit out of him and made him look like a jerk in front of his best agents. Why he hadn't spanked her on sight he didn't know.

Yet, after everything, with a single word and that wounded look, she'd managed not only to undo his rage but make him feel guilty as well. And his stomach was killing him.

"Damn," he muttered as he started back across the street, "it's only day one."

* * * * *

It had been coming on gradually, lurking like a stalking predator waiting its chance to strike. He'd tried to ignore it, force it away but it had continued its slow, inevitable march and he knew now for sure. He was going to be sick.

Never prone to car sickness, even as a child, the combination of the huge, greasy meal, the anger and adrenaline of her vanishing act and the increasingly steep, winding road had converged and descended on him.

Terrific, he mused, not only did I take the bait about breakfast, but she knew about this lousy snake road. She made me look like an idiot and now she gets the satisfaction of watching me heave as well.

Get off it, stupid, another voice piped up in his head. Sure, she dared you to take on that Godzilla-killer snack, but you're the one who fell for it. And you should have known by the scenery and the climbing road you were headed into the mountains. What did you expect? An eight-lane super highway? Granted, she might be a bitch, but you're a jerk so I guess we're even all around.

"There's a rest area up here on the right," she told him without looking at him. "I'd like to stop, please." They were the first words she'd spoken since the sidewalk in French Creek.

"Sure," he responded, trying to sound casual but secretly overjoyed. If he could get to the restroom, at least he wouldn't have to pull off the road and put up with her smirking.

Slowing the SUV into the large, empty lot, he parked in a spot directly in front of the small restroom building. His stomach rumbled like an active volcano but he still had to play it cool. Waiting as she retrieved her paper bag and a blanket from the back seat, they exited.

"I'm going to sit over there on the grass," she nodded to her left, "under the trees."

"Okay. I'll be right back. Don't go wandering off."

Thankfully, he had the men's room to himself. Kneeling on the surprisingly clean but chilly cement floor, he leaned over the toilet and stuck his finger down his throat. A gag and the volcano erupted.

In about five minutes, shaken and slightly dizzy but the load in his gut lifted, Harm came back out into the bright sunshine, slipping his dark glasses on, as much to hide his pale face and red watery eyes as for protection from the sun.

She'd spread the blanket just under the shade of the towering trees but facing out on a vista of pine-carpeted mountains and foothills rolling back toward the flat farmland stretching to meet pale blue, cloudless sky at the horizon.

"This is a beautiful spot," he remarked as he sat down on the small blanket, his leg only about six inches from her.

"It is," she agreed, reaching into the bag beside her. "But you'll probably enjoy it more with these." She handed him a plastic quart bottle and a small box. "Those little pink pills really do relieve the nausea and the seltzer will help settle your queasy stomach."

"How long have you known?" he asked, surprised by her gifts but braced for the razzing he felt sure would come.

"I didn't. Not for sure anyway. But after that Country Breakfast and knowing what this road is like...well, actually I expected you'd be sick before this."

She pulled her legs up, circled them with her arms, set her chin on her knees and considered him for a few silent moments.

"I didn't actually think you'd order it after you read what it came with," she said slowly, "and after you did, I thought for sure, even as big as you are, you couldn't, wouldn't finish it."

A smile lifted the corners of her mouth a little.

"After you did, you looked, as Mimi, my little Jewish friend would say, like you were about to *plotz*. You know, explode from overeating. When you got up to go to the men's room, I thought maybe you were going to be sick then."

The smile disappeared.

"I...I felt sort of responsible so I figured the least I could do would be to get you something for the indigestion. I didn't want to say anything to you because I didn't want to embarrass you about the breakfast. Make you think I was rubbing it in. I thought I'd run across to the store and be back before you missed me. Then, if you did start to feel bad I could just whip out the tablets and seltzer and tell you I always carry them into the mountains, just in case. I even thought of suggesting we lay over in French Creek until you were feeling better but..."

"But I came charging at you like an angry bull," he finished, popping a couple of the pink tablets in his mouth, chewing them and washing them down with the bubbly seltzer.

"No, you were right. I should have waited and at least told you where I was going. I could have told you I just needed something. It never occurred to me that you might worry."

An apology. Not the words exactly, but the sound of her voice, her body language.

Stunned, he took several sips of water and turned his head as if studying the view.

It was totally unexpected and she'd caught him off guard. Again. Why did it seem that just when he thought he had her figured out, she'd turn into something else?

"I guess I shouldn't have yelled at you," he admitted without looking at her. "I should have known you were okay. I mean, I didn't see anyone following us and I checked the rearview mirror pretty carefully."

He turned back to face her then.

"Almost as carefully as you did."

Her smile, warm and genuine, lit up her whole face, even, he imagined, those beautiful eyes still hidden behind the sunglasses.

"Was I that obvious?"

Almost in spite of himself, he smiled back.

"Only to someone paying close attention. For the most part, you look cool, calm and collected."

Elgin laughed, triggering a pleasant tingle from somewhere south of his belt buckle through his entire body.

"I wish. Inside, I'm just one raw, exposed nerve ending."

"You hide it very well."

"Something I learned as a child but I wonder sometimes if it's a blessing or a curse. All I know right now is that I just want to sit in the sun and read and not think ever again, about anything. I'm so tired of being scared all the time."

Without thinking, he laid his fingers gently on her arm. Instantly, the tingle became a lightning strike, welding him to her.

"You don't have to worry about being scared," he assured her. "You have my word on that."

* * * * *

"Take the next off-ramp," she told him, a small note of excitement in her voice. "State Route 2. At the light, make a left and pull into the vista point."

Doing as she directed, Harm pulled the SUV off the road and into the parking lot of a scenic overlook. Elgin jumped out of the car almost before he could get it stopped. She almost ran to a low rock wall running around the lip of the flat area.

"I love this place," she sighed as he came up beside her. "Isn't it gorgeous?"

Below them, the same textured green-black carpet of pines that had surrounded them since they'd left French Creek, flowed down to the very shore of a huge lake, lying in a bowl of rugged mountains like a polished sapphire. The sun, hanging in a cloudless pale denim sky, sparkled off the calm surface like a spotlight on the facets of a perfectly cut gem.

"It's called Haunted Moon Lake," she said. "Just beyond that curved point over there, off to the left, is where we're going. Spirit Cove. The western side of the lake has been developed and has gotten quite ritzy. Several very trendy, upscale little tourist trap villages. But Spirit Cove is the only thing on this side of the lake that passes for civilization. We'll pick up some supplies and then the cabin's about another ten miles up the road."

She seemed giddy, almost childlike. Far removed from the cool, sophisticated bit-…woman, he knew.

And the scene was lovely. It reminded him of the place where he and Jeanne had spent that last…

Stop it, he barked internally, unnerved by the unexpected and unwelcome bit of flotsam dredged up from his memory, momentarily catching his mind and his heart on its sharp point.

That time, that place, everything about that lay gone and far away. Buried. Only the trees and the water and the sky had momentarily brought them back. With an effort, he forced the thought back down and slammed the mental compartment shut again.

The place she'd pointed to from the lookout had seemed very close, but the two-lane blacktop road snaked and meandered casually down the mountain, the lake playing peek-a-boo with them through the pines. It took more than a half-hour for the SUV to crawl out of the woods and suddenly into a large open space between the water and the lake. A small sign, painted yellow letters carved into brown wood announced, "Welcome to Spirit Cove."

Bigger than French Creek, it sported rows of little shops on the left hand side of the road while the lake and snug-looking vacation cottages, small, old- fashioned motels and open public beaches clung to their right. Several cars were parked along the street in front of the shops and the traffic had swelled to perhaps ten cars creeping through as the tourists rubbernecked, cameras and children's heads stuck out the windows.

"Spirit Cove Mercantile is up on the left," Elgin directed, "right after the Skywood Lodge. It used to be a local bar. You know, beer on tap, whiskey out of a jug under the bar and a pool table. Not a bad place 'til the tourists started coming. Next thing you know, the owner's stocking white wine and imported beer. Stuck a sofa in front of the fireplace and got cable for the television. Now, instead of baseball scores and football, you get stock prices and golf. Yuck!" She shuttered in disgust.

Harm grinned. "I dunno. I would have said you were definitely more white wine spritzer than beer. And I can't imagine you risking breaking a nail playing pool."

"Funny," she shot back, her smile and teasing tone matching his, "I would have said you were Chardonnay and golf myself. Even in blue jeans, you still have that faint but distinctly unpleasant stench of Yuppie superiority about you. Of course, I could be wrong. You might just be a plain, garden variety, obnoxious alpha male."

Precisely the sort of barb she'd been needling him with since they'd met, now, devoid of venom, it seemed actually sort of funny.

They passed the bar and turned immediately into a small parking lot. A single story, house-sized building, with pine log exterior and picture windows crammed with merchandise, sat wedged snuggly against a steep cliff. Along the entire front of the building ran a wide, deep covered porch, complete with soda vending machines and an assortment of ladder-back rockers. Above the porch, a small sign announced, "Spirit Cove Mercantile" in red lettering across a bright white background.

Inside, Harm gazed in surprise at the amount of merchandise the deceptively small building held. To the right, aisles of groceries from snack foods to staples ran the entire length of the store, big refrigerator cases taking up the back wall. Beer, soda, wine and dairy products of all kinds sat side by side. To his left, the aisles combined drug, hardware, camping and marine supply store.

"Elgin, my love!" shrieked a blur racing from the back of the store. In an instant, she became wrapped in pale blue arms and darker blue designer slacks, her face disappearing in a huge, wet kiss.

"Oh my God, El," the voice continued, letting her up for air, "why didn't you tell me you were coming? You look gorgeous. How long are you going to stay? Are you working on a book? I hope you're staying for the Fourth. Fireworks are going to be absolutely fabulous this year. Helped plan the program myself. Well, you've absolutely got to stay. That's all there is to it. I'm having a little get together at my place and when I tell people Gillian Shelby's going to be there…well, it will be *the* event of the season although up here that's not really saying much. Oh, and I just got a whole rack of your books in and I'll absolutely die of gratitude if you sign a few. Give you an extra ten-percent off anything in the house. So how have you been?"

Elgin laughed. "I'm fine, Marty, just fine. But give me a chance to catch my breath. I just got here."

"Oh, of course, I know. You must be exhausted after that drive. Supplies, right?"

"Uh-huh. I'm just going to pick up a few things now but we'll be staying the whole summer. Right through Labor Day."

Pale white hands with a trace of pink polish clapped together. "Labor Day? My God, that's absolutely wonderful! We'll go picnicking and take 'The Belle' over to that alpine road company, Vegas and see a show and…did you say 'we'?"

"Yes, Marty." She pointed to Harm, standing about a foot behind him. "This is Campbell Harm. He's my secretary. I'm working on a book and he's helping me."

Marty turned a round, pale face to Harm. Only then did he realize Marty was a man. Well, perhaps man might be too strong a term. Male. Probably. Pale blond, almost white hair hanging in a sort of shag around his moon face, pale gray eyes, thin nose, unnaturally pink cheeks and full lips in that ghostly body.

He put out a long hand and gave Harm a limp shake, running those eyes up and down him like an expert appraiser of horseflesh.

"I thought your secretary was a lady named Martha," he said suspiciously.

"That's right," Elgin agreed pleasantly. "Martha Jackson. I'm surprised you remember her. Well, Martha is a city girl. Hates all this fresh air, and pine trees give her hives. She's taking the summer off and Campbell kindly offered to fill in."

Marty sighed. "I suppose he's unbearably straight?" Disappointment coated his words like a child who's just discovered there's no more chocolate ice cream.

"Sorry, darling," she sympathized, putting her fingertips on his arm, "Gillian Shelby likes her men a little kinky, but definitely straight."

"Oh well," he sighed. "You get on with your shopping. I've got to go over and stand behind my new cashier to make sure he doesn't sell the cash register. Morgan Brantly's son, Byron. Home from college. Begged me to give him a summer job. Great ass, but if he were any dumber, he'd be getting plant food through a tube twice a week." Marty rolled his eyes, made a martyr's face and walked away.

Elgin grabbed a small cart and began slowly going through the aisles. When they were sufficiently out of earshot, Harm leaned down.

"What was that?" he asked in a conspiratorial whisper.

"Martin Van Scoyk. Marty to practically everyone. He owns the place. Don't worry. He's harmless."

"He sounded like my great aunt Clara at Christmas. I was waiting for him to pinch your cheek."

"That's just his way. Marty and I go way back and he's just glad to see me, that's all. Besides, Marty lives over the top. You'll get used to him."

"Don't bet on it."

At the check-out counter, Marty scooted Byron out of the way as Harm reached for his wallet. Elgin beat him to it.

"Be a love and put this on my account, Marty, would you? And while you're ringing up, I'll sign those books."

Once more in the SUV, the supplies stowed safely in the back, Harm turned and glared at her. "What was that all about?"

"What?"

"First you pay the restaurant check and now you have 'The Fairy Prince' put everything on your tab here."

"So?"

"So, I'm perfectly capable of paying my own bills."

Tickled, Elgin giggled.

"What's so funny?" he demanded.

"You are. That is so typically male."

"It's embarrassing," he responded, his anger rising. "I don't like being embarrassed. Especially in public places and especially by a woman."

"You don't need me to embarrass you," she told him caustically, "you do a bang-up job of that yourself. Besides, the money you use comes out of the money Sheila's paying you, which comes out of her share of the money I make writing, so I don't see what the difference is."

"The difference is, what the hell do you suppose people are thinking when they see you paying our bills."

Elgin's smile returned. "They'll think you're a big, dumb jock, gigolo. The women are green with envy and so, I can assure you, are the men. I can also assure you that Spirit Cove's grapevine will not lose a moment getting this tasty little piece of gossip on the wire. By tomorrow noon, everyone within fifty miles will know that city lady who writes those dirty books is keeping a man at her place for the summer. Marty will probably have to re-stock my books a dozen times before Labor Day."

Harm blinked in disbelief. He'd been so concerned with his trap, he hadn't considered anything else. Of course, that would be the first conclusion people were going to leap to. Calling himself her secretary wouldn't help. In fact, it sounded lame even to him. People were naturally going to assume...

Oh swell, he thought as he turned the key, *what else?*

Chapter Eight

"Get ready to make a right up here," she pointed. "Just beyond that wooden bus shelter up there you'll see a sign that says 'Moon Lake Road'. Slow down and be careful or you'll miss it."

Harm slowed a bit and watched as the little wooden lean-to loomed on his right. Almost immediately, he saw a row of about ten mailboxes and the asphalt branching off the two-lane road they were on. Nailed to a tree, a handmade wooden sign, the white paint faded and peeling, announced, "Moon Lake Road. Private. Slow."

As they drove, the road dipped gently toward the lake, smaller branches of asphalt and gravel and even dirt leading off.

"There's a gate across the road up here. Stop so I can get out and open it, please."

A metal gate materialized from barbed wire on either side of the road. Elgin hopped out, unhooked the gate and walked it to the side of the road. With Harm through, she closed it and got back in the SUV.

Another quarter of a mile and around a sharp bend. The road ended in a large open space. Just beyond, the lake shimmered like dark blue glass, the pine trees growing almost to its edge.

"Well, this is it."

"Your friend called it 'a shack'," Harm commented, looking around at the beautiful setting and rustic house up a short stone path from where they were parked.

"Sheila thinks anything smaller than the White House and decorated less lavishly than Buckingham Palace is a 'shack'," she laughed.

They moved to the back of the SUV to start unloading.

"Actually, it was built as a honeymoon cottage and summer retreat in the Thirties. They were just about the first people to build up here. They named it 'Moon's End'. Named the road too. Loved the place so much, they paid a fortune to run a sewer line down from the road all the way here so they wouldn't be flushing into the lake. Come on, let me show you around."

Boots crunching on the gravel, they went up two small steps to the broad, green shingled porch, much like the one in front of the grocery store except that instead of vending machines and rockers, there was only an old wooden porch swing, hanging from the roof by two hardy-looking chains. The clapboard siding that covered the two-story building had weathered down, not to a chilly gray but a warm coffee brown. Above the rough-hewn door, a smiling Man-in-the-Moon gazed down on them, "Moon's End" carved below it.

"I called the propane company about two weeks ago," Elgin told him as she fumbled with the key and her grocery box. "They assured me they'd fill the tank before we arrived and put us on their weekly route, but we better make sure, just the same. Their driver, Les, has a special little truck he drives to the really out-of-the-way places like this where they can't get in with the big truck. Of course, they charge an arm and a leg for this 'extra service,' but until someone gets around to running gas and/or electricity up here, they know they've got us over a barrel."

Pushing down the big, old-fashioned metal handle with her thumb, Elgin pushed the door open wide and stepped in as Harm followed.

He let out a long, low whistle of approval as his head swiveled in all directions. Prepared for a one room wooden cabin with a dirt floor, the reality literally bowled him over. The main room where they stood was big, at least fifty by fifty he guessed. Windows took up most of the wall to his left, blinds covered by lacy sheer curtains covering them. In the corner, a floor to ceiling rock fireplace loomed over the room, a hearth tall enough to sit comfortably on and an opening big enough to roast a pig in. Before it sat a simple wood frame and dark blue cushion sofa, simple end tables and matching pine coffee table. Glass doors made up the rest of the wall, opening he could see to a broad wooden deck facing out on the lake, which filled the view like a living mural. To his right, an open kitchen and small dining table. Just off the door, narrow wooden steps ascended to the second floor.

Elgin grinned as they moved to the kitchen and set down their boxes. "I'm glad you approve."

"It's…it's beautiful."

"Let's get the bags and I'll show you the upstairs."

With their luggage retrieved from the SUV, Elgin led the way. Six steps rose steeply up the well, making a sharp left turn at a slightly larger landing and six more, equally steep steps, put them in a hall running the length of the building.

"This is the master suite," she said, pushing open the door. It took up at least half the upper floor, a huge four-poster bed dominating the room. A wall of windows looked out over the lake and trees.

With a grunt, she dropped her bags on the floor by the bed, carefully laying her laptop on the plump patchwork quilt. "There are two bathrooms which is nice. You're over here."

Directly across the hall, she opened a second door and stood aside for him. Not much smaller than the master suite, the only difference he could see, the scale of the furniture and that his windows looked back on the pine forests instead of the lake.

"Bathroom's through there." She nodded to a closed door on the right. "No closets but the wardrobe and bureau should give you all the room you need. House's been closed up since last year but everything, including the linen, should be clean. If you need anything, give me a holler."

"Thanks."

Elgin turned to leave, pausing at the door.

"Oh, and in case you're wondering," she grinned maliciously, pointing her index finger straight down, "both bedroom doors are *very* sturdy and bolt from the inside. See you downstairs."

Funny, he thought as he dropped his two bags on the bed, when she wasn't being a total bitch, Elgin Collier wasn't too bad to be around.

Unzipping the larger of his two bags, the first things Harm retrieved were his cell phone and holstered automatic. He punched the "on" button, afraid for a moment that the isolated area might have cut off the signal. But the screen came almost instantly to life. By now, the GPS beacon had told his people they were stopped. Later tonight, he'd call and set up a regular schedule of check-in times and begin the flow of necessary information. He already had one name to be checked on, Martin Van Scoyk, and there would undoubtedly be others.

During the day, they'd remain hidden in the bureau under his clothes. At night, he'd put them on the bedside stand, the tiny green light of the recharging stand marking its location, the automatic at the ready beside it.

The bathroom, while large, seemed comfortable. Sunlight from windows on either side of the medicine chest and heavy white pedestal sink let in lots of light. Toilet and a big cast-iron, blue and white claw-foot bathtub and shower, ringed by a Thirties style shower curtain. He didn't need to be an expert to know it was genuine.

Downstairs, all the blinds had been pulled up and the windows opened, washing away the stale, closed-up smell, the air replacing it crisp and clean as freshly washed sheets. As he moved across the room, he noted that the boxes had been emptied, the faint hum of the refrigerator the only sound.

Harm stopped at the French door, his hand on the knob, the tempo of his heart speeding up a little.

She'd changed out of her jeans and turtleneck into a skinny little white tank top and a pair of bright red cut-off shorts. With the emphasis definitely on *short*. Lying back slightly on a redwood chaise, the fat emerald and white striped cushion making a perfect backdrop.

No denying it, he heard that voice in his head again, that's one good-looking woman.

Shaking his head a little, he turned the knob and stepped onto the sunny deck, deliberately moving past her to the railing and scanning the scene before him. With her sunglasses on, he couldn't tell if she was awake or not, but he didn't want to risk her noticing that she'd had a definite, if unnerving effect on him.

Trying to ignore the discomfort behind his fly, he concentrated on the view in front of him, not in back.

From the flat parking area, a worn dirt path followed the gentle slope of the land to a small sandy patch of beach where aquamarine water, clear as glass, lapped quietly, spreading itself outward to a blue topaz and finally the mysterious, rich sapphire of deep water. Thick pine forest hugged the lakeshore as far as he could see except right here. And there didn't seem to be any other houses on this side of the barbed wire and gate.

An ideal spot. The view would give him an excuse to carry his binoculars and with them, he could sweep the entire lake for ten miles around. Later, he'd go hiking in the woods around the cabin to locate hiding places for motion activated cameras and microphones.

"'Come into my parlor,' said the spider to the fly."

"What?"

Her voice startled him and the remnants of his erection caught between his body and the railing.

Shit!

"What?" he repeated, turning his head but not his body.

"Did you say something?"

"No. Why?"

"I thought I heard you say you'd seen a spider or something."

"Just mumbling to myself."

"Oh."

"This is a great view," he commented, forcing his eyes away from her. She didn't have a bra under that tank top. Almost in spite of himself, he wondered if she had on panties under those shorts. "How much of it is yours?"

A blur of movement made him turn his head just in time to see Elgin swing her legs off the chaise and answer his unspoken question about her underwear. Another flash of heat surged up from his re-awakened cock and its growing size made his jeans more and more uncomfortable.

She came up beside him, casually brushing her arm against his as she leaned her forearms on the railing and bent forward, pulling the neck of her tank top out just enough to give him a quick peek of round, white breast before he managed to jerk his wayward eyeballs back to the water.

"My lawyer tells me I have about two hundred acres, give or take, but that doesn't really mean much to me." Elgin tilted her chin up a little and the simple beauty of her smooth, freshly washed skin, plain except for a natural pink glow on those lovely cheekbones struck him, as if he'd never really seen her before.

"Actually though," she continued, "it's easier for me to remember that I own everything from the gate down to the water's edge and from 'Eagle's Rock,' that sharp, pointy little spit of land out there with the gnarled old pine tree at the end, all the way down to 'Robber's Roost'." Her outstretched hand made a line from left to right, her bare arm resting for a fleeting moment against his shirt as she pointed.

He took a deep breath and felt his body filling up with her sweet, warm, sensual musk, wrapped in the tangy, crisp air and the faint scent of wild flowers.

"Oh look," she cried excitedly, pointing out toward the water, "it's 'The Belle'."

Squinting, he could make out a small white box with moving sides and two tall black chimney's puffing out a billow of white smoke behind it.

"What's a bell?"

"The Belle of the Lake," she responded merrily. "It's a wonderful old paddle-wheel steamer. Nowadays of course, it just takes people out on the lake for sightseeing cruises but originally, it was the workhorse of the whole area. Built in the eighteen hundreds in St. Louis as a small river trader but when they discovered gold out here, an enterprising gentleman named Crockett saw the potential profits in a steamer for the lake. So he went back east, bought her, had her disassembled, crated up and shipped overland by wagon and reassembled here. The only place for a landing on this side of the lake was at what's now Spirit Cove and on the western side, Crockett's Landing. From there, he managed to carve a little spur railroad to hook up with the mainline to points west. Mostly carried miners and timber and supplies to the camps and gold and silver back. For ten years, virtually anything that moved on the lake, moved on 'The Belle'.

"After the mines played out and the timber all got cut down, she fell on hard times, mostly just eking out a hand-to-mouth existence for her owners. Then people re-discovered the place in the Twenties and the Thirties. Started building summer homes and coming up here to camp and fish. Crockett's Landing changed its name to West Shore and legalized gambling and the rest, as they say, is history. Water sports in the summer, skiing in the winter and casino hotels the year around.

"And just like Crockett before him, some enterprising young man bought 'Belle,' put a new coat of paint on her, polished her brass and sent her back on the lake to haul tourists. In fact, you and I will have to go out on her. You really can't appreciate the lake unless you're on it."

"Sounds like fun," he agreed, trying to ignore the growing problem in his jeans. The feel of her ass through her thin cotton shorts as they rubbed against his thigh wasn't helping.

"Okay," she began, turning back to him. Abruptly she stopped, seeming to search his face.

"You better go up and take a shower and change into something else," she told him. "You're sweating like a pig."

* * * * *

She could feel his heat through his shirt as she pretended to brush her arm accidentally against his chest and while he'd pushed himself against the wooden railing, she'd glimpsed the bulge pressing firmly on his fly. Not satisfied, she'd turned slightly so that her ass touched the hard muscle of his thigh.

After the long car ride, the quick shower had refreshed her and as she'd stood toweling herself in front of the bathroom mirror, she'd suddenly imagined his naked body tight against her own. She wanted that strong, handsome, arrogant man but not until she'd played with him. Made him suffer for his bullying, overbearing behavior. On his knees, begging for her favor, kissing her pussy and making her come.

Her own heat had risen then, coursing through her with a fiery demand that she take him as quickly as possible. That he fill her and quench the longing that she had only so suddenly become aware of.

Quickly, she finished drying herself, lingering perhaps a moment longer than necessary as she moved the towel between her legs. And then into the bedroom where her bags still sat on the bed. Without thought to bra and panties, she slipped on a pair of red shorts, the legs flared and cuffed just enough to give a glimpse of dark curls and white skin if she moved just so. A thin white tank top with a scooped neck completed the outfit. Revealing only what she wanted him to see, leaving his imagination to finish the torture for her.

Downstairs, she'd put the groceries away, popping the top on a cold bottle of hard cola and then settling herself nonchalantly on the chaise. The trap baited, she had only to wait.

Now, beside her at the rail, she could hear his breathing, labored and heavier than normal, feel his mounting desire. If she turned around, she'd be in his arms.

She did want him. Trapped in the car all those hours, the look, the smell, the imagined feel of him, had taunted her. Right there and yet not. Seeming to ignore her while his whole body seemed to entice her, silently telegraphing his own need. They'd passed the game playing...from here on everything was for keeps.

A tickle of wet heat rippled up from her pussy, as strong yet as hidden as the fist in his jeans.

With a great yawn, she stepped back to the chaise, stretching out, her arms at her side, her crossed ankles keeping the legs of her shorts open just a fraction.

"You really ought to shower and change clothes," she commented, watching him intently from behind her sunglasses. "Maybe get something cold to drink. Might cool you off...a little."

"Maybe I'll do that," he murmured.

"I know it did me a world of good," she continued, pretending calm disinterest but actually determined to throw as much gasoline as possible on the smoldering heat. "Getting out of those heavy clothes. Letting that cool, refreshing water splash all over your hot, sticky body. The sweet, warm mountain air on your wet, naked skin. A towel rubbing briskly over you, making your flesh all pink and healthy."

Carelessly, she raised her arms and stretched again, folding them over her head. The movement pulled up the hem of her shirt, showing creamy skin and pulling her breasts up.

He needed a cold shower now.

"Yeah, well, that sounds good," he mumbled. "I think I'll go up and do that now."

"Could I ask you to do me a favor first?"

"What?"

"I forgot my suntan lotion. It's on the kitchen counter. Would you bring it to me, please? I'll get deep-fried without it."

"Sure."

Dashing inside, he grabbed the plastic tube and walked quickly back outside.

"Here." He held it out to her.

"Could I ask you one more little favor, please?"

Standing there, he couldn't hide his cock. God, practically in her face. In her mouth.

"What?"

"Would you please put some on my neck and shoulders? I can't reach back there." She scooted to one side making room for him beside her and turning her back to him.

Shit, why not? At least this way he didn't have to watch her watching him.

Cool and white, the lotion squirted into his palm and he began to rub it on her pale, surprisingly warm, soft skin. And no doubt sweet-tasting. His cock twitched uncomfortably.

"Hmmm," she purred, "that feels heavenly. You have very gentle hands for such a big, burly guy."

"And you have very soft skin."

The feel of him made her flesh tingle and the heat between her legs spread in ever increasing waves through her body. His warm breath on the back of her neck made her dizzy.

She felt his hands move down to the hem of her shirt and slide up her back, his thumbs running up the ridge of her backbone, his big open hands covering her like delicate wings. A tremor ran through her.

"I want you," he growled in her ear. "I think I've wanted you since the first moment I saw you."

"You called me a bitch," she reminded him, turning to look at him over her shoulder.

"And you called me a bastard," he grinned. "I guess we deserve each other."

She grinned too. "I guess we do at that."

In one fluid motion, he turned her, sliding her tank top off and dropping it on the deck.

Pausing, he drank in the picture of her creamy body against the striped cushion, like a rare alabaster statue laid in a perfect, velvet nest. The dark, pinkish-brown of her nipples stood erect on the peaks of her soft, white breasts, not huge but a pleasant handful.

She could tell by the expression on his face, the look in his eyes, that what he saw pleased him and it pleased her to know that she hadn't disappointed him. Carefully, she reached up and undid the two small buttons at the front of his polo shirt and tugged gently on the bottom edge. In a moment, it had joined her shirt on the deck.

A dusting of soft, dark brown hair covered the area between his nipples, coming together in a narrow line down his chest and stomach, disappearing beneath the waistband of his jeans. She'd never cared for "hairy-chested" men, but the feel of his down under her fingers aroused her in a way she'd never known.

"Come here," she commanded lightly, wiggling her index finger at him.

Dutifully, he leaned forward, their lips meeting in a hard, passionate kiss, filled with fire and lust and need. His hands found her nipples, caressing them, fondling her tender, swollen peaks. A startled cry escaped her but he stopped it with his exploring tongue.

Fumbling with the brass fastener at the top of his jeans, she felt him suck in his stomach a little so that she could get a better hold. A moment later, his zipper fell and her soft, smooth hands were gliding along his skin as she pulled his jeans and boxers down toward his knees. He stood up to step out of them, stopping for her appraisal.

"Very nice," she told him. "Very nice, indeed."

"I'm glad you approve," he answered, settling back down as he brought his hand to the snap at the waist of her shorts. "You're very beautiful."

They completed the heap of clothing as he slid back beside her and took her in his arms. His thick, erect cock pressed itself against her thigh, the heat of him like an iron against her flesh.

"You'd better be careful," she whispered between kisses. "I don't know about you, but I burn like cheap steak...especially parts of me that don't usually see the sun."

"I know just how to handle that," he replied, pecking the tip of her nose and sitting up.

"What are you up to?"

"Just lie back and relax."

Taking the bottle of sunscreen, he squeezed another large dollop into his palm and moved to the foot of the chaise. Sitting down, he picked up her feet and began massaging the thick, white cream into her sensitive skin, beginning with her toes and moving gradually up the ball and arch to the top and ankle. She shivered with a sensual tingle that prickled over her entire body.

His hands continued leisurely up her legs, pausing only for more sunscreen and to gently kiss the top of her knees as his hands moved underneath.

"Did you know that the back of a woman's knees are among the most erogenous zones on her body?" he whispered hoarsely, his fingertips just barely touching her skin, his hot breath raising goose bumps.

"I...I didn't know that..." she answered, barely able to breathe.

"Uh-huh," he continued, "and if you nibble just so on the kneecaps..."

She felt his lips and the edges of his teeth around the bones, nipping and sucking on the thin flesh, his tongue marking a zigzag path across the top. A tremor of unexpected pleasure rippled through her. No one had ever played with her like this before, the sensation both whimsical and sexy.

Up her legs, covering her skin with the lotion, her rising heat under his hands fueling the fire in his own body. But he wanted…needed for this to be the best, most intense sex she'd ever known. To raise her to heights she'd never known before or would ever know again. Except with him.

She'd parted her legs for him and he saw the pink slit of her pussy surrounded by short black curls and skin like fine china. It glistened, wet and inviting and his cock strained to it. Gently, carefully, he bent his head down and kissed her hot, engorged clit.

Like an electric jolt it shot through her, expected but more powerful, more thrilling than she'd imagined. Closing her eyes, she bit her lip a little, not quite stifling the small cry of physical pleasure that escaped her.

But she got only the kiss as he moved up her body, his slick, smooth hands gliding effortlessly over the ridge of her pubic bone, across and around her stomach and thighs. They grabbed her ass, kneading the firm flesh and pushing her pussy to his burning cock. It struggled, trying to gain entry to her, but he wouldn't allow it. Not yet anyway.

As his hands attacked her breasts and nipples once more, his mouth traveled up to her neck, nipping and biting the soft flesh, feeling her squirm beneath him.

Pinwheels of fire danced in her blood and her pussy screamed for him.

"What are you waiting for?" she mumbled anxiously, putting her hands on his ass and pushing down.

"For you," he replied, moving back down to her pussy.

Pinning her thighs securely, he took a last look at her clit, swollen with blood heated by desire. Desire for him, mirrored by his own cock, full of desire for her. She filled him with the outrageous lust Hefner's forbidden magazine dolls had inspired in the days of his supercharged, hormone dominated teens. Except she was real and here. For him.

The sensations engulfed him. A touch of short curls and damp, silky skin. The scent of sunscreen and aroused female musk. Sweet, hot, wet pussy on his tongue. Blood racing and pounding in his ears, keeping time to the primal beat in his cock and sac as they ached for their own release.

He ran the flat of his tongue over the whole area, pulling back her lips and exposing her entrance. Reaching her clit again, he tickled it with the point of his tongue, feeling her writhe under him, squealing with delight.

Her pleasure fired his own, his pace quickening. Tiny moans rose rapidly to cries of ecstasy as she crested, her juices flooding out for him to capture and savor, her body clenched in the grip of its own passion.

Having satisfied her, at least for the moment, his barely controlled need pushed past endurance and he raised himself, bringing his iron hard cock to the mouth of her glistening pussy.

"Uh-uh," she giggled, moving her fingers to cover herself. "I want to watch."

"What?" he answered incredulously.

"I want to watch you come."

"And just how do you propose we do that on this narrow little chaise?"

"Simple. You stay right where you are and play with yourself."

He snorted. "Now why in God's name would I want to jack off when I'm inches from a warm, desirable woman with the most beautiful pussy I've ever seen."

Her fingertips moved across her wet clit. Raising them to his face, she brushed them lightly along his lips. "Because I want you to," she purred. "Because I want to watch your cock and your body and your face when you come. And because it would make me even hornier than I am right now. So much that I'd want you so badly I'd probably do *anything* you asked."

Torn, he hesitated. His cock blazed with the need of her. He had only to slide forward a few inches and he'd be home. She wouldn't deny him, he knew. And lots more sex awaited them. This silly whim would be swept away on the riptide of passion and satisfaction he'd give her.

Still, that single word, "anything" held such delight, such promise…

Rising to his knees, he readjusted his position to give himself better balance as he hovered over her.

Squirting sunscreen in his hand, he wrapped his fingers around the head of his cock, the thick white lotion oozing out between them as his fist moved slowly down its length to his balls. The coolness of it did nothing to quench the fire roaring through him.

"Slowly," she ordered, her voice ragged.

Obediently, he slowed his tempo despite the complaint of his cock, eager for release. His hand traveled to his balls, caressing and separating them, showing them to her in all their fiery glory.

He watched her now, as caught up in her passion as his own. The tip of her tongue moved along her lips as his fingers traveled up and down his cock. Her breasts rose and fell in time to his shallow, noisy breathing. Ivory skin tinged pink with her internal heat, covered, like his cock, in a sheen of lotion and sweat. Those dark, hungry eyes, hypnotized by the rhythm of his writhing snake as he charmed it. And that beautiful pussy, pink and swollen and inflamed just by the sight of him.

The orgasm tore him, ripping a bellow that echoed in the still afternoon sunshine like something wild, spilling through the tall pines and out to the calm water. His fluid spurted out, splattering like lotion on her pussy and curls and sleek stomach.

Spent, he collapsed forward, covering her carefully, feeling her arms and lips and smooth flesh.

"You're beautiful," she mumbled. "So very beautiful."

"And you'd do anything for me?"

"Anything…"

Elgin frowned as she finished reading the scene for the third time since she'd completed it a little more than an hour ago. Vague dissatisfaction gnawed, although the exact cause eluded her. The opening gambit in these woodland sex games would set the tone for the rest of the book and somehow, this scene had failed to strike the right note with her. She knew what she wanted, but the right words just weren't coming to her.

Ah well, she sighed, shutting down her laptop and glancing at her bedside clock. The day had been long and tiring and she really had intended to take a long, relaxing bath as she'd told Harm when she'd retired upstairs. But the sight of her laptop on the little table in the corner of her bedroom had beckoned to her.

The clock gleamed after eleven now and time for bed. She'd deal with the book and Campbell Harm tomorrow.

Elizabeth Stewart

Chapter Nine

"I have a present for you," he told her as they sipped their coffee on the deck. The early sun filtered through the pines and the cloudless sky promised a beautiful day, but a chill hung in the air and they had both put on heavy overshirts before coming out.

"A present?" she repeated in mild surprise. "For me?"

"Uh-huh."

"It's not going to explode or anything, is it?"

"Nope," he grinned, sticking his fingers in his shirt pocket. "Here."

He opened his fist to reveal a beautiful gold locket, carved with a delicate Celtic knot and hung on a short, sturdy looking gold chain.

"Oh," Elgin gasped, completely shocked by the jewelry and the unexpected gesture. "It's...it's beautiful. But why?"

"Don't worry about it. Just take it." His open hand moved closer to her across the table.

Tentatively, she reached out and ran a finger over its surface, feeling the almost imperceptible design. "Not unless you tell me what the catch is."

"What makes you think there's a catch?"

"Because there's always a catch," she assured him.

"Suppose I told you I just wanted you to have it?"

"I'd ask how come you just happen to have a gold pendant on you?"

He looked into those deep, intelligent dark eyes and knew again she wouldn't settle for anything but the truth.

"It's a homing device," Harm sighed. "It gives off a signal." He held up his watch and punched one of the little buttons on the outer rim. Immediately, the numbers vanished and a tiny pulsing dot on a grid appeared. "I can track you anywhere in a two mile radius. That way, we don't have to spend every waking moment together. Give us both a little breathing room."

"And...and you honestly expect me to wear that...that electronic dog collar?" her voice hardened to steel.

"It is *not* a dog collar," he corrected, his own voice growing colder, "electronic or otherwise. It's a necessary precaution for your own safety. It weighs next to nothing, it's very attractive and if you'd stop being such a stubborn bitch, you'd wear it and be grateful I don't get a real collar and leash. And a muzzle while I'm at it."

"You stupid bastard..." she began but he stopped her.

"Look, wear the damn thing or don't," he growled, dropping it on the table in front of her. "It's no skin off my nose. Me? I'm gonna take my binoculars and go for a long walk. There's gotta be more to look at around here than your grumpy face." Pushing back his chair, he stood up, grabbed his field glasses from the table and stomped down the deck steps toward the woods on the other side of the parking area.

Fuming, Elgin picked up her coffee mug, slouched deep in her chair and considered both the situation and the pendant shining on the wood tabletop.

A homing device, she thought angrily. Disguised as a present...a beautiful piece of jewelry to flatter and trick her like some idiot six-year old. Well she'd show him! She'd throw it off the dock into the lake. He could listen to the fishes on his Dick Tracy watch and be damned.

Don't be silly, countered the rational part of her mind, it makes perfect sense. After all, you don't know that the stalker hasn't managed to follow you up here. It's a small enough safety measure to take. And it will give you a certain amount of privacy, freedom. That is why you came up here, isn't it? That and to write your book. You can even make the pendant a sort of 'love token' from the hero to the heroine. 'Keep me close to your heart' sort of thing.

Well, since you put it that way...

Elgin considered the small gold circle on the table. Very pretty, she admitted grudgingly. She didn't normally wear necklaces, but she could slip it under her clothes and no one would know she had it, including she surmised, even herself.

The sound of a twig snapping echoed through the trees like a gunshot, bringing her out of her mood. No doubt he'd walked off his pout, and she'd agree to wear the necklace as a safety precaution only.

She heard the bottom step creak and the thud of a heavy boot on the wooden stairs. Inexplicably, she felt glad that he'd decided to come back. Not that she'd missed him exactly...

An unfamiliar shape, large and heavy materialized, moving rapidly up the steps. In the instant she recognized Harm hadn't returned, a short, frightened yelp escaped her as she dropped her coffee mug and stood up, turning over her chair in the process.

He stopped dead, blinking in surprise at the sight of her.

"I...I'm sorry," he told her anxiously. "I...I didn't mean to startle you. I didn't realize anyone was here. Forgive me, please. Are you all right?" He took a step toward her and instinctively, Elgin backed away, almost tripping over the chair.

"Who...who are you?" Her voice, filled with panic, little more than a squeak.

"Chad Comstock," he replied. "I...I really didn't mean to break in like this. I'm sorry. I promise I'll leave. I just want to make sure you're okay."

Tall, lean and muscular, he stood blocking the stairs and the French doors. Black hair worn slightly shaggy, a square, rugged face, his eyes hidden behind dark glasses.

"What are you doing here? This is private property. Didn't you see the gate across the road?"

"I'm sorry. I climbed over the gate. I bought the Graeters' house, up by the road about eight months ago. I'm an artist." He held up a large sketchbook and wooden box she hadn't noticed before.

"This is just about the only place a fella can get down to the lake near here. I'm afraid I've been coming down here to sketch. The dock, the beach, even I'm afraid, your deck. The sunsets are marvelous here. Marty...Mr. Van Scoyk said you lived in the city and didn't come up very much. I'm afraid I sort of took advantage of the situation. Forgive me, please."

Those full lips parted into a shy, boyish grin as he pulled off his glasses. Granite colored eyes, dark, intense mirrored that grin.

Elgin felt her initial fright melting like spring snow.

"It's all right," she managed, "really. You surprised me, that's all. I...well, I didn't expect you."

"At least let me help you clean up the mess." He took another step toward her.

"There's no need," she told him quickly. "It's just coffee and most of it will just go through the deck spacers."

"I feel terrible," he told her quietly. "You could have burned yourself. Or cut yourself. Fallen over and broken your neck. It would be a shame for anything to happen to such a lovely neck."

For a moment, Elgin had that giddy roller coaster dropping sensation that leaves you breathless and lightheaded. Terrifying and exhilarating all at once. His very presence raised goose bumps of excitement and prickles of something she couldn't quite name.

Color raced to her cheeks and she bent down quickly, pretending to concentrate on the smashed fragments of mug. Even squatting down beside her, she felt overwhelmed and small, not just by his size but by his being there, so close she could feel the softness of his navy blue flannel shirt as his arm brushed against her.

"Well, I think that's all of them," she commented, trying to regain her composure as they stood up again.

"Here, let me have those," he insisted, taking the heavy ceramic pieces from her and cupping them in his own large, strong hands. "Show me where the garbage is so we can get rid of these."

"You don't really…"

"Yes, I must really. Soft, lovely hands like those shouldn't do anything more strenuous than peel the occasional grape. And since it's my fault the mug got broken, if anyone deserves to bleed, it's me."

"All right, if you insist."

"I do."

In the kitchen, he deposited the pieces in the garbage pail under the sink.

"Well, I think that about takes care of everything," he smiled. "I'll get out of your hair now and, much as I enjoy sketching from here, I promise to stay on my side of the fence. Cross my heart. And I really am sorry about scaring you. If I'd known the house belonged to such a lovely lady, I would have arrived on your doorstep with roses and champagne instead of barging in with big feet and sketch book."

That smile seemed to wrap itself around her.

"Don't worry. I'm usually not so jumpy. I guess I haven't shed my big city nerves yet."

"Well, I'm usually not so unbelievably boorish. It's just this is such a terrific place to come and work. The light. The view. The peace and quiet.

"The first day I found it, I actually did come to the door and knock but the place seemed to be empty so I went down and sat on the dock. In no time, I found myself here almost every day. Like something pulling me back. I'm going to miss it."

"There's no reason you can't come down and sketch," she smiled. "I'm usually out walking or on the lake or even upstairs working. No reason we can't share the place."

"That's very kind of you. I'd like to come back. Maybe now that I know the owner, I could even get you to open the gate so I can drive down. Bring my easel and paints and do some real painting. Try for one of those gorgeous sunsets. Or something else of great beauty."

"I think that can be arranged. I'd love to see your work."

"Well, I've got my sketchbook. Charcoals mostly, but a lot of this place. I'd like for you to see them."

"Good. How 'bout I get us some more coffee and you can show me what you have."

* * * * *

"Ahoy there!"

Elgin peered over the railing in the direction of the hail. Marty stepped onto her dock, the mooring line of a small sailboat, in hand.

"Ahoy, Marty," she called back, waving and smiling. She watched him secure the boat and thread his delicate way to the deck.

"Oh." His voice, face and body registered surprise at the sight of the strange man sitting so close beside his friend, a sketchbook open on the table in front of them.

"I...uh...hope I'm not interrupting anything."

"Of course not, Marty," she assured him, getting up and exchanging hugs and kisses on the cheek. "I'm always delighted to see you. Marty Van Scoyk, this is Chad Comstock. Chad, Marty."

"We've spoken at your mercantile, Mr. Van Scoyk." Chad smiled as he stood and extended his hand.

"Marty, please," he replied with an unenthusiastic shake. "Mr. Van Scoyk was my father. And yes, I remember you now. Bought a place up here about a year ago."

"The Graeters house, yes, eight months ago."

"Sit down." She pushed him toward a chair. "Can I get you some coffee?"

"No, no, I'm not staying. Actually, I would have called if you had a phone like normal people but since you don't and you keep that damn gate locked, I had to bring the little boat up here. If you're not going to have civilized communication up here, the least you could do would be to dredge out a channel big enough for me to bring the motor runabout up. It takes absolutely *hours* by sail."

"It takes less than forty minutes from your dock to mine," she teased. "And one of the reasons I come up here is to get away from telephones. Not to mention that I love having you come to visit. Now come sit down and have some coffee and look at these wonderful sketches Chad does."

"I really can't stay."

"You can spare me enough of your valuable time for a cup of coffee," she continued. "And I think you really ought to look at these sketches. I think they'd be a wonderful item for you to carry in the mercantile. Original, one-of-a-kind sketches of the lake, signed by the artist. You know as well as I do that these Yuppie tourists would eat them up with a spoon. You could have a whole display on that back wall where you keep all your other overpriced tourist crap."

"Well, maybe just half a cup. And I suppose I could look through the sketches. You know I absolutely adore art."

* * * * *

He'd made a complete circuit of the property, moving silently through the heavy pine forest along the rocky shoreline to a barbed wire fence where her property ended just short of Eagle Point, following it up to the top of her property, across the gated road and down to the other end. Hiking back toward the house, he felt surer than ever that he'd stumbled onto the perfect layout for his snare.

The first detector would be at the gate. A young man, athletic and determined would have no trouble getting over the gate but there he'd have no place to leave a vehicle on the main road or anywhere along this road. Anyone arriving would have to leave his or her car at the gate and proceed on foot.

Where the fence had been cut into the forest, a narrow band of scrub oak, thorny weeds and man-high poison oak bushes had taken over making the barbed wire doubly difficult to get over or through. Still, he'd make sure that detectors were positioned on each side of the road, just in case his quarry had an adventurous streak.

He'd seen nothing on either side of the barbed wire fence on each side of her property but thick pine forest. Following his exchange of e-mails on his PDA late the preceding night, he knew the agency was busily running down all the information he needed about the owners of the adjacent property and Martin Van Scoyk. When he turned on his mini-computer at the appointed hour tonight, he'd be able to download that information and give detailed instructions for the motion detectors' placement.

That left only the lake itself.

Except for the little sandy patch and dock in front of Moon's End, there didn't seem to be anywhere a person could bring a boat, even a small one, ashore. The trees grew down to the shoreline and in most places the bank had eroded to sharp, almost vertical bluffs. A strong, determined swimmer in a wetsuit against the cold water might make it and he'd picked a couple of potential landing sites for detectors, but only to cover all bases.

A motion detector would be placed just where the dock met the land and in a tree overlooking the little stretch of sand. Several in strategic places around the house and the electronic trap would be set.

Of course, he'd have to get her out of the house for most of a day so that his people could come in and set things up. Perhaps a day's hike to show him the land. Or a picnic. Or even a day spent sightseeing on that ridiculous little boat. Whatever, it would have to be done in the next day or two. As soon as he received word that the men and equipment were ready.

Harm heard the laughter even before he emerged from the trees into the parking lot. Not just Elgin's warm, feminine laugh but a deeper, baritone guffaw. Sprinting just short of a run, he heard unfamiliar voices as he closed the distance to the deck.

"So anyway, I said, 'Well what did you expect, Bill? Didn't I always tell you never trust a woman with a big mouth?'" Gales of laughter met him as he reached the deck, stopping dead at the sight before him.

Elgin, the little gay guy from the mercantile and a large stranger sat around the table, coffee cups and a half-empty tray of breakfast pastry in front of them. The man sat next to her, the arms of their chairs touching, his arm draped casually over the back of her chair.

"Hmm...hmm," he cleared his throat.

Immediately, the laughter died away and all eyes turned nervously to him. He flashed back to his days as a beat cop, catching couples in parked cars. Anger and something else flickered inside.

"Oh, Camp, I didn't know you were back." Her face turned beet red and she could barely look at him.

"Hmmmp," he grunted.

"Camp, you remember Marty Van Scoyk from the mercantile?" Her voice fairly quivered with anxiety. "Marty, my...my secretary, Campbell Harm."

"Mr. Harm."

"Hmmmp."

"And this is Chad Comstock. He's one of my neighbors from up the road. He's an artist. He's been using the place to do some wonderful sketches of the lake." She pointed nervously to a large sketchbook on the other side of the table.

"In fact, Marty liked them so much, he's going to put them up for sale in the mercantile. I think I might like to have a couple for the cabin."

Comstock stood up and extended his hand, a skin-deep smile flashing. "Harm, nice to meet you."

"Hmmmp," punctuated this time by a single shake.

"Would you like some coffee?" she offered, "or a bear claw? You must be famished after your walk. You've been gone for ages."

They stared at each other for several long, uncomfortable moments. Finally, Marty roused himself.

"Well, I really must be running along," he told them, rising to his feet. "I've got absolutely tons of work to do and I have to spend the afternoon babysitting with Byron. You won't forget now, will you Elgin darling?"

"No, Marty, you *can* count on it."

"Good. Well, ciao everyone." Turning, he stumbled right into Harm who took a single step to his left to allow the little man to make his escape. Harm watched him trundle quickly down to the dock, untie the little boat, set sail and turn for home.

The shallow water around the dock rippled and the sailboat didn't make any noise as it maneuvered nimbly back toward the lake. He filed it in his brain under 'potentially useful information'. Then he turned back to the stranger.

"Well, I guess I better be getting along, too," he announced, reaching for his book and box. "I've got a lot of things I need to do and I've gabbed the morning light away."

"I'm sorry," she told him, gazing up into his face. "I feel bad for keeping you from your work."

Comstock smiled a genuine smile this time. "I don't know when I've enjoyed myself more. And now that I know I'm welcome you'll probably get tired of having me around."

She laughed again, a warm sound filled with real joy. Harm felt his stomach tighten and his mouth turn down even further.

"I'm sure that won't happen. Feel free to bring your easel and oils down anytime. Maybe if I'm nice to the artist, he'll give me a break on a sunset painting for the fireplace."

"Consider it done."

They hung there for a moment more, her face turned up to his, their lips only a few inches apart.

Harm plopped down in the chair, still warm from the little man's butt and reached for a pastry. The spell shattered and the moment passed.

"Well, I'll see you later, Elgin," Comstock told her reluctantly. "Goodbye. Oh, and goodbye to you, too, Harm."

"Mmbllemm," he answered, raising his hand.

"Goodbye, Chad."

She stood at the top of the steps and watched until he disappeared up the drive. Enraged, she turned on Harm.

"How…dare…you!" she snarled.

"Me?" he managed after a slug of left over coffee washed down the pastry.

"Yes 'you'. I can't believe even you'd be that rude to my guests. That was utterly unforgivable, even for a crude, selfish lout like you. You practically chased them away physically."

"Yeah, well, what did you expect? You keep forgetting that my job is to keep you from being killed by a guy who may have already committed one murder and who tried to run you down in the street. So what do I get for my pains? Appreciation? Cooperation? Shit no! All I get is attitude.

"Not only are you a pain in the ass, you're a stupid pain in the ass in the bargain. You wander away in a strange town without telling me where you're going. You won't wear a simple little homing device so I can keep track of your skinny little ass without having to put a leash on you. And then, after I take my life in my hands to go out in the woods to make sure there's no one waiting for you with an axe, I come back and find you cheerfully coffee-klatching with your friendly neighborhood gay and a guy you never laid eyes on before!"

"Chad is not a stalker."

"Oh? And you know this for a fact?" Harm's voice dripped acid and ice.

"He's much too...too nice, too normal to do anything like that."

"When the police were hauling body bags out of John Wayne Gacy's basement, his neighbors stood across the street and couldn't believe that 'nice, normal' guy was a sexual sadist and a murderer. Trust me, if guys looked like stalkers and rapists and murderers, Ted Bundy wouldn't have racked up eighty kills."

Her body froze then, the color draining away from her face, her lower lip curling over her teeth. He didn't need to see her eyes behind her sunglasses. He could feel the fear and uncertainty. Like so many times lately, without a word, she'd made his rage boil away to embarrassed sorrow.

"I...I hadn't thought of that," she whispered, dropping heavily into a chair beside him. "I have to admit he did frighten me when he first showed up out of nowhere. But he's so nice and an artist and we have a lot of things in common and...and he's been up here a lot longer than this...this person's been stalking me. I've never met him before. We don't know any of the same people. It...it just couldn't be..."

"Look, I'm sorry I growled at you. And you're probably right. He's probably just what he seems to be. Only please promise me you'll be a little more careful? This job is tough enough without you inviting home strays. Okay?"

She smiled then and Harm felt lighter.

"Okay," she agreed, reaching under her shirt and producing the pendant. "See? I'm wising up already."

"Good," he told her, his anger gone. "Maybe we can get through this summer in one piece after all."

* * * * *

"Ellie!" he cried, scooping her up in his arms like a child and spinning her around.

"Jim." They exchanged warm hugs and a kiss that seemed to Harm a little too long and a little too enthusiastic.

"Let me look at you." He set her down and took her in from head to toe.

"My God but you just get prettier every time I see you."

"Thanks, Jim," she laughed, putting her fingers on his huge forearm. "It's nice of you to say, even if it isn't so. But you look terrific. I think you've lost a few pounds since last year."

"Put on some during the winter. Always do when things slow down but now that the tourist season is here I drop it and then some. Nothing like hard work to keep a body fit." He paused and surveyed her again.

"God but it's good to see you again. When Marty called and told me you were back up at Moon's End and that you wanted to rent a boat to go out on the lake, I got number eight ready myself. Packed the cooler with hard cola although you watch it. A little alcohol and a lot of sun can be a mighty dangerous combination."

"Don't worry, Jim," she told him playfully. "You know I never have more than two at a time. And anyway, I brought along company."

Turning, she nodded to Harm standing behind her about three feet.

"Jim Fisher, this is my secretary, Campbell Harm. Camp, this is one of my oldest and dearest friends, Jim Fisher. My aunt and uncle used to bring me up here every summer for a couple of weeks. Jim practically adopted me."

Harm stuck out his hand and it disappeared in the huge paw. "Camp, please," he panted as the vise closed on his fingers.

"And I'm Jim," he replied good-naturedly.

"Glad to meet you."

Massive leapt to Harm's mind. At least three inches taller than his own six foot two, a whiskey keg head, bare but for a steel gray buzz cut, black eyes like gun ports in the rock hard battlement of his long, square face. The eagle beak bent slightly to the right and a telltale lump on the bridge told of at least one break. Full lips, even pulled up in the delight of seeing Elgin gave him a hint of hardness. A heavyweight's body, all broad shoulders and muscular arms, callused, scarred hands, legs like tree trunks, stretching the denim of his jeans seemingly to the breaking point.

"Jim taught me to sail, water ski and fish," she continued brightly, squeezing Fisher around the middle. "Even bait my own hook. Also gave me my first hard cola and taught me to slow dance. Remember?"

"Fourth of July," he responded almost wistfully, "year you turned fifteen. And I didn't give you that cola. You stole it while I was talking to Dolly Biggs."

He grinned down at her and then at Harm. "Scrawniest little kid you ever saw. Tomboy. All bony elbows and skinned knees."

The rugged face softened and he ran a finger lightly down her cheek. "Summer you were twelve, you were a barefoot kid in raggedy cutoff jeans, swingin' from the trees and shaggin' flies in the outfield. Next summer, you were sportin' boobs and sandals and worryin' about the freckles on your nose. Seems like yesterday."

"I don't even want to think about that long ago," she laughed. "But I still do freckle."

"And they're still cute as the dickens," Jim told her, planting a quick peck on her nose. "But you didn't come all the way up here to hang around reminiscing with this old fart. Boat should be ready by now."

Turning back toward the end of the dock, Fisher shaded his eyes and squinted.

"Yo," he called.

About a hundred feet away, a figure shuffled toward them, waving his hands and seeming to be engaged in an animated conversation with the air. At the sound, he paused, looking quizzically to each side and behind him. Fisher raised a giant hand and motioned him forward.

"That's Tom," he explained. "Don't know his last name. Showed up about three weeks ago askin' could he work for some food. Looked like a skinny stray dog so I told him to go on up to the snack bar and get a burger and fries and coke but he told me he wouldn't take nothin' less he worked for it. Well, I know what it's like to have nothin' but your pride so I told him to get a broom and kinda sweep up. Few minutes later he comes back and tells me he saw an outboard engine and if he fixed it, could he get somethin' to eat and stay the night.

"I knew that engine couldn't be fixed. Gonna strip it down for parts. But I figured it'd give the old guy somethin' to do for a couple hours and then he could eat without feelin' guilty so I said, 'sure'. Well, in about three hours he had that thing purrin' like a contented kitten at its mother's tit.

"Told him if he wanted to stay on for the summer, he could use the spare room out back a the boathouse and I'd feed him and give him walkin' around money 'til Labor Day. Only rules are no booze, no drugs, no women and be polite to the customers. Talks to himself and I got a feelin' he's about two deuces shy of a full deck but he keeps to himself pretty much, nobody's complained and he knows more about engines than anybody I ever saw, includin' me."

"Yes sir, Mr. F?" the old man croaked as he sidled up to his boss.

"Number eight ready?"

"Sure is. Just put the poles an' bait in myself. Tank's full an' she's rarin' to go."

Jim gave Elgin a last squeeze. "Bring in whatever you catch. I'll build a campfire out back and roll 'em in corn meal and pan fry 'em in butter."

"With greasy homemade French fries, and corn on the cob baked in aluminum foil in the fire, and pork and beans?" Harm thought she sounded like a delighted child.

"And fresh strawberry shortcake with extra whipped cream if you eat all your dinner."

"Oh," she squealed. "An old-fashioned fish fry. Just like old times."

"Just like old times," he agreed softly. "But right now, you and your friend better git or those lake trout'll all be home for their afternoon nap."

He held out his hand again. "Nice to meet you, Camp. You take good care of my Ellie."

"I'll do that, Jim."

They followed Tom down the wooden dock, listening as he continued muttering and mumbling to himself.

"Well, here she is," he announced gesturing to a sleek white and blue runabout, perhaps fifteen feet long with a deep "V" nose, open with cushioned seating.

"Doesn't look much like a fishing boat," Harm commented as he surveyed her.

"Ain't," the old man replied. "Just about the fastest little critter we got. Most folks rent it ta ski er ta go ta that gamblin' den 'cross the lake. Little outboards is fer fishin'."

"Well, eight has always been my lucky number," Elgin laughed. "And it's nice to have if we decide we don't want to fish anymore."

His thin shoulders went up and down once. "Suit yerselves."

Harm stepped into the boat, helping Elgin aboard and then sliding automatically into the driver's chair, putting both hands on the wheel and turning it a couple of times.

"So, where to?"

"If you'll get out of my seat," she told him coolly, "I'll show you."

He stared at her, blinking, mouth open. Elgin thought he looked like a surprised guppy. It took a couple of seconds for her meaning to sink in.

"Your seat?"

"Of course. I know this lake like the back of my hand."

His fingers tightened on the wheel.

"You can tell me where to go."

"I intend to," she shot back, "but after you move so I can take us to the fishing spot."

"I got us up here following your directions. I think I can navigate this lake."

"Look, I'm not attacking your manhood, just your lack of experience with this lake. I've been boating up here since I was ten. It makes sense that I should drive the boat."

A loud guffaw made them turn back to the dock. Tom stood, mooring line in his bony hand, laughing heartily.

"You two sound just like old married people," he said between chuckles. "Squabblin' an' bickerin' and carryin' on. You best put yer jacket on an' move young fella. You ain't gonna be in this boat ferever an' when it gets cold tonight, you might want her ta do you a favor." He dissolved into more laughter as the rope landed in the open bow and he moved away.

Without another word, Harm cranked up the engine and edged slowly away from the dock. At the entrance to the little marina, he turned a questioning face to Elgin.

Frowning, she pointed to their left. As soon as he cleared the marina, Harm opened the boat up, feeling the cool spray and the slight bounce of the hull under them.

"Where are we going?" he shouted over the engine.

"To the lee of that little island out there." He followed her outstretched arm to a barren piece of rock sticking out of the sapphire water a few miles away.

In a few more minutes they'd anchored a few yards from the island.

"Welcome to Captain Jack's," she told him as she pulled off her skimpy tank top and shorts. "Best fishing on the lake. But first things first."

Harm felt his lungs intake and his heart speed up at the sight of her. Creamy white skin and a small but thoroughly respectable fire engine red two-piece swimsuit that covered her only enough to show her body to its best advantage.

His cock stirred, demanding he slip out of his jeans and T-shirt to the freedom of his own swim trunks. They too were respectable but would probably not cover his growing...interest in her.

"Could you reach into the cooler for me, please? There should be a pint bottle of whiskey in there."

Dutifully, Harm opened the cooler and sure enough, tucked in the corner sat a small whiskey bottle. He reached in and handed it to her.

"Is this thing waterproof?" she asked, holding the pendant away from her skin.

"To about a hundred feet deep," he answered, handing her the bottle, his curiosity getting the better of him. "Why?"

"Don't want your high tech dog collar electrocuting me."

She moved to the side of the boat, the bottle clutched in her fist.

"Hey," he yelped, "what the hell do you think you're doing?"

"I'm going up to the top of the island to pay my respects to Captain Jack." Nodding to the island, she continued. "There used to be a little wooden dock but now...well, it's the old-fashioned paddle method."

"You can't swim over there," he insisted, moving quickly to where she stood. "That water's freezing and you'll kill yourself getting up that sheer rock."

"Lot you know. I've been doing this forever. The water's cold but it's only about twenty yards to shore and there's a path that winds up the other side. It's a little steep but by no means treacherous."

"What does this have to do with fishing?"

"It's hard to explain. You wouldn't understand."

"Try me."

Elgin sighed. "Please just take my word for it that it's important. I'll be back before you get the lines in the water."

"You're not going anywhere until you tell me."

"All right, but you better sit down and get comfortable. Might even want to get a beer. It's a long story."

With a nod, he turned back and reached for the cooler lid again.

Splash!

By the time he'd stepped back to the side, she was already swimming quickly for shore, her strokes and kick strong, barely disturbing the surface as she moved.

"Come back here, damn it!" he yelled futilely.

For another second he watched her, stripping off his jeans and shirt as fast as he could. He braced himself for the cold as he jumped into the dark water after her.

An instant of body-numbing cold engulfed him as he plunged under the water, the shock literally taking his breath away. Breaking the surface again, his lungs frantically gulped in air and it took several more moments for him to gather himself and set out after her.

With the slight head start and her swimming skill, Elgin came out of the water, threw a quick look behind her and disappeared around a rocky outcropping.

Panting from the cold and the unexpected exertion, Harm had to stop for a few seconds on the little beach to catch his breath.

Beyond the little point, a path wide enough for a small cart began winding up the side of the small island. He couldn't see her but her tracks were clear in the layer of fine dust over the compacted surface of the trail.

Rounding a sharp bend, he found himself at the top of the island, perhaps a hundred feet above the sparkling water.

Elgin stood beside a large gray boulder lying like a huge block by itself in the middle of a large clearing. Other boulders lay strewn around and on the right side of clearing, almost at the cliff's edge, stood a huge pile of jumbled gray boulders, almost as if some giant had heaped them there.

"What the hell is...?" he barked as he approached.

"...and to show our gratitude," she murmured softly, "I leave this small token for your patience and good will." With a twist of the cap, she put out her hand and poured the smoky amber liquid on the top of the stone, pooling and running off both sides.

"Rest in peace Captain Jack. And thank you." Elgin shook the last few drops out, replaced the top and turned to face Harm.

"It's cold. Let's go sit over here in the sun."

They walked over to the pile of rocks, Harm feeling again slightly amazed, first at her swimming ability and now as she climbed over the large rocks to a flat one, warmed by the sun and overlooking the water, by her athleticism.

"Now do I get to hear the story?" He no longer felt anger. Only curiosity and a chill. The sun would take care of one and he waited for her to take care of the second.

"There lies Captain John Crockett, late of the Grand Army of the Republic. Gambler, entrepreneur, father of Crockett's Landing, now known as West Shore and, if local legend is to be believed, drunkard, womanizer and general, all-around scoundrel.

"Came here penniless during the gold rush. Apparently didn't take long for him to decide taking the gold from the miners would be easier than panning for it himself. So, he opened the first gambling hall/saloon/whorehouse in the area.

Became known for honest tables, clean women and not watering the beer. Overnight, he was the richest man in the territory.

"For twenty years, he was King of the Lake. Nothing happened, big or small, for fifty miles around that Jack Crockett didn't have his hand in. Had a huge mansion overlooking Crockett's Landing. Built a little castle right where we're sitting and this island became his private playground. Every Fourth of July he'd load up 'The Belle' with beer and food and fireworks and he and his family and cronies would come out here and party.

"Rumor also had it that he liked to bring ladies not his wife out here for private picnics and nature frolics."

"Sounds like he had it made."

"Most people thought so. Then, one night the people in Spirit Cove saw fire coming from the castle. At first, they thought Jack was over here having a little moonlight fun, but pretty soon they realized something was really wrong. By the time they got out here, the castle was ablaze and there wasn't anything they could do.

"They found Jack's body, *au natural*, right over there, near that big rock in the clearing. His head had been blown off by a double barrel shotgun at close range. Only other thing they found was a scrap of lace from a lady's unmentionable snagged on a bush down by where the dock used to be."

"Died with his boots off," Harm chuckled.

Elgin ignored him. "No one ever found out what happened although the stories flew fast and fierce. Most people thought he'd run afoul of a jealous husband or an angry father and pretty much got what he deserved."

"What about his family?"

"Mrs. Crockett never actually said anything but she made it clear enough what she thought, though. First, she buried Jack right here on the island. Almost the exact spot where he died. Took ten men to move that big old granite boulder over his grave. Only marker she gave him. Then she sold everything he owned for whatever cash she could get, took the children and disappeared."

"Doesn't explain the whiskey."

"Most local people avoid this place like the plague. Down through the years, people have even claimed to have seen Jack's ghost up here, wandering through these ruins of his castle, imprisoned for all eternity for his black deeds."

"You believe that superstitious clap-trap?" he asked cynically.

"About the ghost? I'm not sure. I mean, I don't have enough evidence one way or the other to make a rational decision. I do believe firmly that the soul or the spirit or the life force or whatever you want to call it survives this plane of existence although what happens after, I haven't the faintest idea.

"Jim always told me that since people can be trapped in this life by their decisions and beliefs and acts, it didn't seem all that far-fetched to think a person's soul could be trapped by the same things in the hereafter. If Jack believed he deserved to be imprisoned here because he'd screwed some other man's woman, or that he'd hurt his own wife and family or even that this is heaven or hell and he never made any effort to get off…well…it's just complicated.

"So whenever we came here, Jim always brought some whiskey. 'A neighborly gesture' he called it. Let Jack know we weren't trespassing and that we'd appreciate being left alone and to pay him for the fish we took."

"That is the silliest, stupidest, most ridiculous crock of bull I ever heard."

Before she could answer, a cold gust of wind whipped up, seeming to circle around them from out of nowhere.

Elgin shivered and stood up. "Come on. Let's get out of here." She scampered off the rocks, Harm following her quickly down the path and back into the water toward the boat. He remembered thinking that the water seemed colder than it had when he'd first jumped in.

Climbing into the boat, they grabbed towels and began rubbing themselves dry.

"That's better," she told him when she'd finished. "I'm going to put my pole in the water and see how long it takes to catch my limit."

"Sounds good."

"I wouldn't bother if I were you," she chuckled. "After the way you pissed Jack off up there, I don't think you're going to have any luck at all."

* * * * *

"A coincidence," Harm insisted flatly, taking another sip of his coffee. "That's all. End of story."

Elgin and Fisher exchanged quick, knowing glances.

"I dunno," Jim replied thoughtfully, stroking his chin stubble with his long fingers. "Sounds to me like Ellie could be right. I mean about you pissin' Captain Jack off like that. Talkin' so disrespectful right there in his castle, practically on top a his grave. That wind comin' up when there hasn't been a breath all day and then you not catchin' any trout in the best fishin' spot in the lake."

"Not even a bite," Elgin chimed in giggling.

"Well, doesn't sound natural to me," he concluded.

Harm continued to sip his coffee and glanced out to the vast black expanse of lake and listened to the other two laughing and talking.

Coming in from the lake, Elgin had run right to Fisher, showing him her creel packed with the limit of beautiful lake trout and losing no time in spinning her ghost story. They'd laughed about it as he'd gutted and cleaned the fish for her, bringing them down to this gorgeous spot by the lake as he'd made a campfire and prepared their dinner.

He had to admit that the fresh trout, French fries made right at the fire, baked corn on the cob, and even the canned pork and beans had been a wonderful meal. Strawberries fresh from a neighbor's garden and heavy cream whipped by hand, and not out of an aerosol can, had completed the perfection.

Now, under a canopy of stars sprinkled like powdered sugar and a second cup of fresh coffee, he could almost forget the humiliation of the afternoon. And he could understand Elgin's need to flee here to this peaceful, safe place.

"Moon'll be up in a little while," Fisher commented, looking toward the east. "Full too. Air'll be full a souls tonight."

"What do you mean by that?" Harm asked, instantly interested.

"Didn't you tell this slicker *anything*?" Jim teased Elgin.

"What's the point?" she sighed wearily. "He doesn't believe in things like that. He's thoroughly modern and scientific."

"Which makes me all the more curious about your primitive superstitions."

"Well, we wouldn't want to hamper your scientific research," she giggled.

"You go on and tell him, Ellie. You can explain it better than this poor old, ignorant hillbilly."

They both laughed and Harm felt the pang of an outsider barred from some kind of "inside" joke.

"The Indians who lived around the lake and traveled by canoe and fished and traded, noticed that when people drowned, especially out in the very deepest parts, the bodies never came back up. They believed the drowning victims had actually been snatched up and enslaved by an evil monster, who lived at the bottom of the lake.

"Because the lake's dark and cold, the prisoners couldn't find their way to the next world and the Great Spirit wept for his children lost to the monster. Finally, he had an idea. In the summer, when the days were long and the air warm, he asked the Full Moon Goddess to travel over the lake, laying down a path of silvery light to slice through the darkness down to the monster's lair so that the souls could follow it.

"She said she'd try and so, after a long summer day, while the monster slept, she crept across the lake, marking a wide, bright silver trail. The souls saw it and began following it silently up, finally reaching the lake's surface. On the shore, the Indians saw the wispy, gray spirits moving along the water until they were gradually picked up and taken to the next world by the Full Moon Goddess.

"When the first white men came here and heard the story, they didn't believe it. They were camped at a little beach and one night they sat up with the Indians, and sure enough, they saw the Moon Goddess collecting the souls from the lake and began calling it 'Haunted Moon Lake'. And since there seemed to be an awful lot of activity in the water just off from their camp, they called it 'Spirit Cove'."

Harm snorted. "The lake is very deep and very cold. I'm sure that when someone drowned, especially in the really deep part, the body didn't decompose and release gases and therefore, didn't come back up to the surface. And the 'spirits' on the lake are nothing more than foggy mist created by warm air on a cold lake. An interesting tale to tell the tourists around the camp fire."

"You're a pathetic cynic," she told him, trying to be serious but already past her two hard cola limit.

"And you're drunk. I think it's time to take you home."

Elgin stuck out her tongue and made a raspberry.

"Camp's right," Fisher agreed rising to his feet and pulling her up with him. "You're tanked and it's past my bed time."

"What a pair of party poops you are."

"Yeah, well tomorrow is another day young lady, and we have the whole summer."

"Poops," she retorted, throwing out her lower lip in a childish pout. "The pair of you. Poops."

Fisher and Harm took a place on each side of her and guided her gently back to the SUV. Carefully, they got her buckled securely into her seat.

"Good night, Camp," he beamed. "You come back real soon. I'll give Ellie another bottle of whiskey and you can stay in the boat, sorta hunkered down where Jack can't see ya. Catch yer limit the next time."

"Okay, Jim, you got a deal. Good night."

As he moved around to the driver's side, Ellie rolled down the window and reached out to the big man like a small child. "I had a wonderful time, Jim," she told him. "It's been a long time since I've been this happy."

"That's what I want," he whispered, leaning his face close to hers, brushing a wisp of hair from her forehead. "That's what I've always wanted. Since you were a little girl."

She stretched up and put her lips on his, feeling the warmth of his body and the prickle of stubble and the tang of Irish Coffee.

"I love you, Jim," she mumbled.

"I love you too, Ellie."

* * * * *

"Let's stop at the Lodge for a nightcap," she suggested brightly.

"It's late. You should be in bed."

"It's only early evening and I don't want to go to bed."

"What happened to your 'two hard cola limit'?"

"I'm fine."

"Yeah, well I'm exhausted. I've had a lot of sun, a lot of exercise, a lot of good food and more than my share of beer. I need to go to bed."

"Good. You're no fun anyway. You can drop me at the Lodge. I'll call Marty. Unlike certain other people I could name, he is *definitely* not a poop."

"Okay, lean back, close your eyes and rest. We'll be at the Lodge in about ten minutes."

"Now you're talking."

She was fast asleep by the time he reached the gate. Turning the wheels to the right, he set the emergency brake and put the SUV in "Park". Quietly, he opened the door and slid out, striding quickly to the gate.

The full moon peeked through the trees, giving him enough light to walk and find the gate chain. Concentrating on the gate and the ground as he walked it inward, Harm didn't hear anything until the wheel crunched on the gravel behind him.

Looking up, horror washed over him as the SUV rolled down the hill toward him. Pete's mangled body flashed through his mind. This vehicle wasn't moving at break-neck speed, but its nose pointed downhill just a few feet away. He had neither time nor space to maneuver.

Without thinking, he darted behind the gate, stepping back as far as he could, pulling the heavy metal gate to his chest.

As the car rolled past him, gaining speed, he saw Elgin, her head resting to one side, still asleep.

The instant the car passed him, he bolted across the narrow road, racing to catch up with it. Somehow, the driver's door had swung shut and the big vehicle picked up speed as it gained downward momentum. And just beyond them a few hundred feet, the road made a sharp curve. Traveling straight would put it into the thick forest just beyond the road. If that happened, even with her seatbelt on...

A surge of adrenaline pumped through him, prodding him to more speed.

He pulled even with the driver's door, catching his fingers under the handle and jerking it open, losing his balance and almost tripping. If he fell now, he would almost certainly be caught under the back wheels.

Barely hanging on, Harm jumped into the driver's seat, grabbing the wheel with one hand, stomping on the brake and forcing the gearshift into Park.

Unable to get a grip in the loose gravel, the anti-lock brakes struggled as the SUV slid toward the shallow drainage ditch, transmission whining in protest. Slipping and bumping, it finally came to rest, the front end about forty-five degrees to the left, the engine stalled.

Shaken rudely back to consciousness, Elgin sat up, blinked groggy eyes and looked around. "What happened?"

"It's all right," he lied, gripping the wheel with sweaty palms and forcing his voice to remain calm. "I got out to open the gate and I guess I didn't set the brake right. Car rolled down the hill a little. Stomped on the brakes too hard and kind of fishtailed in this gravel. Everything's okay now."

Taking a deep breath, he restarted the car and they drove the rest of the way in silence.

"You go on up and go to bed," he told her, "I just want to check and make sure everything's all right."

"Okay. Good night."

"Good night."

With Elgin safely in the house, Harm turned on the overhead light, illuminating the interior of the car. The emergency brake lay flat against the console. Except that he'd pulled it upright when he'd set it before getting out of the SUV to open the gate. And he'd had to jam the gearshift from "Drive" back into "Park" to stop the car. Except that he'd left the car in "Park". Having turned the wheels to the right, even if both the gear and the brake had failed, the SUV should have rolled into the ditch after only a few feet, the driver's side door remaining open.

The realization sent a cold chill through his body, and he shivered.

He was here, and Harm had been careless enough to let him get within striking distance of both of them. Lulled by the peaceful beauty and tranquil surroundings, he'd let down his guard and Elgin had almost paid the price for his blunder.

But he'd tipped his hand. Tomorrow, under the pretext of taking the car in to be checked for damage, he'd make sure his forensics people gave it a good going over. A fingerprint. A stray hair, fiber sample. Anything that might give them a clue. And he'd personally search the area by the gate. A footprint, a cigarette butt. Anything that didn't belong.

Yes, the stalker was here. But now, he was in Harm's Way.

Chapter Ten

"Greetings, neighbor," he grinned. "I hope I'm not disturbing you."

Elgin smiled warmly. "Of course not, Chad. I hoped you'd drop by. Please, come sit down. Can I get you some coffee?"

"No, thanks," he told her, taking a seat at the deck table where she'd been finishing a second cup of coffee. "I just came by to give you this." He brought a medium-sized package wrapped in bright yellow paper from behind his back.

"For me? What is it?"

"Open and see."

She ripped open the paper and squealed with delight when she saw the contents, a pastel drawing of her house as viewed from the lake. About eighteen by eighteen inches, it showed the deck and windows and the trees.

"Oh Chad," she breathed, "it's beautiful! I love it!"

"Look on the back."

Turning it over, Elgin saw he'd written something. "To Elgin," she read. "The beautiful lady of the lake."

Crimson rushed to her cheeks. "That's very sweet, Chad."

"Well, it's the least I could do. I gave Marty a whole slew of the charcoals and watercolors I did from your dock and he put them up in the mercantile and he said they all went right away. He wants to know how soon he can have more and he's already had several inquiries about whether there are any large oils for sale. Marty says the stench of money dying to be spent is absolutely overwhelming."

"That sounds like Marty."

"As I told you that first day, I'd like to drive down here with my oils and easel and use your beach and deck to do real paintings. The light on the water and definitely a couple of sunsets. They're gorgeous from here. I promise you the pick of the litter."

"You don't need to do that, I'm happy to have you here. Just drive down and open the chain. But be careful when you get out. We almost had an accident last night coming home from the marina."

"Oh? Nothing serious I hope?"

"No, nothing like that. It was late and Camp'd had a couple of beers and I'd fallen asleep in the car. I guess he forgot to set the emergency brake properly and when he got out to open the gate, the car sort of rolled down the hill."

"Are you both all right?"

"Yes, we're fine. I slept through all of it except when Camp slammed on the brakes to stop us. Now I know how James Bond's martinis feel. Shaken, not stirred."

Comstock grinned. "I'm glad you weren't hurt. That gravel slope up there and that sharp curve...it could have been serious. You should tell your secretary to be more careful. By the way, where is he this morning? Out walking again?"

"No, he said he thought the SUV was fine but he wanted to be sure so he took it into town to have it looked at. Said he had some errands in town and would probably be gone the rest of the day."

"Excuse me, but I need to avail myself of your facilities. Could I ask you for a quick tour of this wonderful old house?"

"Sure," she told him cheerfully as they both rose. "Both bathrooms are upstairs. Don't know why they didn't at least put a half bath downstairs, but they didn't and I've never quite been able to figure out where to put one after seventy some odd years."

Inside, he stopped to admire the huge stone fireplace.

"God, I love this," he gushed, gazing around the room. "And this fireplace is magnificent. Now I know I have to paint you a sunset. On cold winter evenings you can sit in front of a roaring fire and remember the beauty of summer."

"I'm afraid I don't get up here in the winter. I actually haven't used the cabin very much since I bought it. Work keeps me pretty busy. This summer trip is the first time I've been here in almost a year and it's the longest I've stayed."

"So what is it you do?" he asked, as they made their way upstairs.

"I'm a writer," she replied as they came into the master bedroom. "Bathroom's through there."

"So what do you write?" he continued, his business in the bathroom finished.

"Nothing you'd be interested in."

"How do you know what I'm interested in? Come on, tell me."

"I write women's erotica. You know. Soft porn for the lovelorn," she joked lightly but feeling suddenly somewhat embarrassed. "Not exactly Agatha Christie but it pays the bills."

"I haven't read any of it myself," he answered seriously, "but only because I don't have a lot of time for reading of any kind. Personally, I think it's terrific that half the human race is finally waking up to their own sexuality and the enjoyment thereof. You'll have to give me the names of your books so I can get them. Maybe even get an autograph."

"Check with Marty," she laughed nervously. "They're in that little book rack right by the cash register. I autographed a whole bunch of them."

"Done. I'll pick up one the next time I go into town."

He turned and surveyed the room.

"This is a great room," he told her enthusiastically. "Northern exposure. Fabulous light. Be a wonderful place to work."

Abruptly, he dropped into the oversized stuffed chair on the wall facing her bed.

"I'd wake up in the morning, sit right here in this chair with my sketchbook and charcoals and draw a sleeping nude in that very bed."

His eyes locked on hers as he continued. "Black curls rumpled against the white pillow. Childlike face in peaceful dreams. Blankets kicked off during the warm night, soft cotton sheets clinging to her ankles and feet. On her side, facing me. Curves of creamy white shoulders and hips and thighs. Breasts like nesting doves. Black pubic hair and a slit of pink pussy. I'd have to sketch fast to catch her in all her many poses.

"Now she's turned her back to me, one leg over the other. That beautiful black hair pasted to that white neck by sweet summer sweat. Her backbone a little row of white hills on that beautiful expanse of milky back, tracking down to that lovely, heart-shaped, perfect ass."

Elgin's skin prickled as if electricity suddenly charged the air. He sat just out of reach, his implied invitation hanging in the small space between them like a ripe apple. She had only to reach out and take it.

"That sounds lovely," she said finally, her voice raw with emotion, "and I envy the lucky lady. Too bad I'm so shy. Especially around handsome strangers."

He rose, closing the gap until he stood over her, his lips so close she felt his hot breath on her cheek.

"There's no reason to be shy," he assured her tenderly. "We're not strangers. Our souls have known each other always. The bodies may be different but I knew you the first moment I looked in your eyes. And you knew it too."

"Please…" An anxious uncertainty…perhaps even a tinge of fear rippled through her.

His eyes clouded over like thunderclouds and his face grew dark.

"Your 'secretary'…Harm? Is there…more than a business relationship?"

"No. I mean, not what you think."

The big body relaxed and the clouds disappeared. "I'm glad. I wouldn't want to trespass on someone else's property. But it's all right. I'd never hurt you. I want you to want me too. We'll take it slowly, whatever you're comfortable with. I'll go down to the dock now and paint and you won't even know I'm here.

"Maybe though, you'd let me take you to the Lodge one night soon for drinks and dinner. Get to know each other better. Even sit for a portrait…fully clothed for now. Just give me a chance, please."

Longing and need filled those beautiful eyes, that mouth so sensual, so close. The heat of him rolled over her in waves, making her dizzy and hot herself. It had been such a long time…and he wanted her so much…

She felt their bodies being drawn together, his lips brushing hers.

A shock went through her but instead of burning away the last of her doubts, it seemed to snap her out of whatever spell had possessed her. Instantly, they separated.

"I think that would be very nice," she managed, flustered, trying to regain her composure. "I think dinner at the Lodge would be a great idea. Maybe sometime next week."

"That's fine," he murmured. "I look forward to it."

Silently, they walked slowly back down the narrow stairs, Elgin feeling the touch of his warm body on her back as they descended. On the deck, Chad picked up his sketchbook and charcoals and strode quickly down to the beach, settling himself on a flat rock in the shade of a giant old pine and began to draw.

Elgin stood at the railing, watching his every move. Inside, a gnawing hunger wrestled with a haunting uncertainty. This kind, gentle, sexy exterior couldn't possibly hide a monster capable of terror and murder. Certainly not here in her own peaceful, safe haven. Someone who created such beauty would never do such a horrible thing.

He wanted her. Even if he hadn't said the words, his body had been screaming its need, its desire, practically since he'd appeared so unexpectedly on her deck that morning. And she certainly didn't need X-ray vision to see the bulge still pressing against his zipper. A bulge she'd put there without so much as a caress.

That thought sent tiny bolts of lightning coursing through her blood again. He had a gorgeous face and a beautiful body and she imagined him a thoughtful, gentle, skilled lover. There did not need to be any entanglements. A summer fling, and nothing more. And she had to admit he attracted her like no man had in a long time.

Harm.

Elgin frowned and bit her lip. Instantly, the prickles stopped.

He didn't like Chad, she knew. Didn't trust him. He'd made that plain enough after their first meeting. She'd invited him to come and paint but if she took him inside, upstairs, Harm would surely figure out the situation. And there were only so many errands she'd be able to send him on. Going out would only bring on suspicious questions. Not to mention he could always locate her with the "dog collar". Of course, she could "accidentally" forget to put it on, but he'd see through that in a minute.

She wanted to make love again. Feel a hot, hard cock in her wet, excited pussy. Passionate lips on hers, tender fingers on her swollen nipples. Slick, heated skin moving against slick, heated skin in a primal rhythm of need and fulfillment. She wanted to have scorching, animal lust, needy sex. And she wanted it soon.

* * * * *

Harm yawned and glanced at his watch. Almost one thirty. What could be taking so long?

As soon as he'd left Moon's End, he'd headed straight for the secluded storage locker his people had been able to rent on short notice. Fortunately, he'd only had to drive a short distance to find it. Using the code number he'd been given, he'd pulled into the double garage sized unit, a tech had pulled down the door and the forensics team had gone to work.

They'd found smudged prints on the doors, the wheel, the gearshift and the emergency brake. Also hair and fiber trace evidence. From bumper to bumper, they'd gone over every centimeter of the SUV, including making sure that it hadn't been damaged, accidentally or on purpose, by the incident. It had taken several hours and then several more as they'd searched the area of the accident, lookouts with two-way radios posted to warn them of anyone approaching from either end.

Comstock had been on the deck with Elgin, showing her his sketchbook, enjoying a beer and behaving like he owned the place when he'd finally returned late in the afternoon. Even though the thorough background report had showed the artist to be everything he represented himself to be, Harm still didn't like him, either personally with his boyish charm and easy sexuality, or professionally with his hanging around Elgin. Seeing Harm, he'd gathered himself up and made a hasty exit.

He'd grilled steak on the barbecue for their dinner. It had been a long time and he'd been hesitant about his rusty skills, but Elgin had insisted so he'd cranked up the grill and done a pretty fair job. She'd produced mixed fruit and potato salad and they'd watched a gorgeous sunset, lingering over a second Irish coffee before Elgin had gone upstairs about eleven.

Making an excuse that he wanted to watch the stars and enjoy the warm night air, Harm waited for the information about the SUV to arrive. He prayed they'd find some clue, no matter how small, to point him towards his quarry.

Restless, Harm got up and walked around the large main room. He'd had more coffee than he should have trying to stay awake but the inactivity and waiting were taking their toll. Sleep lurked just over the horizon of his mind. His body cried out for him to lie down and close his eyes. But he couldn't risk his PDA's mail alarm going off and waking Elgin and he needed to get the forensic information before morning. Especially if they'd turned up something solid.

Elgin's books were upstairs in her bedroom. Even a sexy romance would have given him something to read, occupy his mind. Perhaps he could find something else lying around. A magazine. A cookbook. Anything.

Absently, he moved to a small desk sitting in an alcove by itself near the front door. He'd never seen Elgin use the desk but it was as good a place to start as any. The drawers contained nothing but dust, an old yellow legal tablet and a fountain pen with no ink. Except the last one on the right-hand side. Lying in the bottom, he found a thick sheaf of paper, covered in faded blue cardstock and held together with two brass brads. Curious, he reached in and removed it.

Another Love, A Novel by Elgin Collier.

Sheila Forbes had told him she wrote under a pen name. Gillian Something. Oh well, better than nothing. Picking up the manuscript, he went back over to the sofa and settled himself under the small reading lamp on the end table. Carefully, he placed his PDA on the table where he could watch the screen. Hopefully, this romantic trash would keep him awake until the forensic boys sent their information.

* * * * *

"How dare you!"

The scream more than the words ripped through his sleep and pulled him to groggy consciousness. Opening his eyes, he sat up and blinked, trying to figure out where he was and what was going on. Before his brain slipped into gear however, something heavy connected with the left side of his head, almost knocking him over again.

"Hey," he yelped, grabbing his throbbing ear. "What the hell...?"

"You miserable, rotten, low down, good-for-nothing, weasel-hearted son of a bitch!" Something came at him again and instinctively he ducked, feeling air whiz by his head. Peeking up, he saw Elgin standing in front of the sofa, her face contorted and purple with rage, the manuscript in both hands, raised to her head and ready to swing again.

"What are doing? Are you crazy?"

"I'm going to kill you, you lying, sneaking, cold-blooded bastard and there's not a jury in the world that would convict me. I'll probably get a medal from the 'Keep America Beautiful' people. Consider it part of the vermin abatement program!" The manuscript flew at him again but he grabbed it and managed to wrestle it away from her.

"Stop it," he shouted, finally getting to his feet. "Stop this crap and tell me what's going on."

Ten bright red claws arched out at his face. Grabbing her wrists, Harm marveled at her strength as she struggled to break free and reach him.

"Let go of me you contemptible prick! You pile of pig shit! When I get my hands on you…"

"Stop this," he ordered again, shaking her like a rag doll. "Stop it."

Suddenly she stopped fighting him, fixing him instead with a look that burned right through him. Theirs had been an uneasy relationship at best and he'd gotten used to her smart mouth and monumental attitude. But this was different. Cold, pure, unadulterated hate radiated out at him like a physical force. He knew if he released her, she'd kill him without a second thought.

"You had no right," she spat, "no right at all. This is *my* house and these are *my* things and most especially this is *my* book. Your Junior G-man license doesn't give you the right to snoop through my things. Through my personal things. And that book is about as personal as my life gets."

He glanced down at the sofa, the little light still on, the manuscript on the floor. The pieces fell into place and a wave of embarrassment and remorse rolled over him. His fingers opened and she immediately pulled back her arms, rubbing the red finger marks on her wrists.

"I'm sorry," he told her softly, his head drooping to his chin. "I couldn't sleep last night. I thought maybe I could find a magazine or a book to read 'til I got drowsy. I found the manuscript in your desk drawer. I...I thought it was one of your romance novels. I wasn't prying but you're right. I shouldn't have been going through the desk."

"Well," she told him, her voice dripping acid, "at least it wasn't a total loss. I mean, apparently it did put you to sleep."

Bending down to retrieve the manuscript, he held it out to her. She took it, pulling it to her, crossing her arms over it in a protective, almost maternal gesture.

"I enjoyed it," he told her seriously. "Really. It's very good."

"You sound surprised."

Like everything else, this wasn't going to be easy.

"I was. I mean, I expected heaving bosoms and throbbing rods. That's the cliché of romance novels. But this," he nodded to the book, "totally blew me away. The story, your way with words. It's a love story but it's more. It's...it's..."

"Literature?" she prodded.

"Yes. Literature. Your descriptions of the ordinary, everyday, almost invisible indignities of a slave's life made me angry and sad and ashamed. You throw the whole, ugly, filthy system in your reader's lap, narrowed down to the laser point of two human beings on opposite sides of it. I hope you'll autograph a copy for me when it's published."

Elgin laughed, a single caustic, ironic chuckle. "Yes, well don't sit by the telephone with a tuna sandwich and wait for that to happen."

"I don't understand."

A deep sigh escaped her, resonating with despair and resignation and frustration. "It's very simple, really. I've been writing as long as I can remember. I never wanted to be a schoolteacher or a nurse or any of the other things little girls want when they're growing up. My mother and I both worked to put me through college.

"Clutching my newly printed degree, I struck out for the center of the publishing world, New York. Worked as a filing clerk in the daytime and wrote like an inspired fiend at night. Haunted agents and publishers, lived in ratty apartments, ate peanut butter and jelly sandwiches and generally suffered for my art.

"One day, I literally bumped into Sheila on the subway. She told me she had a job as a reader at what she termed, 'Pervert Publishing'. 'Alternative fiction,' they called it. But she'd discovered people were buying it up like rainwater in the desert, especially on the Internet. She also discovered the one area these sleaze bags didn't cover was women's erotica. Sex but tied up with ribbons and champagne. She told me they got dozens of inquiries a month asking if they carried that kind of thing.

"So, having maxed out her credit cards for the publishing software and a website, she'd gone into business for herself. Fantasy Publishing…cool stories and hot sex."

"Well, then, I guess you were all set."

"Yeah. Right. I told her she was crazy and that she'd be in the poor house in six months. She told me I was probably right but to keep her card anyway.

"Well, winter came and one morning while covering a hole in my shoe sole with one of my rejection slips, it dawned on me that I'd suffered enough for my art. I rummaged around in my desk for a novella I'd written about a 'soiled dove' in a western bordello and trundled off to see Sheila, who by then had a real office and was printing real books.

"She read the novella, told me to call my heroine a 'whore,' write three more sex scenes and see that she ended up reformed in the arms of the hero and I'd have myself a hit. So I did. Of course, since I was only doing it for the money and didn't want it to reflect on my 'real' writing, I created Gillian Shelby. The book came out and presto! After five years of struggle, I was an overnight success."

"But...?"

"Here's where the irony comes in. I thought that Gillian's success would open the right doors for Elgin. No longer a mere 'wannabe,' I'd achieved 'published' status. Or at least Gillian had. Unfortunately, she'd been consigned to 'romance' hell and publishers and agents didn't take seriously that she might have more meat on her literary bones. And Elgin Collier still couldn't get arrested. So, *Another Love* gathers dust in my drawer."

"You shouldn't just give up like that. It's too good to just sit in a drawer. Why doesn't your friend publish it?"

"Because Sheila's running a business, not a charity. *Another Love* does not fit her publishing criteria or her target audience."

"And she can't broaden that target audience? Even for a friend?"

"Oh, I'm sure she'd do it if I pressed the matter," Elgin responded, "but I believe you shouldn't take advantage of your friends."

"She must know other publishers."

"Sure and they'd be glad to read it. Even publish it...if Gillian Shelby agrees to break her contract with Fantasy Publishing and write three or four novels. Just in case Elgin Collier bombs."

"It's not right. Not fair."

"Maybe not, but that's how the world is. And speaking of fair, I'm sorry about flying off the handle like that at you. It's not very fair of me to go off on you without even giving you a chance to explain. I'm sorry. And I'm sorry I bopped you with the book."

Harm gingerly put his fingers to his ear. "Ouch!"

"Here, sit down. Let me look at it."

"No, it's okay, really. Just a little sore." He grinned. "Now I know what they mean about a book being 'weighty'."

"Please, let me see." Laying the book on the coffee table behind her, she touched her fingertips to his ear, running them softly, slowly around the edge, bending forward as she did so.

Her skin, smooth and cool and the feel of her made him tremble, feel weak in the knees. Warm breath tickled the morning stubble on his cheek, her lips close enough to touch. The feel of thin satiny robe as it rubbed against his chest. The rich, sweet smell of her.

Wordlessly, she pressed herself against him, raising her other hand to cup his head between them as their lips met. Passion, unexpected and intense, engulfed them, pulling them deeper, closer. Grabbing her ass, he pushed into her body, feeling her sudden heat through his hard cock.

Fingers feeling like sausages, Harm fumbled with the sash of her robe as Elgin quickly unfastened the top button of his jeans, yanking down his zipper to expose the python-like bulge in his shorts. They had to part for a moment so that she could slide off her robe and he could pull off the rest of his clothes.

"You're beautiful," she whispered, running her hand lightly up and down his shaft, feeling the rigid heat of him as lust pounded through it with every heartbeat.

"So are you," he answered, running his fingers across her nipples, watching them get hard like his cock, cupping them and feeling their soft weight in his hands. Tenderly, he bent his head, suckling each one in turn, feeling her trembling, her breath catch.

When he took a breath, she lifted his face to hers, enjoying another ecstatic, longing kiss. Parting, she took his hand and they hurried up the stairs to her bedroom.

Soft morning light filtered through the trees and into the room, bathing it in a kind of peaceful glow. The covers lay where she'd pulled them off when she rose, the sheets still wrinkled, a depression in her pillow where her head had lain.

Slowly, she crawled in, moving to the unrumpled side to make room for him. As he followed her, Elgin put out her arms to him.

"I want you," she murmured. "No strings, no expectations, no promises. Just now and for however long it lasts. It's been so long I'd almost forgotten how it feels to want someone as much as I want you. Please..."

"It's pretty obvious how much I want you," he answered quietly as he wrapped her in his embrace, feeling her arms around his body. "I'll do whatever you want, however you want to do it. Just let me be with you, make love with you. You make me feel...well, like I never thought I'd feel again."

"Come inside me, now." She underscored the urgency in her voice by taking his cock in her fist and guiding between her legs.

"Don't you want me to play with you?" he mumbled, surprised by her eagerness.

"Right now," she breathed in his ear, "all I want is you. Inside me. Fill me up and then some with that thick, hard, beautiful cock of yours."

Settling between her legs, Harm slid effortlessly into her wet pussy, a short gasp of pleasure and a tensing of her body under him. And then he felt her relax, matching her movements to his, pushing herself against him, taking him up, the friction of his cock on her swollen clit, sparking new fire in her blood with each stroke.

Her lips and arms and pussy enfolded him, wrapping him in heated pleasure, making him forget everything but her body and the sensations roaring through his own. Far from romantic, fantasy lovemaking, they were two people, filled with lust and bottled-up passion, releasing an animal need as primal as life itself. It didn't mean anything except the pleasure of the moment. They wanted each other and that was reason, explanation, enough.

Elgin moaned softly and he felt the first tremors of her release ripple through her body. Fingernails dug into his skin as she grabbed his ass, kneading and grinding, trying to force himself deeper, harder into her. The muscles inside her, closed more tightly around his cock and his tempo sped up, his own orgasm just strokes away.

Her moans and cries of pleasure mixed with his as they crested and exploded together, rainbow bolts of sensation shooting through them like a perfect electric circuit feeding on itself until the power is spent.

"Oh...God..." she breathed between pants as she struggled to catch her breath. "You're...you're...unbelievable."

"Likewise," he mumbled, exiting gently and collapsing beside her. Elgin curled herself around him, snuggling in the crook of his arm and laying her head on his chest.

Slowly, she ran her fingertips over his chest, tweaking his nipples playfully and exploring the thin, light brown hair sprinkled over his chest, tapering in a straight line to the surprisingly soft nest of pubic hair and his not-quite-resting cock.

"You have a nice body," she told him, her voice still a sultry whisper. "Now that I'm not in such an...excited state, I hope you'll let me examine it in a more leisurely, more thorough fashion."

"Only if you'll let me reciprocate." He took a nipple between his long, hard fingers and felt her tremble against him. Even having just climaxed, he felt his cock stir once more and he knew the morning's delight would continue.

"That feels good," she encouraged him, moving her fingertips down to his inner thighs and fondling his sac.

"Before we get carried away again, don't you think we ought to talk?" She raised her eyes and saw the seriousness in his.

"About...?"

"Well, for one thing, protection." He flushed slightly and glanced past her to the wall. "I...uh...didn't come prepared. I mean... I... You and me..."

The Scout scenario flashed in Elgin's mind and she clenched her teeth to keep from laughing out loud.

"Oh."

He gazed down at her. "I don't make a habit of dropping into bed with every woman I meet. Especially not a client. Most especially not when I'm on a case. I guess maybe I should have figured that a woman like you would just naturally..."

"Excuse me," she interrupted sharply, raising herself on her elbow. "What exactly do you mean, 'a woman like me'?"

"I don't know. Beautiful. Worldly. Sensuous. You probably have hot and cold running guys chasing after you." Those sad dark eyes looked away again, his voice dropped to a whisper. "I haven't been with a woman in almost five years. That's a major reason for my lack of...staying power. That and the fact you're so sexy. I...uh...generally take my time about this."

Gently, Elgin put her fingertip under his chin and turned his face back to hers. "Trust me, you did just fine. It's sort of like gulping your food when you're hungry. And believe me, famished doesn't begin to explain how I felt. It's been more than three years for me. Despite what I write, I don't drop into bed either. I have to feel a connection, something 'special' that I want to share with someone. Like what I feel for you.

"If it makes you feel any better, I had my annual physical four months ago, including the standard blood tests. I'm depressingly healthy. And I've been on The Pill for irregular cycles since I was seventeen."

"I was married to the last woman I had sex with," he told her quietly. "We only used protection because we didn't want to start a family right away. When she died, something in me did too."

"I'm sorry, Camp. I didn't mean to bring up unpleasant memories. I didn't mean to rush into anything...to take advantage of the situation. Of you."

He smiled a little and ran the ball of this thumb gently down her cheek. "Isn't the man supposed to say that at a time like this?"

"I'm the one who came at you, remember? I think on some level I've been attracted to you from the beginning. I tend to be willful and, as Sheila puts it so delicately, damned bullheaded. That, combined with your attitude towards my writing...well, I guess the sparks flew but in the wrong direction."

Harm stared past her again and she had the feeling that he'd gone somewhere else, somewhere she couldn't follow. For long moments, she lay beside him, silently speaking to him with her body. At long last, he looked at her again, the sadness in his face, eyes, whole body, making her heart suddenly ache.

"Jeanne was seventeen when I first met her. She was the oldest daughter of my first partner after I got out of the police academy. Bill invited me to a barbecue one weekend. We'd only been partnering about three months. I rang the bell and she answered. Five foot four, red hair, blue eyes, a body to make a man fall on his face at her feet. I loved her before I even knew her name.

"We waited two years. A lot of necking, a lot of petting, a lot of cold showers, but she wanted our first time to be 'special'. A celebration." Harm paused and Elgin thought he might cry but he managed to go on.

"Our wedding night was beautiful. We spent hours playing and fondling and arousing each other. I wanted her to be happy, as fulfilled emotionally as physically. When she climaxed the first time, I almost came myself, she was so enraptured, so high. From then on, all I wanted was to make this woman happy. Explore all the ways there are for two people in love to show it. Make her body sing and be glad we were together."

"It sounds wonderful."

"It was. For a while. But in those days, I wanted a career as much as I wanted a home. I worked all the overtime I could get. I told her it was so we could save money and buy a house and start a family, and I meant it. But I also wanted to make rank, get ahead. When I wasn't working or studying for the next exam, I was asleep."

"One day I got a chance to try out for the FBI. When I was accepted, it meant uprooting to Quantico, Virginia. She didn't want to leave her family and friends, but I told her that as soon as I graduated and got a permanent assignment, we'd buy a house. Have kids. And I'd put in for a transfer back 'home' as soon as I could."

"And that never happened?"

He shook his head and bit his lip. "The training took every hour of the day, every ounce of strength I had. It made my police days seem like a paid vacation. I don't even remember when we stopped making love. It just seemed to…to sort of dry up and…"

"That happens in long-term relationships," she offered. "It's called 'reality' and afflicts lots of couples."

"I don't know," Harm sighed. "All I know is that I spent a lot more time with my career than my wife. It wasn't that I didn't love her…didn't want to be with her. I did. I even told myself I was doing it for us. That as soon as I got 'ahead', I'd slow down and we'd do all the things we planned. We never got the chance."

"It wasn't your fault she died."

"I didn't shoot her or push her off a cliff, if that's what you mean," he answered bitterly. "But I might just as well have. I just stopped being there for her. I killed her and I didn't even know it. Hell, I didn't even know she was going out. I was never home at night and when I was home in the daytime, I was usually asleep.

"I came home from an undercover operation. I'd been gone the best part of three months. I found her lying in our bed."

Tears pooled in his eyes and slid down his face. "She was in labor."

The word hit Elgin like a physical blow and she felt herself flinch.

"The sheets were soaked and she was barely conscious. I called an ambulance and we drove to the hospital. All the way there, I couldn't understand why she hadn't told me. I would have been happy to have a child. A piece of us.

"She didn't make it to the hospital. The baby came in the ambulance and the paramedics rushed both of them into emergency. After a while, this teenage kid in a white coat came out, told me he was Dr. Such-and-Such and how sorry he was but that Jeanne hadn't survived. He told me the baby was in a bad way and needed an emergency operation to survive. Said the baby had a fairly rare blood type and that if I could give blood, it would save time trying to locate some. Asked me if I wanted to donate blood.

"My wife had just died…of course I wanted to do anything I could to save our child, so I said of course. At that moment I was so shook up, I totally forgot that I'm A positive. Only after the blood work came back that I wasn't a suitable donor did it dawn on me. The reason she hadn't told me about the baby was because it wasn't mine. She'd been too ashamed even to get pre-natal treatment."

"Oh Camp…"

"Turned out it didn't really make any difference. He died on the operating table."

Harm wiped his face on the corner of the pillowcase.

"I don't remember very much about the days after that. I buried Jeanne and the baby and everyone told me what a tragedy it was. I asked for a transfer. Told people I couldn't bear to be in the same apartment, the same town… While I was cleaning out Jeanne's things, I found a whole box full of paperback romance novels. The kind you write with lots of hot sex and happy endings. Most of them looked like they'd been read and re-read. I couldn't believe it. My wife's stash of porn. Flipping through them, I got angrier and angrier as I skimmed the passages. People like you had made her dissatisfied, filled her head with a lot of romantic nonsense about forbidden love affairs and steamy passion. I blamed you for her death."

"I can understand that, Camp. Really, I can."

"Don't be understanding, Elgin. I don't deserve it. Jeanne was a beautiful, healthy woman with all the needs and wants a woman has. Should have. I gave her the gift of sex. I showed her the power and the pleasure of that gift and then I took it away from her. Blaming you and the sexy books was easier than facing the truth. If it was your fault, it didn't have to be mine. Somehow, you'd seduced her away from me. I hadn't let her go. And it worked very well until I met you. Now I understand, about a lot of things."

"Then let it rest, Camp. Jeanne did what she did. If she'd loved you...really loved you...she would have talked to you. Tried to work it out. Maybe you couldn't have stayed together. No one can know that now. But I know that if she loved you...if she *ever* loved you, she wouldn't want you to stop living, to be alone."

"I don't know..."

"Yes, you do. You know that if you'd have been killed in the line of duty, you wouldn't have wanted her to grow old by herself. Nothing but memories to keep her warm. You'd have wanted her to get on with her life, including someone else to share it with. Wouldn't you?"

"Of course, but..."

"No 'buts'. It's time for both of you to rest in peace." Elgin kissed him softly, the salty taste of his tears on her lips. He responded, taking her in his arms and returning the kiss, opening her lips to explore her mouth.

In a moment, his cock had resumed its hot, hard shape, rubbing against her flesh as they embraced.

"I don't think he wants to rest," Harm laughed, pointing downward.

"Well, then, let's see if he'd like to play some more." Elgin slid out of his grasp and out of bed.

"What are you up to?" he asked as she rummaged in her bureau.

"Ah, here we are," she announced, turning around and holding up a hand full of colored scarves. "Let the games begin."

"What are you going to do with those?" he asked warily.

"We're going to play 'Blind Man's Bluff', and you're 'it'. Put your arms up at the headboard."

"Oh no," he told her, shoving his hands under his body. "No games."

"Of course games," she chuckled, dragging the smooth, silky material over his cock. "He wants to play. I want to play. Don't be a poop."

The materials gliding over him sent a chill of pleasure through him. Reluctantly, he raised his arms for her, watching as she tied his wrists securely to a couple of the spiral posts that made up her headboard.

"Not too tight?"

"No, I guess not."

"Good. I use the cotton instead of the silk because it's not so likely to slip and tighten up when you're...ah...moving around."

"Hey, now what?" he barked as she folded a thick, dark blue scarf and leaned toward his head.

"You're 'it'," she explained with a giggle. "You can't play the game without a Blind Man. Now hold still." Quickly she covered his eyes, tying the scarf securely behind his head.

"Okay, now what?"

"I'll be right back," she laughed and he felt her get up from the bed. "I have to go find my camera."

"Elgin!" he shouted. "Elgin, you come back here. That isn't funny." Tugging, he couldn't move his wrists.

"Don't get so excited," she told him as he heard her bare feet pad back into the room. "At least not yet." He felt the weight of her as she climbed back onto the bed. "Hmmm, you look positively yummy. All helpless and totally at my mercy."

"Elgin…"

She took his cock in her hand, grabbing it firmly but not uncomfortably at the base. Something warm and thick touched the head, flowing slowly down like molasses.

"What is that?"

In answer, her lips closed around his shaft, her tongue licking the head, her mouth forming a tight vacuum. The sensation would have sent him crashing through the ceiling had he not been tied securely to the bed.

"I love hot fudge," she sighed, raising her mouth from his cock but leaving her tongue to roll around the tip. "It's so sweet and thick and rich. I like it on just about anything I can get in my mouth."

Her lips moved to the base of his cock, her soft cheeks brushing his pubic hair and sac, her tongue moving around the shaft as it traveled slowly upward, making sure that not a drop of chocolate escaped her.

He'd never known anything like it. Certainly he'd had oral sex, but not like this. Helpless, his sight gone, his whole body seemed more alive, more sensitive than he could ever remember. Fire pulsed through his body, his cock straining at this sweet torture.

"You know what I like with hot fudge," she murmured. "Nice cool, whipped cream."

He heard a raspberry noise and his cock felt the chill of the light froth as it covered him completely again from base to tip.

"Oh shit," he muttered, "that's cold."

"Well then, let me get rid of it for you."

Her pursed lips moved up and down his shaft, sucking the sweet cream up like a vacuum. At the top, her teeth raked gently over the tip as it disappeared, her tongue lapping up every last bit.

"Hmm, you taste good. A little salty, but very good. Let's see what else there is to play with."

Something smooth, cool and silky moved across his thighs and stomach, drifting lightly to snake itself around his cock. A feather tip tickled his balls as her breath blew softly on his pubic hair.

"Oh God..." he moaned, twisting and writhing in building pleasure.

"What a lovely, big, thick cock you have," she cooed, dragging the silk scarf around his shaft like the red stripes on a candy cane. "So hot and full."

Another scarf moved lazily across his throat and down to his nipples, the thin material barely touching his skin but sending icicles of excitement through him like a burst of electricity. The scarves moved around his cock and over every inch of his body. She pulled one tenderly up and down the arch of his foot, relishing the little chuckles they elicited from him.

His rising excitement was firing her own. Watching him squirm as she worked on him, she felt herself growing hot, her desire building. Removing the scarf with a last flourish, she straddled him, brushing her swelled, wet clit and pussy the length of his cock, his fiery, rippled hardness sending flashes of pleasure sizzling through her.

Under her, his cock twitched and wiggled like something alive, seeking her in hot desperation.

"Do you like that?" she whispered, laying herself out on him, her nipples touching him ever so slightly, her lips meeting his.

Groans and whimpers of pleasure answered her, his body moving against her. She watched the big vein in his neck throb as blood pumped through it, hot and horny and anxious for her.

A wave of heat washed over her as she bent down and bit into his soft flesh just where his neck blended into his shoulders.

He whimpered and wiggled beneath her, his body musky and aroused, covered with a salty sheen of passion and exertion. Satisfied that the red marks of her teeth would blossom into a very nice hickey, Elgin traced her tongue slowly down his chest, stopping at his nipples. At her first touch, Harm shuddered, his hips bucking under her in response to the unexpected sensation. Encouraged, she nipped and sucked on the tiny buds, bringing them to their full erection.

She couldn't stand much more foreplay and she knew he couldn't either. Moving backwards a little, she eased herself up, taking him in her hand and guiding him until she sat, fully impaled on him, her clit rubbing on his rough pubic hair, the feel of him filling her to bursting.

Groans and growls bubbled out as she moved slowly up and down his shaft, squeezing and teasing, pushing herself down on him as hard as she could, then easing up until only the head of his cock remained in her.

She watched, eyes half-closed in a dreamy fog as his stomach muscles tightened and relaxed with the rhythm of his pumping, chest hair darkened with his sweat, arms straining and outlined against the bedding and the dark wood spindles.

Sparklers fizzed in her blood and the first shudders of orgasm grew into full climax, rocking her as he came beneath her, their cries and moans mixing and running together like streamers of confetti in the wind.

Quickly, she undid the scarves, tossing them aside as she removed the blindfold and began to massage his wrists and arms.

"Turn over," she ordered. "If I don't rub your neck and shoulders, you're going to feel like you played the first half without your pads."

"Mmm," he mumbled, dutifully turning on his stomach, letting her gently massage his neck, shoulders, back, arms and wrists.

"Okay?" she asked after several moments.

"More like terrific. Come here."

She folded into his embrace and they lay quietly, listening to the morning birds and their breathing returning to normal.

"How 'bout a nice refreshing shower and then a long soak in a warm tub? Help keep those muscles from getting stiff. Just in case..."

"I knew there was a reason they had those great big old tubs," he laughed. "Nothing like a little aquatic hanky-panky for a honeymoon cottage."

"Sorry to disappoint you, Romeo, but the reason the tubs are so big is that according to local gossip, the original owners were both well over six feet tall. Had the tubs made extra large especially for the cabin."

"Makes a good cover story," he insisted. "And after all, what's a little good, clean fun between consenting adults?"

"You think so, huh?"

"Definitely."

"Then what are we waiting for?"

* * * * *

"Mmmm, you taste good," Harm mumbled, nibbling the back of her neck.

"You can't possibly still be horny," she laughed, shaking her head and settling against his chest.

"I never said I was horny," he corrected, "only that you taste good. And look good and feel good and smell good."

"Are we just going to lie here in this tub all day getting wrinkled and pruney?"

"Either that or we could go back to bed. I think there's still some hot fudge left." Circling her in his arms, he leaned back and closed his eyes.

"Whoa, there," she giggled, feeling his soft cock in the small of her back as she cuddled between his legs, "I don't know about you, but I've had more sex in the last couple of hours than in the last couple of years. Better pace ourselves. We're going to be here 'til Labor Day and you don't want to peak too soon."

"I don't care about anything except fucking you, which I intend to do as often as you and Nature will permit, including in this marvelous old tub. Maybe not right this minute, but it's definitely going to happen. With any luck, more than once."

"My God, I've created a monster. A horny, insatiable monster."

Turning her gently, she saw he'd grown suddenly quiet and serious.

"On the contrary," he whispered. "You took a hard, cold, unfeeling monster and turned him back into a caring, needy, *very* horny man again. He just wants to show his gratitude and appreciation for giving him back his life. If he can make you squeal with pleasure, that's just a bonus."

"I didn't do anything. That warm, caring, very horny man's always been there. He just needed to be reminded, that's all."

"Thank you anyway." They shared a long, passionate, slightly awkward kiss.

"Well, I've got to get out of here," she announced. "If I don't, in another ten minutes I really will look like a wrinkled old hag. Besides, if I don't at least get some coffee, I'm going to pass out."

"I guess you're right," he agreed as she grabbed the tub sides and lifted herself up. "You better eat. You're going to need all your energy. The day's still young yet." He flashed her an evil grin.

Rolling her eyes, Elgin padded across the room and grabbed her towel. Pulling the plug, Harm got out and joined her.

"What say you take me to the Lodge for dinner tonight? If you're good, I'll let you pay the check." She smiled slyly. "And if you're *very, very good*, I may even let you get me tipsy and take advantage."

"And how good would I have to be?"

"We'll work on that today. A lot."

When they'd dried, Harm went across the hall to his room to dress and Elgin went to her room to dress, too, taking a little extra time to comb her hair and put on fresh lipstick but no underwear.

Straightening the bed, the memory of their lovemaking replayed itself. With a chuckle, she wadded up the scarves and put them in her nightstand drawer. Since she knew they'd be needed again…soon…no point putting them back in her bureau.

Idly, she wondered what The Mercantile might have in the way of adult toys. Probably nothing but she'd have to remember to buy more hot fudge.

Stepping into the hall, her nose wrinkled up as it caught the welcome scent of food cooking. Following the aroma, she found Harm at the stove, sausage frying in a black skillet.

"Well, well," she teased, putting her arm around his waist, "aren't you just handy as a shirt pocket? I didn't know the FBI had a cooking merit badge."

Bending down, he pecked her cheek. "Watch it, woman," he warned playfully. "I swing a mean spatula. God knows you need a good spanking but you'd probably enjoy it."

"Wouldn't you like to know?"

"As a matter of fact, yes. And I may just find out before the summer's finished, too. Any objections?"

"Who knows?" She shrugged, moving to the coffee maker on the counter. "It's a long time 'til September. Anything might happen."

"Is that a threat or a promise?"

* * * * *

"Gettin' a late start this mornin' aren't you?" Jim eyed the breakfast dishes still sitting on the table as Harm and Elgin enjoyed a leisurely second cup of coffee.

"Well, you know how it is, Jim," Elgin told him, throwing Harm a quick glance, "some mornings you just don't feel like getting out of bed."

Trying to stifle a surprised laugh, Harm began coughing, sipping coffee as Elgin patted his back.

Jim looked from Harm to Elgin and back, suspicion in his eyes, his mouth drawn down a little. Obviously they didn't intend to share the joke.

"Would you like some coffee?" she offered when Harm had regained his composure.

"No thanks. Since you don't have a phone, Marty called me to ask if you two'd like to go out on 'The Monkey' tomorrow. Says he's gotta go over to West Shore on business and thought you'd like to ride over, lose a few bucks in the casinos and gawk at the tourists. Late lunch and then back here before sunset."

"What's 'The Monkey'?" Harm asked.

"Marty's boat," Elgin replied happily. "Actually, 'The Brass Monkey'."

"That's a strange name for a boat."

"Marty's sort of a strange guy," Fisher chuckled. "If ya get my drift. Never owned a boat before he bought her. Big, ocean goin' thing. Not exactly huge, but twice the size of anything up here. Had it brought all the way from the coast.

"Well, soon as I saw it, I asked him what the hell he intended to do with it when winter come. He looks at me with those big sad eyes of his and say, 'whataya mean?' I told him the lake gets too cold and too rough to leave a boat in the water all winter. I take all mine out and put 'em in storage. Told him livin' up here all his life, he should know that in winter, even the brass monkeys come inside.

"Well, he looked at me and my little runabouts and back at his yacht and says, 'Oh.' That's all. Just, 'Oh.' Two days later a crew a workmen arrived up at his place. Built a big old shed up behind his place where ya couldn't see it from the water or the house. When winter come, he hired a crane to come down, pull that thing outta the water and haul it up to that shed. Next year, he had 'em come back and put her in the water. Had a big christenin' ceremony and named her 'The Brass Monkey'. Everybody had a good laugh includin' Marty."

"Oh that sounds wonderful," Elgin replied excitedly. "You'll love it, Camp, really."

"Sure. Sounds like fun."

"Figured you wouldn't turn it down," Fisher smiled indulgently. "Marty said he'll meet you at the 'Monkey' 'bout nine-thirty. Better set yer alarm. Don't wanna over sleep."

"No need for that," she assured him. "We'll be there with bells on."

"Well, I better get goin'. Us workin' people can't afford to lounge around all day. 'Sides, don't wanna tax poor Tom's brain by leavin' him in charge too long."

"Let's face it, Jim," she teased, putting her arm around him, "you think anything after five a.m. is sleeping in."

"And you think anything before nine is gettin' up with the chickens. Damn good thing you're a writer and don't have to punch a time clock like the rest of us."

"You know I never worried about having a job. You promised me as a child I could always come work for you."

"Offer still stands. Any time you wanna give up that city crap and come home, Ellie, you know you're always welcome."

"I know Jim," she told him quietly. "And you have no idea how much that means to me."

He gazed down at her fondly. Finally, he kissed the top of her head.

"You and Harm be sure to come by and say 'howdy' tomorrow. Might be able to rustle up a beer er even a hard cola."

"Bet on it."

"Okay then. Bye Ellie. Harm."

"Bye Jim."

The two of them settled back to the breakfast table.

"I, uh, don't mean to be rude, but where the hell did he materialize from? I'd hate to think of someone sneaking up on us if we'd been otherwise occupied."

"Oh, I keep forgetting. You're a stranger here. You don't know the territory. Jim lives just on the other side of that knoll over there. Sort of catawampus to the upper corner of my property.

"This whole area is honeycombed with old logging roads and trails. Some of them go all the way back to the gold rush. Jim knows them all and in that great big old truck of his with those big wheels, four-wheel drive and high ground clearance, he uses them as short-cuts to get around. In fact, there's an old trail that goes past his place and sort of doglegs down to the lake and comes out just below my gate. Moon Lake Road used to be part of the logging system. You wouldn't see it if you didn't know where to look. Grown over mostly now."

Elgin's voice dropped and she looked away toward the lake.

"Jim's wife, Cissy, liked to hike the trails around here. Did it practically every morning, rain or shine. Especially the one down by the lake.

"Jim and a buddy of his came home from fishing one day and she wasn't there. It was getting late and dark so he and his friend went out to look for her. They found her body floating face down in the shallows just below the trail."

"I'm sorry. That must have been awful for him."

She nodded. "It was terrible for everyone who knew her. Cissy was kind and gentle and just about the best person I ever knew. The police figure she was walking along, tripped, fell, hit her head and tumbled into the water and drowned.

"That happened the autumn after the summer I turned fifteen. Marty got a letter from his folks and he told me. I felt really bad and wrote Jim a letter, and he wrote back to me telling me how much he appreciated the sympathy and how he looked forward to seeing me again in the summer. I didn't go back the next year. Not for a lot of years as a matter of fact. Not until I bought this place." She paused as if in thought.

"Funny…" she mused.

"What?"

She turned back to him then. "Oh, I don't know. I hadn't thought about that trail or Cissy for ages. In fact, after she died, no one ever used it anymore, including Jim. I just thought how funny he should use it to come visit me after all this time. Guess it was just quicker than going all the way around and down the road and opening the gate. Now, what do you want to do with the rest of the day?"

"Oh," he answered, pulling her to him, "I'm sure if we put our heads together, we can think of something."

Chapter Eleven

"Holy shit!" Harm breathed as he pulled the SUV to a stop and got his first look at "The Brass Monkey" rocking gently at the end of the longest dock at Fisher's Marina.

Elgin grinned. "That's the general reaction when people first see 'The Monkey'," she told him. "I know it was mine. Come on."

"She must be...what? Fifty...sixty feet?"

"Sixty-five."

Sleek, winter-white fiberglass with a broad fore deck, flying bridge and sparkling blue awning covering the after deck. As they came along side, Harm noticed a little brass monkey sitting just over the railing, grinning a warm welcome.

"Elgin, darling." Marty beamed, grabbing her hand and helping her aboard, hugging her as her feet landed on the polished teak-look deck. "I'm delighted you could make it. Absolutely delighted."

He extended a polite but less than enthusiastic hand in Harm's direction.

"And of course you too. Harm, isn't it?"

"Camp, please."

"Yes. Well, sit down, get comfy and we'll get underway." He shooed them toward the plump, bright blue cushions ringing the deep well of the after deck.

"Paul?" he called into an intercom.

"Yes sir?" came a voice from the box.

"We're all set. Cast off and get underway whenever you're ready." Flipping the "off" switch, he came over and made himself comfortable next to Elgin.

"So, what sort of mischief have you two been getting into?"

Harm bristled silently at the nerve of his host. And he was sitting entirely too close to Elgin.

"Nothing but soaking up the peace and quiet," she replied, patting him gently on the knee.

"Knowing what a fidget box you are," he sniffed, "of course I don't believe that for an instant. But whatever it is, it definitely agrees with you. You're glowing. Absolutely radiant."

"It's the fresh air and being around my friends."

"I don't believe that for an instant either, but if you're going to be mysterious, I shall just have to badger you unmercifully until you break."

The engines roared to life, the boat shuddering like a living thing as it moved slowly away from the dock.

"She's a beauty," Harm remarked, anxious to steer the conversation in another direction.

A young Hispanic man in white steward's jacket and Bermuda shorts appeared, coming to a respectful stop beside Marty.

"I'm having Mimosa," he told them, "unless you'd prefer something else."

"No, that's fine."

"Same here."

Marty nodded once and the young man disappeared. A moment later, he reappeared with a silver tray bearing three tall, slender glasses of orange juice, a slice of fresh orange on the rim.

"Oh, that's good," Elgin sighed. "I couldn't tell you how long it's been since I had Mimosa. Especially with fresh squeezed orange juice and just the right amount of champagne."

"That's because you've chosen that urban rat race," he scolded lightly. "Now that you're rich and famous and could live anywhere you want, you should come home. Back to simple things like fresh orange juice and the people who love you."

"I like the urban rat race," she laughed. "I always said that I enjoy the lake in the summer but that at heart, I'm a city girl. John Denver not withstanding, I've always thought living in the country was vastly overrated, especially in the dead of winter with six feet of snow on the ground and no propane because the truck couldn't get through. Nope. Give me concrete and electric lights any day in the week."

"And what about you Mr. Harm?" Marty asked suddenly, focusing those pale eyes on him as he sipped his drink.

"Oh, I don't know," Harm stalled as he tried to recover. "Never spent much time in the country. I like it well enough but I guess I'm just a city boy."

"Well, you never know what you might like until you try it."

The face remained impassive but those eyes continued to watch him...study him almost. A cold breath prickled the hairs on the back of his neck.

"Breakfast is served," announced the young man, holding open the salon door.

"Ah, good." Marty rose and waited for Elgin and Harm.

"A little light buffet," he told them, taking Elgin's arm. "Nothing elaborate. Just had the cook throw together whatever he had. Hope you don't mind potluck."

Harm felt as if he'd stepped into a fine restaurant. Rich, dark wood blended perfectly with glove soft-cream suede and brass accents. Instead of portholes, large windows on each side gave a view of the passing scenery.

A buffet table ran along one wall for perhaps ten feet, an older man in a tall chef's cap at one end and a middle aged gentleman in the same kind of outfit as the young Hispanic, stood at the other end.

Marty gave Elgin and Harm a mock bow and stood aside for them. The large table, covered with thick white tablecloths, fairly groaned under the weight of all the food. Lox, bagels, cream cheese and even caviar. Fresh strawberries, blueberries, raspberries, melon and pineapple. Pastries, muffins, biscuits, English muffins. Covered trays of bacon, sausage and ham. Crisp hash browns.

"Joseph makes pancakes, omelets and a Belgian Waffle that is absolutely decadent."

"Ohhhhh," she breathed, "that sounds good."

The chef smiled. "Thank you, Miss. Would you care for fruit on it?"

"Oh yes, Elgin," Marty urged. "Have the apples. Trust me, you will absolutely weep with ecstasy."

"All right. Apples please."

"And you sir?"

"A couple of eggs, over easy please."

"Ah, a simple man of simple tastes. I like that." Harm thought he detected just the faintest note of sarcasm in the other man's voice.

"I'll have the usual, Joseph."

"Well, we can sit down now. Ernesto will bring everything to the table."

"So, how is it that you and Elgin know each other?" Harm asked.

"You mean Elgin hasn't told you about us?"

Harm's fork stopped halfway to his mouth and he stared at Elgin.

"Oh, Marty, stop that," she giggled, tapping his arm lightly and turning a little crimson. "Camp isn't interested in such ancient history."

"No," Harm told her, "I'd be *very* interested."

"Well, there really isn't very much to it."

"Nonsense," Marty objected. "There's a great deal to it and since we've an hour to kill between here and West Shore, I think you should absolutely tell Camp all about us."

"I agree."

"All right. Marty's great-great-grandfather came here during the gold rush hoping to make his fortune. He didn't find any gold but he opened the first general store on this side of the lake. Had to have everything shipped up here by mule train and later on 'The Belle'. Eventually, he built a little cabin on the bluff just overlooking the store and got married."

"Had twelve children," Marty interjected. "How they managed that in a single room log cabin escapes me absolutely, but they did. My great-grandfather, being the eldest, naturally inherited the mercantile."

"That's kind of how it went," Elgin continued. "Every generation improving their lives. Built better houses and expanded the mercantile. Every parent wanted better for their children. Rebecca, Marty's mother, made up her mind that he should be the first college graduate in the family."

"She read to me as long as I can remember. Played the phonograph. Bought one of the first televisions in the area. Taught me to read and write and do numbers before I went to school."

"She was also the first one to realize that Marty wasn't just bright, but gifted. He finished high school at ten. At twelve, he had a full scholarship to Winston Technical University, but his family couldn't close the mercantile and go with him."

"At that time, Elgin's aunt suggested to my mother that I go and live with Elgin and her mother. They lived less than six blocks from the campus, they had a spare bedroom and with Elgin's father departed, her mother needed the money a boarder could provide. I knew Elgin slightly because she used to come up here summers with her aunt and uncle. So, clutching a suitcase and a book bag, I went to live at Elgin's house and began college."

"It must have been rough."

"A masterpiece of understatement, Mr. Harm," Marty responded acidly. "Oh not the academics. I thrived on the challenge and the opportunity to expand my horizons. But the social milieu was hellish. There I was, thirteen years old, showing up so-called men twice my age in every academic area but totally isolated. Friendless and totally alone in an alien environment. Add to that the fact that my budding sexuality hardly fitted the norm and you have the makings of a nightmare. I should no doubt have killed myself if it hadn't been for Elgin."

"Oh Marty, really…"

"No, it's true. Younger than I, she didn't care about my IQ or my sexual problems. She was warm and funny and loving and absolutely accepting of me. We listened to music and talked about the kinds of things children talk about, and I did her algebra homework so she wouldn't flunk out of eighth grade."

"I graduated at fifteen, took my first Masters at seventeen, my Doctorate at nineteen. All those years I lived with Elgin and her mother. In the summers, she and I came back here."

"At twenty-one," Harm interrupted when Marty paused, "after receiving his second Doctorate, M. Van Scoyk founded Pine Box Computers utilizing a chip of his own design. The third generation of that chip is the foundation of most PC's running today. Rarely photographed and said to be an eccentric recluse, Van Scoyk spent most of his time behind the scenes. At thirty, he sold the company, retaining a healthy chunk of stock and disappeared."

"Business bored me. Even computer research became confining in the face of a universe to be understood. So I took the money and ran. Here in Spirit Cove, I'm still Fred and Rebecca's only son, Marty. Made some money but still runs his father's mercantile. Even give you credit in the winter if things get a little thin. They talk about me and laugh behind my back, but they're family so I forgive their trespasses as they forgive mine."

He glanced at Elgin and back to Harm. "Sometimes there's no security like home."

Ernesto arrived with their breakfast and the conversation drifted to other matters.

"So how long does it take to get across the lake?" Harm asked.

"About an hour, give or take," Marty told him, spooning caviar onto a thin slice of toast. "If I'm in a hurry, I have Paul run her wide open. On a day like today, when I have guests whose company I wish to enjoy, I have him take it easy. Don't want any queasy tummies now do we?"

"I wouldn't know," Harm responded casually, "Navy myself. Carrier duty in the Pacific. Two typhoons in one cruise. You know what a wave looks like breaking over the bow of a ship eight stories high?"

"Large, I would imagine."

After breakfast, they went back out on deck, enjoying the beauty of the lake, a second cup of coffee that even Harm had to grudgingly admit was excellent, and small talk. Well, mostly Van Scoyk talked, Elgin giggled and he sat quietly, watching the hotels and casinos rising out of the thick pine forests grow larger on the opposite shore.

"Well," Marty announced finally, "we'll be docking in about ten minutes. I assume, Elgin my dear, that you'll want to adjourn to the powder room before we land."

"You know me too well, Marty. I'll be right back."

"So Harm," Marty began, turning those pale eyes on him again, his voice serious, "I don't want to sound like a meddling old Auntie, but Elgin is very special to me in ways you couldn't possibly understand, even if I were so inclined as to explain them to you, which I am not. If this...this *thing* is merely a summer dalliance, a passing trifle on her part, so be it. She's a grown woman and certainly entitled to take up with whomever she desires. I have only to look at her to see how happy she is.

But should this turn out to be more serious to her than to you, I wouldn't like it. I wouldn't like it at all."

"Which means?"

"Just this. I've checked you out very thoroughly. You're educated, successful in your chosen profession of keyhole peeping and comfortably well off. You seem to be a man of reputable character, not given to excesses of wine, women or song. Nevertheless, hurt Elgin, no matter how slightly or even inadvertently, and you will have to deal with me. I know you think me a foolish, silly little fag but make no mistake. I am very rich and very powerful. My feelings for her run deep. Rest assured Mr. Harm, I would make a formidable enemy."

Chapter Twelve

God but he was gorgeous. Just looking at him sleeping made her horny. Broad shoulders and smooth back, flat ass, long legs pulled up slightly. The calm, reassuring rhythm of his breathing.

The days had flown by on a magic carpet of sun, water, pine scent and the best sex of her life. Mornings began with lazy passion, punctuated with giggles, sighs, moans and shrieks. Long afternoons sunning nude on the deck, a newly installed motion activated brass bell alerted them to approaching visitors. Warm nights on a blanket by the water, covered with nothing but stars and the watchful Moon Goddess.

July Fourth.

As a child, it had both excited and saddened her. Spirit Cove, decked out in its most festive, most patriotic red, white and blue, the daylong festivities in the park. Hot dogs and sack races and Sousa marches filling the air. Fireworks lit the sky, reflected like fountains of multi-colored falling stars in the still, black water.

But in her child's mind it had also signaled the halfway point, the beginning of the end of summer. Like a roller coaster creeping expectantly toward the first rise and then rocketing down the other side to Labor Day.

Labor Day.

Pack up her summer fantasies and return to the real world. Work. Duty. Obligation.

No strings she'd told him, whatever there was for however long it lasted. Swept up in the desire and need of the moment, she hadn't considered anything beyond the prospect of his cock in her yearning, aching pussy.

But that had been before she'd loved him. Before he'd touched her heart as well as her clit. He'd wrapped himself around her body and slipped into her soul as easily as he slipped into her pussy.

She wanted to tell him how she felt. Whisper it to him in their most intimate moments. Say the words as they sat on the deck watching the sunset. Run through the world screaming it at the top of her lungs. Paint it on the clouds so that everyone would know.

Something stopped her though, the words sticking in her throat like a cork in a bottle of wine.

He hadn't told her he loved her. For all she knew, this might be nothing more than a summer fling, a pleasant way to combine business with pleasure. When he unloaded her gear in front of her condo back in town, would he simply drive away and never look back? Perhaps his plans did not include her at all.

A knot formed in her chest and she put out her fingertips to touch him. She needed to reassure herself he was still really there.

What if she told him? Just said the words out loud?

"I love you Campbell Alexander Harm. I can't tell you exactly when or exactly how it happened. All I know is that it did."

Perhaps he'd smile, take her in his arms and say the words her soul thirsted for, "I love you too, Elgin Collier."

Or he might gape at her, shock, uncertainty, and fear replacing his smile. Warmth and closeness giving way to distance and chill.

"I'm...I'm sorry, Elgin," he'd stammer helplessly. "I don't know what to say. I never meant to hurt you... I thought we both agreed. No strings..."

His words ripped into her gut, the pain so strong, so real, she had to squeeze her eyes shut tightly to keep the tears from coming.

Elgin felt him stir, turning his body and reaching out to pull her to him.

"Good morning," he mumbled in her ear and she felt his steely cock, already solid and hot against her thigh. Hot need immediately rose up in her, pulsing out from between her legs like ripples in a pond.

She had him now, she told herself desperately. Now mattered. Here…this moment counted, not some maybe, some Labor Day that might never come. He wanted…needed her now. The heat of him melded with her own.

"Why do men always wake up with a hard-on?" she teased.

"Can't speak for all men," he answered, nuzzling the back of her neck, "but I wake up horny because you're here. I also walk around horny all day and go to bed horny for the same reason."

"I don't think it's me, I think it's you."

He curled himself around her like spoons in a drawer. "Uh-uh. It's definitely you."

"And what makes you say that?" She snuggled her ass against him, feeling his cock press like a hot iron rod on her soft flesh.

"Well, for one thing, you have all these great tasting parts that I like to nibble on. Like your ears…" He took a tender lobe in his mouth, raking his teeth across it and nipping a little. Her shivers of delight rewarded him. Sticking out the tip of his tongue, he moved it quickly along the outer shell and pushed it into the canal, tickling as he went.

"Ohhhh," she breathed, her body tensing with pleasure.

"And there's that beautiful, slender, sexy neck of yours." His lips moved down the side, barely touching her. Waves of heat rolled across her.

"Melting into those creamy, round shoulders that just beg for me." Gently, she felt the tips of his teeth brush the soft flesh, combined with vigorous sucking, his fingertips gliding from neck to shoulder and back.

A jolt of electricity shot through her, making her start with its force, but he held her firmly as he continued his travels, turning her to her back. Through dreamy eyes, she saw him eagerly taking in the sight, relishing and savoring her.

"Those beautiful, perfect breasts," he breathed, cupping one in each hand, feeling their round smoothness. When he'd first seen them, they'd been white as milk. But the nude sunbathing had turned them to a beautiful light brown, gold almost, blending into the dark pink of her nipples. Playfully, he grabbed them between his fingers, twisting and rubbing them as they became as stiff and erect as his cock.

"I like your all-over tan," he chuckled. "Makes you look like a wild native virgin."

"Yes, well considering how much time you spent covering me, I'm surprised I got any sun at all."

"What can I say? I've always been a sucker for wild native virgins."

Harm straddled her on his knees, his muscled thighs tight against her hips, his cock taut and red against his tanned stomach, growing like one of the forest pines out of tangled dark brush. The sight of him, horny and needful, heightened her own desire for him.

"No doubt a holdover from your Navy days in the South Pacific."

"Uh-uh. When I was twelve, I found an old copy of *World Travel* magazine. Had a story about some island in the tropics somewhere. Don't even remember which one now. But boy I sure remember the pictures. White sand, blue water and lots of golden brown skin. Which reminds me. Turn over."

"Why?"

"Don't argue. Just do what I tell you."

"Harm's Way?" she needled.

"Exactly." He moved a little and put his hand on her thigh.

Slowly, she complied, turning on her stomach. "Now what?"

"Now I give you a relaxing massage and look at your beautiful back and that incredibly sexy ass," she briefly paused, "and make you so horny you come all over my cock."

"Mmmm, sounds like a plan to me," she sighed and closed her eyes.

"You feel so good," he told her softly, leaning forward and putting his big hands on her shoulders, kneading gently. Instantly, she felt herself melting. "I could just stay here and touch you forever."

Leaning down, Harm nuzzled the back of her neck, running his tongue across her smooth flesh, gently nipping and biting as his hands moved up and back along her shoulders.

She trembled beneath him as he brushed his erect cock in the crease between her cheeks. Hot and hard, his desire fanned her own and she wriggled her ass, pressing him between their two excited bodies.

Gently, he moved his hands under her, lifting her up and back until her ass presented itself to him, round and hot and waiting.

"You taste so good," he murmured as his lips brushed over the curves of her cheeks in a prolonged, passionate kiss. As he did so, his fingertips slid under her and found her dripping pussy and swollen clit. The wet heat of her bolted through him like lightning.

Pressing harder against him, she whimpered like a needy child. "Please, please come inside me," she begged.

Bringing his fingers to his lips, Harm licked them slowly, relishing the sweet taste and aroused scent. His cock glowed red with its own heat, straining like a leashed animal toward its prize, just inches away.

"Well, since you asked so nicely," he murmured, guiding his cock to her pussy, feeling it swallowed up by her anxious, hungry body.

They began a leisurely, rhythmic dance, Harm balanced on his knees, his hands gripping her hips as she moved easily back and forth, now smearing his balls with her essence, now holding nothing but the head. Squeezing him the length of his shaft, up and down or letting him glide at his own pace. Frantic pumping and almost stopping, they changed their timing and movements like they'd been together forever and not merely a few weeks.

Elgin had never experienced this passion, this intensity. She'd written countless love scenes...torrid casual sex and white-hot committed love. Erotica was her specialty, indeed, her reputation. The excuse she'd given herself for coming here with him. But she understood now how hollow all that had been, why her heroine's sex scene with Kemp Harmon hadn't struck the right note. She'd been trying to seduce him as an act of power and domination, not love.

What she'd mistaken in Campbell Harm for arrogance and self-importance had turned out to be fear and need and pain, disguised as aloofness and an edge of superiority. The same fear and need and pain she'd covered independence and disdain. Something strong enough to break through their mutual barriers had found them, translated itself into yearning, desire and a physical force that rocketed them past orgasm to a melding of their beings.

Fire screamed through her blood, pounding in her ears, making her gasp for breath. Her fingers clenched around the pillow as she streaked skyward, small moans and meaningless sounds escaping her.

Behind her, she felt his strokes quicken, his hands digging into her cheeks, growls and moans as the first shudders of climax bubbled up.

It tore through her, liquid fire shooting up from him like exploding lava, shaking her physical body and trembling the foundations of her very self. She hung for an eternal, glorious moments in a web of pure, crystal pleasure like a sunlit dewdrop on a silken spider's web. Her writer's mind was suddenly devoid of words to describe this wonder.

A few more hearty bangs against her ass and he stopped, sagging against her, his hot, ragged breath and soft lips on the flesh of her back.

"God," he sighed, between shallow pants, "you are the best lover a man could ever have. I just hope you don't kill me before Labor Day." He pulled out and dropped beside her, curling her in his embrace.

"Oh no," she assured him with a kiss, "I have no intention of letting anything happen to you before Labor Day."

* * * * *

"We need to get up," Elgin sighed, not moving or even opening her eyes.

"I've already been up," Harm replied wryly. "Although if you play your cards right, I might manage to get up at least once more."

"I meant out of bed."

"Okay. How 'bout the deck? Or the rug in front of the fireplace? Maybe the kitchen counter?"

She sighed again. "In case you've forgotten, today is the Fourth of July. Spirit Cove party's all day, then we're invited to Marty's for a barbecue and then out on 'The Monkey' for the fireworks."

"I have a better idea," he answered, taking her in his arms. "Why don't we stay home and make our own fireworks?"

"You're not only a satyr," she pretended to grumble, "but a poop as well. I don't know which is worse."

"Poop?" he declared, his eyes popping open. "What do you mean, 'poop'?"

"I mean you. You're nothing but a great big old party poop."

"You didn't seem to mind my great big old party favor just a while ago. Or were you faking those screams?"

"Ohhh, I can assure you, the screams were absolutely, positively, one hundred percent authentic. You do nice work."

"I'm glad you approve," he beamed at her, "but it's the inspiration. I've never felt this way about anyone. Even Jeanne." Harm gazed into her face, his eyes filled with pain, searching it seemed for something. For a fleeting instant, he held her, his lips moving as if he intended to say something.

Please dear God, she thought anxiously, please let him say the words.

"You're right," he told her finally, "I guess we should get up. I've never seen a real, old-fashioned, small-town Fourth."

As he turned his back and moved to the other side of the bed, Elgin released a breath she hadn't realized she'd been holding. The moment had come and gone and he hadn't told her what she wanted so much to hear.

Putting her feet on the floor, her chest tight, her heart a rock, she knew now that the words would never come. That he'd told her what she needed to know with his silence.

Well, she had until Labor Day and she meant to hang on to every moment like it might be the last.

* * * * *

"Holy shit!"

Elgin giggled as the SUV rounded the last curve of the long circular driveway and pulled up in front of Marty's house. Immediately, two young men in bright red vests opened their doors.

"Valet parking?" Harm's voice brimmed with amazement.

"As you may have noticed," she laughed, taking his arm and starting up the wide granite steps, "Marty likes to do things in a big way."

"I've noticed. First that sea-going yacht and now this steroid-enhanced Adirondack hunting lodge. What does he do for an encore? Stage moose hunts in the parlor?"

She laughed again as they reached the veranda and stopped so he could gawk. Two solid panels of glass rose in graceful triangles three stories high, bisected by a wall of some dark, rich wood that ran up to the peak of the blue shale roof, supporting both the glass and making a place for two massive doors. The same color as the wood, they were unadorned save for huge gold door handles and the enormous lion's head knocker. They stood wide open to the warm late afternoon air, the hum of conversation mixing with laughter and the clink of ice in glasses floating out to greet them.

Slowly, they threaded their way through the crowd of people that began in the huge foyer and stretched unbroken down the long, high-ceilinged main hall, into the cavernous living room and spilled through the wall of glass doors out onto the deck, which ran the length of the house and out for at least thirty feet.

Harm had thought the view from their deck grand. This was nothing short of breathtaking, more than one hundred eighty degrees of lake, mountains, pine forests and sky. Across the water, almost to the horizon, he could just make out the dots of the West Shore casinos.

"Champagne?" asked a liveried waiter, juggling a large silver tray of long stemmed crystal flutes.

"Uh, no, thank you," Elgin smiled.

"No thanks," Harm added.

"Well, if you'd like something else, the bar is in the living room by the fireplace." He smiled and moved away.

"Listen, I'm gonna fight my way through this mob and see if I can snag a beer. No sense both of us getting trampled. Find someplace out here to sit and I'll bring you a hard cola. If I'm not back in fifteen minutes, send up a flare or get the bloodhounds." He gave her a quick kiss. "And for God's sake, try not to wander off."

"Promise."

She watched him melt back into the crowd and then turned toward the railing, hoping to find a place for them to sit and watch the sunset with a modicum of quiet and privacy. A few moments later, she came upon an empty glider off to the side. Most of the throng milled around the industrial size barbecue set up on the other side of the deck, watching two men in jeans and cowboy shirts turn ribs, steaks and burgers on giant grills that looked like fifty gallon oil drums cut in half and laid on their sides.

"Hello."

Glancing up with a start, Elgin found Chad standing in front of her.

"Hello," she answered as he sat down, causing the glider to rock slightly.

"It's good to see you." He smiled, his eyes scanning her up and down. "You look terrific. The tan becomes you and I think that's the first time I've seen you in a dress. The bright red goes with your dark features."

Elgin felt herself blush, embarrassed as much by his presence as by his compliments.

"Thank you. It's good to see you, too."

"I stopped by a couple of times to check on you...do some sketching down at the beach and see if you were free for dinner, but I haven't seen much of you and when I noticed you'd installed the motion sensor and the bell...well..."

"I'm sorry," she apologized, putting her fingers lightly on his arm. "It's just that...I mean..."

Chad patted her fingers, feeling a tingle down his spine as he did so. "It's all right, really. If you'll remember, I asked only if you were...free. Judging by the look on your face, you're obviously not. While I'm disappointed and more than a little jealous, I understand completely and I'm very happy. I suppose there's no chance?"

She grinned and shook her head.

"Well," he sighed in resignation, "you can't hang a guy for trying. But I do want to drop by and give you the oil I promised. Sunset off your deck."

"Oh no, Chad, that's not necessary."

"I didn't say it was. I'd like very much for my friend Elgin to have a remembrance of me. After all, if it hadn't been for your view, I wouldn't have had anything to paint to begin with."

"All right. I'd like that very much."

"Good. Can I come by early tomorrow with it? Say about nine? I have a plane to catch at two and with all the security nowadays, I want to make sure I get there in time."

Her smile faded. "You're leaving?"

"'Fraid so. You see, after I couldn't paint at your place anymore, Marty insisted I come up here. The morning light is spectacular. He sold one of my paintings to a guy who, it turns out, owns a gallery on the coast. Wants me to come out there and discuss a possible showing, maybe in the spring."

"That's wonderful, Chad, really. I'm so happy for you."

"Well, I have the niggling suspicion that Marty may have had more to do with this than just selling a painting, but he insists that it's my talent and nothing more."

"Sounds just like Marty. He loves to do things for people, the more anonymously the better. And even if you catch him red-handed, he still won't own up to it. But it sounds like a great opportunity and I hope it's just the beginning for you."

"Thanks. By the way, who's your friend?" He nodded at the foot tall stuffed animal, a baby polar bear dressed in a crimson and silver clown suit, complete with jester's cap and covered in silver sparkles.

"He doesn't have a name yet," she laughed, holding the bear up for him to get a better view. "Camp won him for me this afternoon at the picnic over at the games area. You put a quarter on a color and then they spin a wheel and let a mouse loose on it. He runs down a hole and if you pick the color of the hole, you win. Camp told me he could just tell it was a green sort of mouse and he was right."

"I like him," Chad grinned, reaching out and flipping the pompom on the bear's cap. "I…"

"Hi."

They looked up to find Camp standing there, a beer bottle in one hand, a dark brown hard cola bottle in the other and a combination of distrust and questioning on his face.

"Oh, Camp, you startled me."

"Harm."

"Comstock."

"I was just showing Chad the bear you won for me."

"Very cute," Comstock added. "I've never heard of betting on mice before."

Holding the hard cola bottle out to her, he felt a twinge of something. Not quite anger but he definitely didn't like finding Comstock sitting there, Elgin practically in his lap.

"Personally," Harm told him coolly, "I don't like mice. Sneaky little bastards. Always trying to slink in when your back's turned and make off with your goodies. But Elgin really wanted the bear so…" he shrugged his shoulders and smiled at her. "What's a guy gonna do?"

Elgin didn't know whether to be appalled or amused. They were behaving like stray tomcats circling a mouse or a fresh fish. Why did men always think women found these displays of possessiveness and jealousy flattering? Especially in a situation like this where Chad knew how she felt about Harm and Harm had not expressed any serious, long-term intentions to her.

Yet there they stood, Chad deliberately baiting Harm and Harm fairly twitching for a fight. If she'd been watching two other idiots and another woman, the ludicrous scene would probably have made her laugh and ended up in one of her books. Happening to her though, reduced its comic value considerably.

"Howdy everybody."

Jim Fisher strolled up and stood beside Harm, a bottle of beer in his hand, Tom trailing behind like a bewildered puppy, clutching a can of soda and gaping in all directions. He'd put on a clean pair of jeans and a white T-shirt with a waving flag on the front. His hair had been combed and slicked into place. The difference made him look almost handsome, she mused.

"Jim." She smiled, glad for the interruption of the tension. "Happy Fourth."

"Same to you Ellie. Camp. Mr. Comstock." He turned slightly. "You remember Tom? Works for me down at the marina."

"Of course. Glad you could make the party, Tom."

"Thanks, Ma'am," he answered quietly. "Mr. Marty, he invited me hisself. Came right up ta me an' said, 'You be sure ta have Jim...Mr. F., bring ya along ta my party. Gonna be lots a food an' drink and afterwards we're gonna go out on 'The Monkey' an' watch the fireworks.'" He gazed at all the people and shook his head.

"Didn't know there was this many people in the whole a Spirit Cove. Guess that's why Mr. Marty had his shindig here at this hotel. Too big fer just a house er even 'The Monkey'. I think I'm gonna go over an' look at the cowboys."

"All right, Tom," Jim told him gently, "but you be careful to stay out of the way and don't get too close to the fire. And don't go wanderin' off."

"Yes sir, Mr. F.," the older man assured him like an obedient six-year old. "I won't get inta nothin' an' I'll stay close." With that, he ambled away toward the grills.

"It was nice of Marty to invite him," Chad commented, watching the little figure disappear into the crowd."

"Ah hell, Marty didn't invite him," Jim replied with a laugh. "Marty wouldn't know Tom if he ran over him. Just one a Tom's fanciful ideas. He's seen Marty down at the marina and heard all the talk about the party and he sort of 'imagined'

Marty talkin' to him. But everybody knows Marty just throws open the doors on the Fourth so I knew he wouldn't mind. Made sure he cleaned up enough to be presentable though. Speakin' a which, I just wanted to say how pretty you look, Ellie. That sun dress looks real nice on you."

"Thank you, Jim, that's very sweet. I bought it especially for this party. I just hope it doesn't get too cold out on the boat tonight."

"Marty wouldn't let that happen. You think he's gonna let a little thing like Mother Nature screw up his big Fourth of July party? Hell no. He's probably paid off the old gal to go to Florida or somethin'. Even the full moon doesn't come up 'til almost midnight. Wouldn't dare show her face before that."

They all laughed heartily.

"Well, I've got to be moving along," Chad told them. "I promised Marty I'd check to make sure all the canvases were crated up properly. The truck will be here tomorrow to take them to the airport. You know what a stickler he is."

"Canvases?" Harm asked.

"Uh-huh. I'm taking several of my paintings to the coast tomorrow. Meeting with a gallery owner who's interested in perhaps giving me a show. I'm leaving and I doubt seriously I'll be back before Labor Day." He glanced at Elgin and smiled wistfully. "Even though I regret not getting up to the plate, I at least hoped to stick around in the on-deck circle. Just in case you had a change in the line up."

"If I don't see you again tonight, Chad, I'm looking forward to seeing you tomorrow. Leave enough time to have a last cup of coffee."

"I will Ellie, I promise. Good night everyone."

"Good night," Jim called as he retreated. Harm didn't say anything, just quickly moved to the glider beside Elgin.

"What was all that baseball crap?" he inquired, trying to sound casual but not succeeding.

"Nothing," she told him softly. "Nothing at all."

"Well, I don't know about you two," Fisher chuckled, draining the last of his drink, "but I'm gonna see about another beer and see when we're gonna eat. Barbecue's startin' to smell real good." He turned and moved slowly away.

"You hungry?"

"Not right this minute. Even if they are serving, the line will be a mile long and I'm sure they're not going to run out of food. Marty's probably got enough to feed Spirit Cove for a week. I'd just like to sit here with you for a minute and enjoy the sunset." She looped her arm through his and laid her head on his shoulder. The glider rocked slowly and silently they watched the picture postcard scene spread out before them.

Elgin could never remember such peace, such a feeling of "rightness" before. More than anything else, she wanted to stay in this glider, the warm sun hanging low over the blue water, and Camp sitting beside her forever. Make time stand still so that not another day, another moment passed. They'd just stay like this and live happily ever after.

"I think I'll go get another beer," Camp chuckled. "But I think I'm going to have to make room for it. Can I bring you back another hard cola?"

"Well, as long as you're going that way. And since the guest bathroom off the living room will probably have a line, go straight through and down the hall towards the east wing. Second door on the left is a guestroom. The door will probably be closed but you can just go right in. Bathroom's on the right."

"Thanks. When I get back, we'll walk over and see what's for dinner."

"I'll be right here, promise." They shared a kiss and she watched him stride leisurely toward the house. Camp'd been gone only a few moments when a young waiter approached her.

"Ma'am, a gentleman asked me to give this to you." He held out a piece of folded white paper. When she took it, he nodded once and scurried back toward the house.

Curious, she unfolded it.

Snagged a blanket and a bottle of champagne. Meet you in the clearing just north of the house.

Horny rascal, she thought as she slipped the note in her pocket, picked up her bear and turned toward the steps leading down from the deck to the grounds below. The bathroom thing had been a ruse to spring his naughty little surprise on her. In the huge crowd, everyone concentrating on dinner, no one would even notice their absence. Marty wouldn't come looking for them until it was time to leave for the marina, at least another hour and a half. They'd have plenty of time to, as Harm had suggested, make their own fireworks.

Her own desire rising, Elgin hurried across the broad expanse of lawn, checking to make sure she was alone. In a few moments, she reached the edge of the forest and closed the last few yards, breaking into the clearing, expecting to find her lover.

Instead, the clearing stood empty and silent, no sign of an illicit tryst, no sound.

Oh well, she thought, moving to the center, I'll be here to surprise him. After all, she knew Marty's place and could find this spot in the dark. Camp would have to go out one of the doors and then circle almost all the way around the house.

A breath of something chilly suddenly raised goose bumps.

Camp didn't know this place. He'd never been to Marty's house. How would he have known about this clearing? And where would he have gotten a blanket?

Something grabbed her from behind, pinning her arms to her sides and seeming to root her in place. Opening her mouth to scream, something wet and soft pressed itself to her face, clinging like a starfish. She couldn't smell anything but something slightly sweet trailed into her mouth as she sucked in the material, struggling to breathe. But the harder she fought, the tighter the grip on her body, the harder the wet thing clung.

She couldn't get any air. Her whole body seemed paralyzed with fear as the thing holding her squeezed the air from her lungs, deflating her body, leaving her limp and sliding sideways. Legs too wobbly to hold her up, unclenched fingers releasing the soft fur of her bear. Heartbeat and breathing vanishing. Darkness.

* * * * *

"Here you..." Harm stopped, the sight of the empty glider bringing him up short. Craning his head in all directions, he didn't see her.

"God damn it," he muttered, angry that she'd chosen now to play this stupid game. Well he'd been scared out of his wits once too often to be taken in again. Wherever she was, she could just stay there. In a little while, she'd realize he wasn't going to bite and come back. In the meantime, he had a beer to keep him company.

Setting her bottle of hard cola on one of the little wood end tables, he settled into the glider and took a long draw, letting his eyes sweep the area to see if he could spot where she might be hiding.

His hand brushed against something. Looking down, he saw a piece of folded white paper stuck between the cushions, almost hidden from view.

Down the steps, across the lawn and into the clearing at the north end of the house.

E

So, that was it, he grinned to himself, stuffing the paper in the pocket of his jeans. She was hungry but not for barbecue. A little fun and games to work up an appetite. Rising, he walked casually over to the deck steps, his cock, excited by the prospect of a romp in the woods, making his progress uncomfortable.

He wondered what she had planned. A nice, long slow fuck in the pine-scented stillness or a wild quickie, pressed against a strong tree, pumping and grinding like horny teenagers grabbing some before they're discovered.

His steps picked up-tempo across the perfectly manicured lawn, his cock now bulging against his fly. No wonder she'd suddenly decided to wear that sundress at the last moment, he chuckled to himself. Easier than trying to wrestle out of two pair of jeans.

The lawn ended and the forest began as he moved into the trees. It couldn't be very far he reasoned. Probably just a few feet.

"Elgin?" he called, weaving among the trees.

And then he saw it. A flash of red among the green trees and brown dirt.

"Here I come," he growled playfully, "ready or not."

He stepped into the clearing and in a heartbeat, the heat of his need vanished, replaced with icy dread. From the middle of the space, Elgin's bear grinned up at him, its black eyes wide in welcome, its little arms outstretched as though glad to see him. The pendant hung from his left paw like an extended gift.

In three long strides, Harm got to the bear, bending down and reaching for the little stuffed animal.

Behind him, he heard a branch snap and turned his head just in time to see a blur of movement before the bomb exploded in the back of his skull and fireworks lit up the sudden blackness.

Chapter Thirteen

He became aware of the pain, even before he awoke. A fleet of jackhammers pounded out the "Anvil Chorus" in his head while thousands of little people in spiked shoes polkaed through the mush that had recently been his brain. Yellow lights like points of ugly, glaring neon pulsed regularly behind his eyelids.

Slowly, carefully, he opened his eyes a little. The blur in front of him resolved itself into his white polo shirt and just below that, his dark blue denim jeans. He felt his chin brushing the soft, slightly fuzzy material.

To either side, his forearms rested comfortably on the broad, flat, wooden arms of the chair he sat in. Curiously, someone had left their belts looped over the chair arms and his wrists.

Raising his head seemed to speed up and intensify the pain but it also helped clear away some of the fog. Inch by inch, he managed to turn his head, taking in the bare gray walls and floor, the single overhead light bulb and the closed door in the right wall.

Futilely, Harm yanked his wrists. The belts he realized now were thick leather straps locking him to the arms of the large wooden chair. Bending over at the waist, he saw his legs, spread slightly, secured to the chair at the ankles with another pair of straps.

The effort made him nauseous and he leaned back, shutting his eyes and gasping for air. A small line of sweat beads formed at his hairline and he prayed his head would explode. At least then the pain would stop.

Suddenly, the room plunged into darkness. Harm struggled against the leather, adrenaline and fear pounding into his blood and gut.

A light came on in front of him and he found himself looking into another room. On a bed in the center of the other room, Elgin lay on her back, her head resting on a pillow, her arms at her sides. The red sundress in place, even her little red sandals on her feet. But he knew Elgin didn't sleep on her back, at least not so perfectly posed.

"*Noooooo!*" he screamed, everything, including the pain, swept away by the horrible thought that she wasn't merely sleeping.

The light flashed back on as the door opened.

"She can't hear you," Fisher told him calmly.

"I'll kill you," Harm snarled, his surprise at Fisher's appearance erased by his fear for Elgin.

"Oh, she's not dead," he continued. "At least, not yet. Little chloroform to relax her. Get her to come along without makin' a lot a hoo-hah and spoilin' everybody else's Fourth."

"You left the note for me."

"Yep. Waited 'til you were gone and then had the waiter take Ellie a note sayin' fer her to meet you in the clearin'. Had a blanket and champagne. I knew that'd bring her. When she left, I put the note fer you and followed her. Knew you'd come sniffin' after her like a hound after a bitch in heat."

Fisher leaned down into Harm's face, hate filling his body, twisting his face into a horrible caricature of the kindly old uncle he'd seemed.

"I knew the first time I saw you, you weren't anybody's *secretary.*" The word spit out like an obscenity. "I couldn't believe my little Ellie'd bring her cheap lay up here and rub everyone's nose in her dirt. Only thing that's kept me alive all these years was Ellie comin' home...comin' back to me. Not that tramp who writes that trash, but my sweet little girl. But the tramp came back and I knew I had to get rid of you and her so I could have my Ellie back."

"Go ahead and kill me," Harm answered, trying to keep his voice calm but feeling the fear building inside him, "but don't hurt Elgin. She's not to blame."

"Oh, but she is," Jim assured him coldly. "Everything that's happened is her fault and she's gonna make up for it before…before I'm finished with her. I'm gonna bring her in here and let her see you. Touch you. Talk to you. And I'm gonna tell her that if she does what I want, I'll let you both go after a while."

"She'll know it's a lie. She'll know you can't let either of us live now."

"Maybe, maybe not. But she's gonna want to save your skin and hers as well. She'll do it, believe me. Then I'm gonna take her back in that room and she's gonna strip naked and get in that bed and I'm gonna tie her down and do all the things I've dreamed of all those long, lonely nights, years. And you're gonna sit here and watch me while I take her. Over…and over…and over. Listen to her squeal and scream 'til she's too weak to make any more noise. And when I'm finished, I'm gonna drag her back in here and make her watch while I kill you."

Slowly, he reached behind him and pulled out a large, ugly automatic, a forty-five Harm noted almost in passing.

"First the knees." He pressed the barrel against Harm's knee and grinned. "Then the thighs. Lots a meat, lots a blood. Then your arms and hands." The gun moved as he marked his targets.

"Next'll be your balls. That's how they do it in the big city gangs. Finally, your gut." Fisher drove the gun barrel into Harm's stomach so hard he gasped with pain. "Gut shots take time to die and they hurt like hell. I worked in a hospital once as an orderly. Saw lots a gut shots. When you're finally gone, I'm gonna put a bullet in Ellie's head."

"Someone will miss us at Marty's," Harm tried to bluff. "The waiter you had give the note to Ellie will remember you. They'll come looking."

"Probably right. But even if someone does miss you, they'll just think you two snuck off for a little nookie. And if the waiter says I gave him a note, I'll just say you gave it to me to give to him. Won't make any difference, though."

"Why's that?"

"Because in a day or two, one of the search parties'll find what's left of my number eight boat up on 'Devil's Fangs.' Real nasty rocks up toward the north end of the lake. Everybody'll figure you and Ellie took the boat, got drunk or lost or careless. Out there, they won't even bother draggin' for your bodies."

Elgin stirred and Fisher's attention focused back on her. "Well, guess it's about time to get our little party started. You stay right there. I'll get Ellie and then the three of us can get to know one 'nother better."

Harm watched as Elgin gradually came to, Fisher leaning over, trying to talk reassuringly, calmly to her. But by now, she'd figured out that she was his prisoner, not his guest and when she tried to get away, he grabbed her wrists in one big paw, raising his other one and obviously threatening her. Tearfully, she stopped struggling and he dragged her out of sight.

A moment later, the door flew open and Fisher almost threw her at Harm.

"Oh God, Camp!" she cried, clambering into his lap and kissing him. "Are you all right! Oh God, I'm sorry." Her hands remained behind her back and as she cried into his chest, he saw the glint of handcuffs.

"Shhhh." He tried to comfort, her tears like acid on his skin. "I'm all right. Shhhhh. Don't cry, please."

"I...I don't understand Camp. What's happening? What's going on?"

"He's the stalker." The words caught in his throat. Not only had the maniac who'd been terrorizing her turned out to be someone she loved and trusted, he hadn't been able to save her.

She blinked those beautiful dark eyes in amazed confusion. "I don't believe you."

"It's a lie," Fisher told her hurriedly. "I'm not no stalker." His features softened then, his eyes filled with the love and caring that had so carefully hidden the truth.

"I love you, Ellie." The words she'd longed to hear, soft and warm and real but filling her now, not with joy but with bone chilling fear.

"I've always loved you, Ellie. Since you were a little girl. You were so pretty. Remember how we'd go out fishin' er boatin' and you'd be in yer little swimsuit er yer T-shirt and cutoffs? How many times did you fall asleep in my lap, lookin' like a little angel? I wanted you then. Wanted you real bad. Coulda had you more'n once but I knew I had to wait for you.

"God, that summer you were fifteen and a woman's body and all them horny teenage boys hangin' around you. I knew then that you were grown and I'd have you when you came back the next year."

"What about your wife," Harm asked, a cold picture beginning to form in the back of his mind. "What about Cissy?"

"That was her fault," he shot back flatly. "I asked her for a divorce. Told her I didn't love her anymore and that she could have anything she wanted. House. Marina. Whatever. But she wouldn't hear of it. Said we were married and that she didn't care about me makin' a fool a myself over some little slut but she wasn't gonna be made a laughin' stock like John Crockett's wife. I was hers 'til death do us part."

"You...you killed Cissy?" Elgin's eyes grew huge with horror and shock. "You killed her...for me?"

"For *us*. So we could be together. When you came back the next summer, I was gonna tell you how I felt and enough time'd gone by that people wouldn't think nothin' of it."

The dreamy look faded and something hard took its place.

"Only...only you didn't come back that next summer. All those years I waited. Thinkin'...plannin'...dreamin'...lovin'. And one day you did come back. Bought Moon's End and I thought you'd come home to stay. But havin' you here once in a while was almost worse than not havin' you here all that time.

"I saw those books you write down at The Mercantile and I knew that 'Gillian Shelby' couldn't be my sweet little angel, Ellie, so the last time you were up here, I followed you when you went home. Back to that big old fancy buildin' you live in with the fella in the fancy suit openin' your door for you. It was like it was you but it wasn't you."

"So you started sending her things," Harm picked up, a glimmer of understanding for Fisher and his obsession with Elgin dawning. "Things Ellie would understand like the carnations and the candy and things Gillian would understand like the whip and handcuffs and the lingerie."

Fisher nodded, the tip of his tongue running along his lips. "I found a program on the internet that let me break into Ellie's computer. Let me be with her every day, even when I couldn't actually be in the city with her. Let me know how she spent her days and who she saw and even what that whore, Gillian Shelby wrote."

"How did you manage to get in the elevator and fondle her ass without her seeing...recognizing you?"

A proud grin lit up his face. "I knew where she was gonna be all the time. I just followed her into the elevator and then elbowed my way to her back. I wasn't gonna touch her but when I felt her ass through my jeans, I couldn't help myself. You felt so good and I wanted to take you right there if I could have. When the elevator stopped and people pushed out, I just stood in the corner by the buttons 'til you thought everyone'd left."

"And the beggar on the street?"

"He put his filthy hands on Ellie," Fisher growled. "Scared her. Tore her clothes and hurt her arm. I'd bought two new pair of blue jeans, a pint of whiskey to bring back to Captain Jack and a new carving knife for the concession stand. Everything fell into place. Like God wanted me to get rid of that animal.

"I followed him until he went in the alley. I gave him the whiskey and when he turned around, I pulled out my knife and stabbed him and stabbed him 'til he stopped twitching. Changed my jeans, wrapped them and the knife in my jacket, went back to my car and drove home. Went out on the lake and threw the jacket, pants and knife in the deepest part."

"If you loved her so much," Harm pushed, desperate now to know the whole story, "how could you possibly have tried to kill her? Running her down in the street?"

"I wasn't tryin' to kill her," he insisted, "just scare her so she'd want to come back here...back home to me."

"What about the man?"

"That was his fault. I saw him hangin' around her and I wanted him to leave her alone. I woulda missed him clean except he pushed Elgin out of the way and turned back, tryin' to get a look at me and I swerved."

"And the night we came back from the fish fry at your house?"

"I wasn't tryin' to kill Ellie then, either. I was after you. I knew you'd have to go the long way 'round to Moon's End and get out at the gate. Shit, after all the hard cola Ellie'd had, I knew she'd be sound asleep before you got back to the main road. So I jumped in my pickup and took one of the logging road short cuts I know. I waited in the brush 'til you stopped that big fancy truck of yours and got out. Just snuck up, turned the wheels, put the car in gear and took the emergency brake off. I figured the car'd run you over while you weren't lookin' then run into the ditch. Even if it'd run all the way down and into the trees, Elgin wouldn'ta been hurt bad because she had on her seatbelt."

Fisher took a step toward them. "Guess I'm gonna have to finish the job the old-fashioned way." The gun reappeared.

"No, wait!" Elgin screamed, turning to face him. "Please! Don't hurt Camp! I'll...I'll do anything you want. I'll stay with you as long as you want. Anything, but please..."

The two men shared a knowing look, a cold smile touching Fisher's lips.

"I don't know," he pretended to ponder. "I mean, if I let him go, how do I know you'll keep your word?"

"You know me, Jim," she stammered between sobs. "If you let Camp go, I'll stay. I promise."

"What about him though?" He nodded at Harm. "What's to say he'd even go without you? Or that he wouldn't come right back with the law?"

She glanced at Harm and then back to Fisher. "He'll go because I want him to. And even if he does come back with the sheriff, it will be his word against ours. I'll tell everyone that I'm with you of my own free will. We...we can have the life you always wanted."

"Elgin," Harm barked, "don't be stupid. He's lying. He can't afford to let me live because he knows if he does, I won't leave without you."

"Make up your mind, Ellie."

Tears flowed and she buried her face in Harm's chest again.

"Listen to me," he whispered, bringing his lips as close to her ear as he could, "and don't say anything. Just nod if you hear me." He felt her head move slightly and he took a deep breath. There was nothing left to do but make sure she knew the truth and that she had only one option.

"He's crazy, Elgin and he's going to kill me. There's nothing you can do to prevent it. He intends to take you back into that room and...and rape you." She shuddered and his arms pulled against the straps in their need to hold her, comfort her. He didn't want to hurt her, but he had to make her understand the gravity of the situation and how much worse it could get.

"Rape you over and over and make me watch everything. When he's finished, he's going to drag you back here and he's going to kill me...shoot me and make you watch me bleed to death. Then he's going to kill you. Do you understand, Elgin?"

She nodded again, great sobs wracking her body. Harm felt as if a knife were twisting in his chest, but he had to keep going. There was no other way.

"I don't mind dying," he told her softly, his voice catching, his cheek brushing her hair, "except that I won't be with you. But I'm not afraid. What I couldn't stand would be to sit here and watch that monster...hurt you. Put his hands, his cock..." his voice faltered as he struggled against the pictures in his mind.

"You have to try and get away."

Her face rubbed an emphatic "no," in his shirt.

"I mean it," he insisted, his voice a harsh whisper. "Let him take you back to the other room. He won't be expecting you to try anything. Look for something to use as a weapon...your nails or fists or feet if that's all you have. Remember how you took down the homeless guy. Just let yourself go and you can do it."

"I won't leave you," she mumbled.

"You have to. I want you to. You mean more to me than my life. I could die if I knew you were safe. And if you get away, you can make sure Fisher's punished for everything he's done. If we both die, he gets away with it all."

"Don't ask me..."

"I'm not asking, I'm pleading. Please try to escape. For me."

Elgin raised her head and blinked back the tears. His face brushed against hers, their tears running together. "I love you, Elgin."

As their lips touched, Fisher grabbed her and pulled her away. "Leave her alone," he bellowed, the back of a giant hand catching Harm's face at the jaw line, the rough knuckles traveling across his mouth like steel. A trickle of blood trailed from the corner of his mouth down to his chin.

"Come on," Fisher ordered, yanking Elgin by the elbow toward the door. He dragged her next door, pushing her to the bed in full view of the window. Releasing her from the handcuffs, he stood back, almost drooling with anticipation.

"Okay now, strip. Nice and slow for me and your secretary."

Elgin glanced up at the window. She couldn't see him but she could feel Harm in the darkness.

Fear engulfed her and she felt as if she were drowning, her heart pounding, her lungs starved for air. A wave of nausea and she thought for a moment she'd be sick or even pass out.

"Now!" The sharp edge of his voice hit her like a physical slap.

All right, she thought, fighting to regain the upper hand of her mind and body, *calm down. Think. Our lives depend on you keeping your head.*

Trembling, Elgin forced herself to look up, her gaze sweeping the small area in front of her. The slightly rumpled bed. A small wooden nightstand with drawer and an open shelf. Her already racing heart felt as if it would explode in her chest at what she saw.

A vibrator, a little bigger than a regular flashlight lay on the shelf. Cream-colored plastic, a large round knob on one end. From the look of it, Elgin knew it was hard, solid, powered by at least two "C" batteries. If she could take him by surprise...

"Strip!" he barked again, "now."

Slowly, Elgin reached for the button holding the thin strap that crossed over her shoulder and connected to the front of her sundress, just above her breast. She never took her eyes off the vibrator, her mind churning.

She'd have to make a grab for it. How far? Not more than a foot, eighteen inches perhaps, but almost at her knees.

"Turn around," he ordered.

As slowly as she dared, Elgin turned toward him, inching backwards as she did so. Hopefully, he wouldn't notice anything but her front.

Her shaking fingers fumbled with the button a little more. She couldn't breathe, couldn't do this.

The beggar had been a fluke, a purely instinctive reaction, requiring no thought. This meant life and death, literally and had to be planned as carefully as possible in the blink of time she had.

Perhaps if she gave him what he wanted…

His eyes riveted on her breasts, a cold mesmerized look in those now alien eyes, his face filled with naked, animal lust. He wasn't Jim Fisher anymore. He'd become a predator whose only satisfaction would come from blood and pain and death.

With agonizing slowness, Elgin put a hand behind her, fingers stretching, searching blindly until they brushed the front of the nightstand. Fisher, still focused on the dress, didn't seem to notice.

The button gave way and her strap slipped off her shoulder and down her back. He swallowed hard, the tip of his tongue just barely visible between his lips. The predator, having stalked her for so long, enjoying the last moments of the hunt before striking for the kill.

She moved her fingers to the other button, watching his eyes as they followed her.

With a last deep breath, Elgin popped the button. The strap fell, lowering the top of her dress and revealing a flash of breast. Pretending to collapse, she bent backwards, clutching the nightstand as if to catch herself from falling. Almost by themselves, the fingers of her right hand wrapped themselves tightly around the vibrator and she swung her body slightly so that her back stood to him, hiding her makeshift weapon.

"Ellie," he yelped as he came to her. "Are you all right?"

A last dizzy second before she felt his hand on her shoulder, strangely gentle as he turned her. In his eyes, she thought she saw a flicker of concern.

With all the force terror-fueled adrenaline could give her, Elgin brought the vibrator up almost from the floor, her arm rising as she turned, swinging an arc as she came.

Plastic shattered with a sickening "thud," shards splintering, the knob exploding in a spurt of blood, batteries flying like tiny missiles. Impact waves shuddered through her hand, arm and shoulder as the vibrator connected with Fisher's temple.

Startled, he released her and stepped back, the gun slipping from his hand, bouncing once off his heavy boot and skittering under the bed. Putting his hand to the gash in slow motion, he instantly pulled it away, looking first at the blood and then at her, apparently shocked by Elgin's attack.

Oh God, she thought, frozen now with panic. She hadn't finished him, hadn't even knocked him out. She'd only wounded the crazed animal.

Fisher's mouth moved a little but no sound came out. Blood poured down his face, filling his left eye and dripping from his chin.

Wordlessly, he collapsed, twisting slightly as he fell face down almost at her feet, sprawled like a huge sleeping bear.

She stood for a few seconds, paralyzed by terror and disbelief. Perhaps she'd killed him.

Camp!

The thought snapped her back to reality. Not able to take her eyes off the body almost blocking her path, she managed to tiptoe around him and dash out the door.

"Elgin!" Harm screamed as she crossed the room to him. "For God's sake, get out of here. Run. Now."

"Not without you," she answered firmly, starting to unbuckle the first of two small straps holding the larger one in place.

"Don't argue, damn it! I'm telling you to get out. Call the police. I'll be fine 'til you get back."

Abruptly, Elgin stood up and glared at him.

"Campbell Harm, did you mean it when you said you loved me?" she asked angrily.

"This is not the time…"

"Did you meant it?" she repeated.

"Of course I meant it," he replied, totally exasperated that she'd pick now to discuss the subject. "I didn't want to die and not tell you how I feel."

"And if I was tied in that chair, would you leave me?"

"Elgin…"

"Would you?"

"Of course not," he yelled, "but that's not…"

She grinned down at him.

"Of course it's the same thing," she finished. "I love you, too. So why don't you stop wasting precious time acting like a macho horse's ass and let's get the hell out of here."

Bending down, she kissed his lips quickly and went back to the buckles.

"As soon as I get your hand free, I'll start on your ankles while you free your other hand." The second buckle opened, releasing him.

Instantly, she dropped to her knees as he began working on his other wrist.

"By the way, that was pretty clever with the vibrator."

"You'd be utterly amazed at how inventive I can be with my sex toys, given the proper motivation." Elgin laughed as the last strap came off his ankle.

Standing up, he grabbed her hand, helping her to her feet as they embraced tightly and kissed passionately.

"Really? I guess I'll have to file that for future reference. In the meantime, I think you're right about getting the hell out of here." Grabbing her hand, they ran to the door.

Besides the two small rooms, there was only a large, windowless area, dirty gray cinderblock walls and some old cardboard boxes and trunks strewn around. In the far left-hand corner rose a flight of rickety wooden steps.

"Come on."

Crossing the room, Harm took a last look back to make sure they weren't being followed, pushed Elgin in front of him and they raced up the stairs. The door at the top flew open and they found themselves in a small pantry area leading to a large, country style kitchen.

"This is Jim's house," Elgin told him, turning her head in all directions to take in the familiar room. "Cissy and I used to make chocolate chip cookies in here and then the three of us…Jim and Cissy and I would go out on the deck and drink milk and eat cookies and laugh. Sometimes we'd even go up to the meadow across the road and catch fireflies at night."

A pleasant childhood memory flickered in her mind, wiping away the horror of the present moment. It hurt him to bring her back but they didn't have any time.

"Elgin, where does he keep his car keys?"

She looked at him blankly for a moment, the child Elgin caught between the familiar and the foreign. It took her a second to get back.

"Uh…probably in his pocket. He keeps them with him until he gets ready for bed at night."

"Damn! That means he's probably got the SUV keys too." Harm took a deep breath and stood silent. "Okay, where's the phone? We'll call the police, tell them what's going on and then head for the nearest neighbor."

"It…it used to be on a little table by the sofa in the living room. The sheriff and his deputies are probably all out directing traffic and doing crowd control for the fireworks and all the neighbors around here are probably down at the fireworks too." Harm could hear the panic creeping into her voice.

"It's all right. When they hear what's going on, I'm sure they'll send someone. And if we don't find any neighbors home, maybe we can find an unlocked car I can hotwire. We can't stay here."

Nodding, she turned and they ran into the living room, Elgin leading the way to the phone. It was an old-fashioned thing, heavy and black with a rotary dial. Harm grabbed up the receiver and reached for the dial. Instead, a look of confusion and uncertainty clouded his face and he pounded the small black receiver hook several times.

"What's wrong?"

"I don't know. I picked up the phone, got a dial tone and…and then it just went dead."

Terror showed again in Elgin's eyes, the color draining from her face.

"Let's go," he ordered, throwing down the receiver, grabbing her arm and taking a step toward the front door, all it seemed to her in one fluid motion.

Something roared behind them, a great, enraged grizzly roar that filled the room with its deafening power, freezing them in mid-stride.

Instinctively they turned to the roar, fear washing over them like the massive sound waves.

A creature that had once been Jim Fisher stood just in the kitchen door. Fury shook his body, now covered in his own blood, one eye swollen shut, the automatic like a child's toy in his huge paw.

"Bitch!" he screamed. "Whore! Tramp!"

Harm edged himself between her and the monster.

"It's over Fisher," he bluffed calmly. "I called 9-1-1 before you pulled the plug. The sheriff will be here any minute."

"Liar!" he bellowed. "Thief! Whoremonger! You didn't call anyone. But you're right…it is over for the both of you. I don't care about having you anymore, you faithless harlot. You teasing, heartless cunt. You're not my Ellie…you're that dirty book writer, Gillian Shelby. I can't believe that I was taken in by you and your sweet smile and warm caress. I'm going to kill this pretty little cock of yours just the way I said. One piece at a time. Then I'm going to choke the life out of you with my bare hands."

The room seemed to lurch suddenly, swaying with a dizzying wobble, Elgin's knees growing too weak to hold her up, her stomach turning Olympic caliber back flips. She wanted to be sick, to pass out, to scream. All of them seemed to be running through her at once, vying for first chance.

And then the fireworks started. A loud bang and a little bug whizzed by her ear, so close she could hear the whine of it going by. Another explosion and a dart of fire. Elgin could feel the room spinning like a top. Disoriented, she heard firecrackers popping behind her and a crack like shattering glass. The acrid smell and faint haze of smoke filled her lungs. Crowd noises as the fireworks built to a climax. Screams and shouts. People pushing past her. Camp going down on his knees to give her a better view.

"Elgin?"

"Marty?"

"Are you all right, Dear?" he asked anxiously, taking her shoulders and looking her up and down. "You aren't hurt are you?"

"No…I think I'm all right…" She cocked her head quizzically to one side, the reality of his sudden presence just sinking in. "What are you…?"

Behind him, Chad knelt on the kitchen floor beside two long, denim-clad legs.

A soft moan at her feet attracted her attention. Looking down, she saw Tom, although it looked like him but different somehow. Instead of his slow movements and slightly disconnected speech, he squatted beside Camp, ripping his red shirt, speaking quickly, decisively and...

Camp's shirt was white. And why was he lying on the floor?

Screaming, she dropped to her knees, tears flowing like the blood from the hole in his chest, streaming down his side and spreading on the highly polished wooden floor and being absorbed by her dress.

"Shhh," Harm soothed, reaching for her hand and bringing it softly to his lips. "It's okay."

"Camp!"

"Shhh," he repeated. With a grin, he moved his head in Tom's direction. "Elgin Collier, I'd like you to meet Charlie Simons. Charlie, this is the beautiful lady I've been telling you about."

"Miss Collier," Charlie responded politely. "Camp's told me a lot about you."

"Charlie? But I thought your name was Tom." Confusion mingled with panic about Harm, the lingering terror of Fisher and relief at the unexpected, dramatic arrival of the trio. "I...I don't understand. What's going on?"

Chad came up behind Charlie and handed him several folded dishcloths. As he took them, he glanced into the other man's solemn face. Almost imperceptibly, he moved his head from side to side. Charlie nodded ever so slightly and returned to Harm.

"I work with Camp," he explained, rolling three of the cloths together and pressing them to Harm's chest. "He sent me up here before you arrived to scout things out and get settled in. Become part of the scenery so I could keep an eye on all our players without attracting attention.

"Here, press down as hard as you can." Taking her hands, Charlie crossed them and put them on the towel. "Lean on it. You're not going to break anything and we need to stop or at least slow down the bleeding."

Rising, he grabbed his cell phone from his pocket and went into the kitchen.

"Apparently," Marty continued, "Chad, Fisher and I became the prime suspects. Mr. Simons tells me that my summer houseboy, Ernesto, is actually one of Mr. Harm's agents. Pity. Wonderful young man and very efficient. I'd planned to keep him on after Labor Day."

"And," Chad added, "it turns out my housekeeper, Mary, works for Mr. Harm as well."

"Mr. Simons only attended my party to watch Fisher and to keep a pre-arranged meeting with Harm. When he discovered you both gone and being unfamiliar with most of the people there, he had no choice but to reveal himself to me and ask for my help in determining if anyone else had gone missing.

"Having already discovered that your 'secretary' was in fact a private detective and that both of you might be in grave danger, I made a quick circuit of my guests. I discovered Fisher gone and that he'd given one of my waiters a note to give you. Well, it didn't take Sherlock Holmes to figure it out."

"I saw Tom and Marty huddling and looking worried," Chad picked up the story, "so I decided to see what they were up to. Followed them to Marty's den where I eavesdropped and found out everything, including the fact that Fisher might be a homicidal stalker."

"Broke in," Marty smiled. "Demanded to be part of the posse."

"But why didn't you just call the sheriff?" Elgin asked, glancing up from the towels now starting to turn red.

"Because as Mr. Simons pointed out," Marty answered, "we had no way of knowing if Fisher actually had you and if he did, where he might be holding you. Not to mention that if he had abducted you, the sight of police cars might have caused him to do something drastic. So we decided to reconnoiter as it were. Since this place is only about ten minutes from my house, it seemed the logical place to start."

"And Jim?" she asked timidly.

Marty sighed, glancing from Chad to Elgin and back again. "We could see through the window Fisher was armed," he replied quietly. "Fortunately, so was Mr. Simons. He broke the window, shouted at Fisher to drop his gun and put up his hands. Fisher fired and Mr. Simons returned." He stopped, looking again at Elgin, the pain of his story evident in his face. "Before we could do anything, he put the gun to his head and pulled the trigger."

"Oh!" Her eyes went immediately to his body sprawled on the floor. Unaccountably, after everything that had happened, she could only remember her lifelong friend, Jim, and the tears started anew, Harm running his fingers lightly up and down her arm, powerless to comfort her.

Charlie reappeared, pale and drawn. Quickly crossing the living room, he knelt by Harm, wadding up more towels.

"How you doing?" he asked, smiling thinly and replacing the soaked towels.

"Other than it hurts like hell?" Harm managed.

"We have to get him to a hospital," Elgin sobbed.

"Yeah, well you're gonna have to hold a little longer, Pard. We've got a problem."

"What do you mean, 'a problem'?" Marty leaned down slightly.

"9-1-1 says there's a major smash up on the north end of the lake. Chain reaction. At least ten, twelve cars. Most of the sheriff's deputies are either on scene or stuck in the traffic trying to get there. Only ambulance and paramedics on this side of the lake are up there too. They're trying to get another team up there from West Shore right now. And the Life Flight 'copter from West Shore is making an emergency flight to the coast with a kidney for a transplant."

"What about a local doctor?" Chad ventured. "Surely there must be someone on this side of the lake?"

"I'm afraid not," Marty shook his head. "We've been trying to get a doctor up here for years. I've offered to build and furnish a clinic and pay a doctor myself but there's such a shortage and we just can't afford to compete with big cities and rich suburbs."

"Then let's put him in my car and take him to West Shore."

"According to the dispatcher, the fireworks traffic is a solid jam all around the lake. Who knows how long it might take to get there." Charlie glanced down at Harm. "Don't worry, Camp. We'll think of something."

"I know."

They lapsed into silence, watching as the stains on the towels grew larger.

Suddenly, Marty snapped his fingers and dug into his slacks for his phone. "I think I might have an idea." He punched a speed dial button and waited a few seconds.

"What...?"

Marty held up a finger and spoke quickly into the phone. "Paul? It's Marty. Listen, I don't have any time to explain. Is 'The Monkey' ready to go?"

"Yes, sir," the boatman answered. "In fact, everyone's boarded. We're just waiting for you so we can cast off."

"Get everyone off the boat...now...and get her up to the dock in front of Jim Fisher's place as quickly as you can."

"I don't understand..."

"There's nothing for you to understand," Marty snapped, an authority in his voice that Elgin had never heard before. "I'm your boss and I'm giving you an order. Tell everyone that we won't be going out on the lake for the fireworks this year but that the deck and grounds afford an excellent view of the show. I want 'The Monkey' up here and I want her up here *now*!"

"Yes sir. We'll be there in about ten minutes."

Snapping the phone off, Marty looked at the others. "She's the fastest thing on the lake," he told them. "Now, how do we get Mr. Harm down to the dock?"

Chapter Fourteen

"She's here," Marty announced as he hurried through the open front door.

Charlie glanced down at Harm and tried to smile. "Taxi's here, Camp. You ready?"

"Sure," he replied, trying to return his friend's smile. "Just make sure you guys don't drop me, okay?"

"Like I'm gonna let anything happen to the guy who signs my checks. You just lie back and take it easy."

He checked Harm one more time. They'd taken one of Fisher's large, old-fashioned arm chairs from the dining room, laid it on its back and put him in it, securing his arms and legs to the chair's arms and legs with soft towels. Then they'd tied a bed sheet securely around the whole thing and slid one of the sofa pillows under his head.

Being the largest of them, Chad took his place at Harm's head, grabbing the chair back on each side just under the arms. Charlie and Marty each took a side, positioning themselves to carry a back and front leg. Elgin walked along side, keeping pressure on the dressing.

On the count, they lifted the chair and started for the dock, winding slowly down the gravel path.

With Paul's help, they got him on board and settled in the main salon on one of the bench seats under the window. Harm looked up into the silent, star filled sky.

Marty accompanied Paul back to the wheelhouse, watching him for a moment as he fired up the engines and inched away from the dock.

"How long will it take to get to West Shore?"

"An hour maybe. There'll be a lot of traffic out there tonight." He glanced at the clock glowing in the dashboard just above his right hand. "Fireworks'll be starting any time now."

"What's the shortest time you've ever made the crossing?"

"Forty-three minutes. Four years ago. You made that bet with the loud mouth drunk at The Lodge who called 'The Monkey' a scow. Course you were drinking too but it was a hell of a ride."

"There's a thousand dollars for every minute you shave off forty-three," Marty told him calmly. "If you make it under thirty-five, there'll be an extra ten thousand."

"Must be a very special friend."

"She is."

* * * * *

The pain had relented a little but it didn't make him feel any better. Harm knew enough first aid to know the numbing effect of shock. They'd managed to slow the blood loss but he could feel a chill settling in, even under the snug blanket that covered him, another sign that he was losing the race.

Beside him, Elgin sat in the chair they'd used as a litter, checking his dressing every few seconds, clutching his hand and trying gamely not to cry. The pain on her beautiful pale face, the silent anguish in those dark eyes hurt worse than the bullet burning in his chest.

"Look," Chad said, standing behind Elgin and pointing out the window, "the fireworks have started."

What a lovely way to die, he thought idly. The black sky raining cascades and fountains of red, gold, blue, silver and green, and Elgin close to him. He wished for a wider bench so she could lie down beside him, feel her warm body against him, her soft lips kissing him, murmuring sweet nothings. How wonderful to make love with her just once more...to fill their own private universe with sparklers and streamers and skyrockets.

Chad put his hands on the back of Elgin's chair, his fingers brushing her shoulders as he gazed out at the fiery display.

He won't lose any time, Camp thought sourly. Hold her hand through the funeral. Send her flowers and come by 'to see how you're doing'. Long walks in the park, quiet dinners, a friendly shoulder to cry on. She'd be lonely and vulnerable and easy prey for a smooth charmer.

Still, he sighed silently, she was young and beautiful and he didn't want her shutting herself off and mourning him her whole life. Just a 'respectable' period. And certainly not with a two-bit Romeo like Chad Comstock who'd sink to taking advantage of a woman in Elgin's fragile state.

He squeezed her hand and she looked down at him.

"Are you are all right?" she asked anxiously, her free hand going instantly to his dressing.

With breathing so precious and difficult, he could manage only a little smile and a nod.

Elgin tried to smile back. "We're almost there," she told him, trying to sound cheerful. "The old 'Monkey's' fairly flying. I can see the casino lights plain as day. A few more minutes and you'll be safe in the hospital. Just hang on, Camp. Please, just hang on a little longer."

The chill had become a gnawing cold and there didn't seem to be enough air getting to his brain. He felt himself slipping away, the edges of his vision growing dark, Elgin's image as if through a smudged lens.

I love you, he told her softly in his mind. You can be a royal pain in the ass sometimes, but then, so can I. I guess that's just one of the reasons we belong together. Please don't cry. I'm not sorry for anything except leaving you. Find someone else and be happy, love. Just remember me sometimes. Goodbye, Darling.

He looked up at her and with a last squeeze, closed his eyes, his head lolling to one side.

"Camp?" She felt his grip loosen. "Camp!"

"Elgin..." Comstock leaned down to her but she ignored him.

"Oh God," she wailed. "Charlie! Marty!"

"What happened?" Charlie yelled, coming through the salon door followed quickly by Marty.

"I don't know," Comstock replied in bewilderment. "We were watching the fireworks and..."

"Charlie!" she screamed. "It's Camp! Oh God, Charlie, do something!"

Moving her aside, he bent over Harm's body, lifting his closed eyelids and then checking the pulse in his neck.

"Marty, how soon before we dock?"

"About another five or six minutes. I radioed ahead. There's an ambulance standing by as soon as we land. Is he...?"

"No, but it's going to be close. Comstock, find something to put under his feet. We need to raise his legs. Elgin, dig out some more blankets. We have to keep him warm. Marty, we need everything 'The Monkey's' got." He nodded and the rest of them scattered.

Looking out the window, Charlie could clearly see the marina now, the flashing red light of the ambulance visible among all the other bright lights.

"Stay with me, Camp," he urged. "We're almost home."

* * * * *

What was taking so long?

Elgin glanced at the wall clock for the millionth time. A little past one. A new day. Outside, beyond the waiting room's huge picture window, the moon had just arrived from beyond the dark ridge of mountains and had begun her leisurely stroll across the black water.

Why didn't someone come and tell them something?

A full moon, she noted. The Moon Goddess looking for lost souls. But tonight, the lake was empty, nothing but her silver wake to mark her passing.

"'Pass by, Moon Goddess, pass by,'" she mumbled, the words of a childhood chant coming suddenly to her lips. "'You seek those who have gone not those who remain. But know Moon Goddess that we will meet again.' He's mine," Elgin told the Moon Goddess defiantly. "And you can't have him. I won't give him up."

Chad looked up from the magazine he'd been pretending to read. "Did you say something, Elgin?"

"No," she sighed, shaking her head and dropping on the sofa beside him. "I can't stand this waiting…this not knowing."

Gently, he put his arm around her and pulled her to him so she could nestle against his chest. "I'm sure if anyone can find out what's going on, it's Marty. In the meantime, why don't you try to close your eyes and rest?"

"I can't. Not until I know…something."

"All right. How 'bout I go try and round us up some coffee then? I hear hospital coffee is guaranteed to keep you awake."

"That would be nice. Thanks."

He'd just stepped around the corner when Marty reappeared.

"Oh God, Marty, what's going on? How is he? Is he all right? What are they doing? What's taking so long?"

"Good heavens, Elgin," he told her, putting up his hand. "Get a hold of yourself. I can only answer one question at a time. Now come over here and sit back down."

"Marty, tell me!"

"He's in surgery right now. He's lost a lot of blood and it took longer to stabilize him than they thought before they could operate. While they were getting him ready, I put in a call to an old friend, Leland Carswell. Excellent thoracic surgeon. Up here spending the Fourth making a large donation to the local economy via the casinos. He agreed to consult and the hospital graciously consented to allow him to perform the surgery."

"How long will it take to do the operation? When will we know something?" she pressed.

"They couldn't tell me. X-rays and tests can only tell them so much. They won't know what they're up against until they actually get into his chest. And there are a myriad of things that could happen once they start. You'll just have to be patient."

"Oh Marty, this is all my fault," she cried. "Everything. Cissy and that homeless man and Pete Fowler and Jim and now Camp. All my fault." Overwhelmed, Elgin dissolved into hysterical sobs, her body shaking with the force of her grief.

Marty wrapped her in his arms and let the emotions flow.

Chad arrived carrying two white Styrofoam cups. Seeing Elgin, he set the cups down and almost ran over to where they were sitting.

"What's wrong?" he yelped. "Is it Harm? Has something happened?"

"No. He's in surgery right now. We won't know anything until they're done. I'm afraid this is everything just catching up with Elgin at once. It's been a most eventful Fourth of July."

Comstock sighed. "You can say that again."

"Look, Chad, it's late. Since we won't be returning to Spirit Cove tonight...or rather, this morning, I've taken the liberty of making overnight arrangements at the Crystal Pines. They're sending a car, which will pick you up in front of the main lobby in a few minutes. They can provide you with anything you may want or need. Simply tell them to put it on my bill. Tomorrow I'll call our friend on the coast, explain why you were detained and set up another meeting."

"Thanks, Marty."

"Don't mention it. Just go along and get some sleep. See if you can find Mr. Simons. I think he went downstairs to get some privacy and contact Mr. Harm's office."

For several minutes after he left, Marty held Elgin as she cried. Finally, the tears subsided and the shaking stopped. Pulling out his handkerchief, he handed it to her.

"Are you quite finished?" he asked her.

Elgin nodded, wiping her eyes.

"Good. Now you can also stop all this bullshit about everything being your fault." The unexpectedly sharp tone of his voice brought her head up in surprise.

"But...?"

"No 'buts' about it," he continued firmly. "This is most assuredly *not* your fault. If we're going to affix blame here, let's lay it squarely where it belongs, on Jim Fisher. All of this ugliness and violence is the result, solely, of his sick, twisted delusions."

He shook his head. "Make no mistake about it, you are as much a victim of his insanity as anyone else his viciousness has touched. This...this obsession of his has been brewing and fermenting since you were a child. It sickened and rotted and killed him as certainly as any cancer. Even now, from the grave, he's reaching out and trying to hurt you by making you feel guilty...excusing or minimizing his evil by somehow making it 'your fault.'

"Well Fisher's done enough damage. I refuse either to let him do any more or to allow him to escape even the tiniest shred of responsibility for the horrors he's perpetrated. You have far and away more important things to think about than a heinous old man and his demented fantasies."

"Such as?"

"Well...well for one thing, your wedding."

"My what?" she cried in disbelief.

"Your wedding," Marty repeated calmly. "I doubt seriously that a man who would put himself between the woman he loved and an armed, homicidal maniac will flinch at marriage." His face softened and he smiled at her.

"Of course, being both a sentimental old fool and an incurable buttinsky, I'll no doubt end up taking over the whole wedding in the worst, most annoying, meddlesome fashion you can imagine but you'll forgive me when you see what a masterpiece I turn out.

"Now, preparation-wise, you and Harm can't even *think* about anything sooner than spring although knowing you two, you'll no doubt move in together as soon as he's out of the hospital. Speaking for myself, I don't think there's anything more beautiful than a church wedding and that little chapel in Spirit Cove...the one that overlooks the lake...would be perfect. And of course, the reception at my house.

"I mean, unless you're going to have one of those huge, showy things where you invite three hundred of your closest friends. In that case, we can have it in one of those wedding places in West Shore and we can rent out a banquet room, which I think would be extremely tacky for someone of my extraordinary good taste.

"And I have the most absolutely perfect gown," he gushed, now completely caught up in the scenario. "A sort of soft bone color, satin with antique lace and a high collar and puffy long sleeves and absolutely scads of seed pearls and the most gorgeous six-foot train and matching veil. Of course, it will probably have to be altered across the bust..."

"Excuse me, Marty," Elgin interrupted, "but...*you* have a wedding gown?"

"It was my mother's," he explained stiffly, "and if you don't get your dirty little writer's mind out of the gutter, you'll end up being married in the desert by a man in cowboy boots and hat while a man dressed in a white rhinestone and sequin jumpsuit sings 'Jail House Rock' in the background. And besides, I look absolutely ghastly in pastels."

Elgin giggled and Marty embraced her.

"I'm glad to see you haven't forgotten how to smile completely. Now, rather than drink that crankcase oil they laughingly refer to as coffee in this place, I'm going to order us some nice Irish Crème and a tray of snacks from this marvelous little place I know in town."

"Marty, it's almost two. What kind of a place would have Irish Crème coffee and snacks at this hour? And that would deliver on top of that?"

"A very expensive, very private gentlemen's club," he answered. "Members only but open 'round the clock. Just another perk of being obscenely rich."

Pulling out his cell phone, Marty had just begun to dial when the doors opened and a tall man about sixty, wearing surgical garb entered. Immediately, they both stood up.

"Lee," Marty greeted him warmly, "this is the lady I was telling you about. Elgin Collier, Leland Carswell."

"Miss Collier." He put out a soft, surprisingly strong hand to her.

"How's Camp?" she asked anxiously.

"A little rocky, but I think he'll be just fine."

Euphoria rolled over Elgin and she grabbed Marty, kissing him full on the mouth. "Oh thank you, Dr. Carswell," she breathed, feeling a new round of tears...happy ones...well up.

"Don't thank me. I've rarely had a patient with such a tenacious will to live. With the severity of his injuries and the blood loss...well, I'm not that good a doctor."

"When can I see him?"

"Oh, not until tomorrow at least. Or more precisely, later today. He'll be in recovery until we're sure he's stable enough to move and then to ICU. This is a good hospital, but I'd feel better if he could be transferred to some place with a more specialized chest unit."

"I've made arrangements for him to be taken by helicopter to St. Francis as soon as he's cleared to travel," Marty assured him. "It's one of the best places around and in his home city."

"Good. Good. Well, I'm beat. Gonna call it a night. Suggest you do the same. Don't expect any problems but you never know. I've left my pager number in case there's a change during the night and I'm just down at Colton's. Can be back here double quick."

"Thanks, Lee."

"Yes, well don't thank me 'til you get my bill. Should just about cover my losses at the crap table. Don't know how you managed to get me operating privileges on such short notice, Marty, and knowing you, I'm not even going to ask. Good night."

"Well, Elgin my dear, I guess we'll pass on the coffee and snacks. I'm exhausted and I'm sure you are too. I'll call the Crystal Pines and have them send a car."

"You go on, Marty. I want to stay here. In case."

"Absolutely not. You can't see him and even if something did happen, you couldn't do anything but get in the way. And if you spend the night on one of these orthopedic disasters masquerading as a sofa, you'll be too crippled and disfigured to walk, much less…anything more strenuous when you do get to visit. So, it's off to bed we go. Separately, of course."

"By the way," she asked as they walked toward the elevator, "you said the hospital 'graciously consented' to allowing Dr. Carswell to operate?"

"Yes."

"So, how much does 'graciously consented' run these days?"

"Good God, Elgin," Marty sighed. "You have the most foul, suspicious mind."

"How much, Marty? A new wing?"

"You're the one who's in love with him," he sniffed disdainfully, "not me. For you, a new wing. For him, just a new dialysis machine, which I'd been planning on donating anyway so it's no big deal. Now can we get out of here? I'm absolutely famished."

Chapter Fifteen

One more day.

In twenty-four hours, he'd be sleeping in his own bed. Or, better yet, in Elgin's.

Harm shifted uncomfortably and tried to close his eyes. After two weeks in various hospital beds, he still couldn't sleep on his back, no matter how much he fiddled with the bed adjustment. He normally slept on his side or stomach, virtually impossible, first with chest tubes and thick dressings and IV tubes and now simply because of the narrow, hard bed.

Oh well, with visiting hours past now, perhaps the floor would settle down. Tomorrow, his doctor would come after breakfast, sign his release papers and with any luck, he and Elgin would be having lunch on her terrace.

He heard the door to his room open and close quietly. No doubt the night nurse coming to wake him up to give him his sleeping pill.

A pair of lips brushed gently against his, bringing him wide-awake.

"Sorry," Elgin whispered, "didn't mean to startle you."

"I thought you left. Visiting hours are over. What are you doing here?"

"I decided after two whole weeks, I can't wait another day."

"What's that supposed to mean?"

She stepped back, undid the sash of her trench coat and pulled it open. "Surprise," she chirped as he gaped at her naked body.

"Are you crazy?" he asked, not taking his eyes off her.

"Just unbearably horny." Elgin stepped back to the bed, running the fingertips of both hands lightly along the top of the railing. "How do you get these things down?"

"You can't be serious?"

"Why not?" A malicious grin appeared. "I mean, haven't you ever wondered what it would be like to do it in one of these things? See what happens when you press the up and down buttons?"

"In case you hadn't noticed, I'm in this thing because of a gunshot to my chest."

"You're getting out tomorrow. Obviously the doctor thinks you're okay. I think you're hot."

Dropping the coat on the floor, she moved past the rails and hopped up on the bed. "Shove over."

"What if someone comes in?"

She slipped under the thin sheet and blanket and snuggled against him.

"This is a hospital," she whispered brightly, "I'm sure they're familiar with anatomy."

"Elgin…"

Taking his face gently in her hands, she stifled his objection with a passionate kiss, feeling his mouth open to receive her anxious tongue, his body relax as he pulled her to him.

"Ouch!" he yelped.

"Oh, sorry."

"How do you propose we do this? I mean, without both of us ending up in traction."

"I suppose we'll have to do it like porcupines," she giggled. "Very carefully. Here." She opened her hand to reveal a white plastic box about two inches square.

"What's this for?" he asked, taking it from her palm and examining it.

"You'll see."

"I don't know if this is such a good idea."

"Well I do, and so does he." Elgin pulled up the hem of his gown. His fully erect cock lay red and hard against his brown hair and tan skin. "That makes it two against one."

Harm grinned. "Okay, I guess I'm outnumbered. What now?"

Elgin changed her position, settling between his long legs. Gently, she kissed the head of his cock, slowly taking it up in her mouth, nipping lightly at the swollen flesh, feeling his body tense under her. Sucking, she swirled her tongue around the tip, tasting a salty drop of his fluid.

A few more seconds of this delightful torture and she released him.

"Flip the little switch on the top to 'on'," she instructed, "and move the thumb wheel very slowly."

Obediently, he did as she said.

"Oh," she squeaked in surprise, shivering a bit.

"What?" he demanded quickly. "What happened? What'd I do?"

In response, Elgin rose to her knees and spread her pussy lips apart. Sliding her thumb and forefinger slowly inside, in a moment she produced a smooth, shiny silver egg, which she held up for him to see.

"It's a vibrator," she explained with a broad smile. "Remote controlled."

"You mean…" He could hardly believe it.

"Uh-huh, I'm completely in your hands," she laughed, sliding the egg back where it had come from. "Since it might still be a little bit longer until we can resume our more…strenuous activities, I thought it might be fun to explore alternate avenues. Besides, I know how fond you are of gadgets."

"Well, well, well," Harm chuckled, " a remote control pussy. Whatever will they think of next?"

"Yes, well you be damned careful with that thing," she warned playfully. "Don't forget, I may be in your hands but you're in my mouth."

As she worked on him at her leisurely pace, Elgin could feel the egg inside her, now barely running, the next second sending waves of pleasure shooting through her. Nibbling on his balls, she felt a steady flow of energy prickling through her blood like shards of fire. Moving back along his shaft, the current ebbed and flowed like a roller coaster of sweet torment, dipping and rising and plunging and swaying as she moved toward the edge.

His cock, stiff and erect, glowed red hot, wriggling as she played with him, alternating her own tempo just as Camp varied the vibrations for her. But she knew they'd both been simmering, alone, for much longer than they should have been. Like that first frantic time, all that mattered to either of them showed in their revving hearts, rapid breaths and moans.

Grunts and stifled cries signaled the onrush of his climax, pushing the vibrator to its limit as she came too, muffling her shrieks of pleasure with his cock, swallowing as much as she could, the rest spilling out.

Limp, she pulled herself up and collapsed next to him, feeling the egg shut off as she lay back on the shared pillow, unable even to express her joy at being with the man she loved again. Panting, she closed her eyes and reveled in the sheer ecstasy of him.

"I love you," he mumbled contentedly.

"I love you, too."

"I know you've got a contract with Fantasy Publishing for some more of those Gillian Shelby books, but I want you to start shopping *Another Love* around. I've done some work for a couple of the big publishing houses and can probably open some doors. Book's too good and you're too talented to be wasted."

"Uh-huh," she agreed, between yawns. Chuckling to herself, Elgin remembered the book she'd started out to write and how much more wonderful the reality had turned out to be than the fantasy. Oh well, Sheila will just have to settle for something else. She was not about to share even a fictional Campbell Harm with anyone. Gillian's fans will just have to be satisfied with her imagination. Of course, with the kind of inspiration she now had, that might turn out to be very hot indeed.

"I want to find a townhouse for us as soon as possible. Your condo's all right for now and certainly better than my bachelor pad, but after we're married, we'll both want to stay in the city because of our careers and a condo is just no place to raise kids. Need room to spread out. And a backyard."

"Uh-huh." She could barely keep her eyes open.

"And while you'll always be an equal partner in this relationship and I want you to continue your career even after we have kids, I'm still old-fashioned enough to believe that a man should wear the pants in the family. You know, Harm's Way."

Hmmm. Thoughts went running through her sleepy mind.

Mr. and Mrs. Campbell Alexander Harm?

Mr. and Mrs. C.A. Harm?

Campbell and Elgin Harm?

Camp and Ellie Harm?

Mrs. Elgin Collier Harm?

She smiled slightly.

"Yes, dear," Elgin answered softly, reaching over to kiss him good night. "From now on, it will always be Harm's Way."

Enjoy this excerpt from
The Academy

Chapter One

"Daria! Daria!"

Pausing uncertainly, the young woman swiveled her head in the direction of the voice and peered groggily through the airport throng. Above the crowd, about thirty feet away, a raised hand waved wildly, and a head bobbed like a jumping bean at the end of a long, thin pole as the body wound its way hurriedly toward her.

Wearily, she set down her travel bag and waited the few seconds for the other woman to reach her. Almost immediately, a massive bear hug engulfed her and a rain of fond kisses began to fall.

"Oh Daria," she squealed delightedly, looking her friend up and down, "it is so good to see you even if you do look like something the *fenises* dragged in!"

"Cat, Analet," Daria corrected gently, extracting herself with some difficulty from her friend's embrace. "It's *cat*. I've told you a hundred times, if you're going to use human adages and proverbs, you've got to try not to mangle them. It's good to see you too."

"Yes, yes, 'cat,'" she repeated in mild frustration. "There are too many of your languages. And they're too hard to learn and remember. You humans should just pick one and stick with it. On Carus, everyone speaks the same language and understands one another. Perhaps that is the reason your people have had so many problems in their history."

"Perhaps, but I'm too tired to argue galactic politics with you right now."

"Ah, I understand. The luggage claim is this way. I assume that for the length of time you're probably going to be here, you brought more than that teeny travel bag." She pointed a long, pale blue finger at the small black bag at Daria's feet.

"I have two larger cases," Daria agreed, picking up the bag. "I didn't know exactly what I was getting into so I thought I should err on the side of overkill. Lead on."

"So," Analet asked as they threaded their way through the crowd, "the trip was pleasant?"

At barely five foot three, Daria gladly trailed her Amazonian friend as she parted the crowds like a huge luxury cruiser amidst a harbor of toy boats. Like all the women of Carus, Analet stood over six feet tall, board-straight hair falling like a snowy waterfall to her waist, amber eyes and blue skin the color of a sun bleached August sky back in Daria's native home of California, Earth.

"As pleasant as these things ever are," Daria answered wearily. "Except for a few short jaunts to Mars on business, I haven't traveled very much. I don't like getting into those little hibernation chambers at the start of the trip, and I always feel like I'm still half-suspended until I can get a proper night's sleep after we land."

"Well, you needn't worry. Your audience with The Sildor, Minsee, isn't until tomorrow afternoon."

"The Sildor." Daria recited aloud. "'Hereditary ruler of the planet Utan. Minsee, current ruler, the fourth in her dynasty, having been on the throne for the equivalent of twenty-six Earth years. Considered to be progressive and forward-thinking, especially in comparison to her recent forebears. Seeks expanded contact with other planets and civilizations.'"

"You've done your homework well, little friend," Analet laughed, draping her huge arm around Daria's small, thin frame. With Daria's honey-colored hair falling in thick waves around her oval face and her emerald green eyes, the women made quite a sight as they traveled down the long moving sidewalk to the luggage claim area.

"But then, you always do. The proposal you wrote for Unitech to enter into an agreement for the exclusive mineral rights to Utan's north sphere was nothing short of brilliant."

"Thank you. But my position as New Projects Analyst has always been behind the scenes. I've never had any desire to be in the spotlight. To tell you the truth, I'm more than just a little frightened."

The other woman threw back her head and literally roared with laughter. Several people in the near vicinity jumped at the massive sound and turned to see where it was coming from.

"Daria Evans, afraid? I can't believe that. You, who've engineered some of the biggest deals in the history of the biggest conglomerates in the known universe? Ridiculous!"

"Those 'deals' as you so blithely refer to them, resulted from months, sometimes years of careful planning; assembling every scrap, every detail of information. Plotting every conceivable scenario and every conceivable permutation of every conceivable scenario." Daria shook her head and frowned. "There are any number of people at Unitech who could and should be making this presentation."

"Well, that's not how The Sildor does things. She is smart and she is tough and she does not care about the smooth talk and the smiling faces. She wants to see for herself, what kind of mind thought this project up. Who will be, in large part, responsible for making this thing a reality, and that, Daria my friend, is what you do best."

They arrived at the luggage claim as pieces disgorged from the transporter into their individual bins. Joining a group of others from the liner just docked, they waited while everything was unloaded.

"Analet," Daria turned cautiously to her friend as they waited, "how long have you been on Utan now?"

"Uhm…six, no, seven years as you humans measure time."

"And most of that has been with the Carusian delegation to the palace?"

"Correct."

"Well…" Daria could feel pink rising in her cheeks and she stared down at her feet. "In my preparations for coming here, I was reading up on Utan. You know, its history, culture, customs. That sort of thing."

Knowing by the slightly embarrassed tone of her friend's voice where the conversation was leading but determined to make Daria actually say what was on her mind, Analet feigned ignorance.

"A wise idea," she commented simply.

"Apparently, the planet has been in the grip of an Ice Age for some thousands of years and that thanks to geothermal energy, the civilization was able to move underground."

"That is true."

"But before the transition could be completed, most of the women and children died from the freezing weather and a plague."

"Uh-huh." Analet stifled a giggle.

"As a result, there's a tremendous shortage of women, even now, and they hold a great deal of power. Not just political, but economic and social as well." Daria cleared her throat. "I…uh…understand that many women here have…multiple husbands." She could barely get the last words out.

"Exactly," Analet agreed. "Most women who can afford it have at least four. In fact, The Sildor, being the most powerful woman on the planet, is reputed to have a harem of some one hundred mates, although the exact count is not known because no one, save The Sildor and her servants—all males—are allowed access to them."

Daria's head popped up, a look of astonished disbelief on her face. "Four?" she practically shrieked. "A harem? That's…that's…"

"That is the way of Utan," Analet laughed.

"But it's wrong," Daria insisted. "Marriage is a sacred institution. To be shared by *two* people. Not some state-sanctioned orgy. It's just not right."

"You humans have your ways," Analet shrugged. "We Carusians have ours. And the Utanians have theirs. They are not 'right' or 'wrong.' They are simply different. It is the way of the Universe."

"But..."

"A word of advice my friend," Analet told her quietly. "If the Utanians came to Earth, you would expect them to abide by your customs as well as your laws. It is the same here. And here, the matters of men and women and the pleasures of the flesh are as they are. You would do well to keep your opinions to yourself."

"Well, fortunately," Daria told her friend firmly, "I'm not going to be here long enough to find out about the Utanians and their customs. Tonight, a good soak and a long sleep at the public accommodation center, tomorrow the audience with The Sildor, a few days to get all the paperwork signed and then back to Earth on the first liner..."

About the author:

Liz began her career at age three when she started telling her own stories to her dolls and favorite stuffed bear. Her older sister taught her to write at six so she immediately began writing down her stories and reading them to her family. At seven, she decided to become a writer. She won several creative-writing contests in grammar school and by the time she'd moved on to high school, she was working on the school newspaper and had a "lending library" of her popular stories that circulated amongst her peers. Her first paying writing job was in her teens working for the local newspaper, interviewing celebrities who appeared at the local theater-in-the-round.

Liz married, had children, and took a "real" job while she went to college at night, finally earning her degree in Business but never giving up her writing. During this time, she continued to learn her craft and hone her skills. Five years ago, she decided to devote herself to writing seriously. In that time, she's had several short stories published and finished four novels. Her work ranges over several genres from romance to the paranormal.

Elizabeth welcomes mail from readers. You can write to her c/o Ellora's Cave Publishing at 1337 Commerce Drive, Suite 13, Stow OH 44224.

Why an electronic book?

We live in the Information Age—an exciting time in the history of human civilization in which technology rules supreme and continues to progress in leaps and bounds every minute of every hour of every day. For a multitude of reasons, more and more avid literary fans are opting to purchase e-books instead of paperbacks. The question to those not yet initiated to the world of electronic reading is simply: *why?*

1. *Price.* An electronic title at Ellora's Cave Publishing runs anywhere from 40-75% less than the cover price of the <u>exact same title</u> in paperback format. Why? Cold mathematics. It is less expensive to publish an e-book than it is to publish a paperback, so the savings are passed along to the consumer.

2. *Space.* Running out of room to house your paperback books? That is one worry you will never have with electronic novels. For a low one-time cost, you can purchase a handheld computer designed specifically for e-reading purposes. Many e-readers are larger than the average handheld, giving you plenty of screen room. Better yet, hundreds of titles can be stored within your new library—a single microchip. (Please note that Ellora's Cave does not endorse any specific brands. You can check our website at www.ellorascave.com for customer recommendations we make available to new consumers.)

3. *Mobility.* Because your new library now consists of only a microchip, your entire cache of books can be taken with you wherever you go.

4. *Personal preferences are accounted for.* Are the words you are currently reading too small? Too large? Too…ANNOYING? Paperback books cannot be modified according to personal preferences, but e-books can.

5. *Innovation.* The way you read a book is not the only advancement the Information Age has gifted the literary community with. There is also the factor of what you can read. Ellora's Cave Publishing will be introducing a new line of interactive titles that are available in e-book format only.

6. *Instant gratification.* Is it the middle of the night and all the bookstores are closed? Are you tired of waiting days—sometimes weeks—for online and offline bookstores to ship the novels you bought? Ellora's Cave Publishing sells instantaneous downloads 24 hours a day, 7 days a week, 365 days a year. Our e-book delivery system is 100% automated, meaning your order is filled as soon as you pay for it.

Those are a few of the top reasons why electronic novels are displacing paperbacks for many an avid reader. As always, Ellora's Cave Publishing welcomes your questions and comments. We invite you to email us at service@ellorascave.com or write to us directly at: 1337 Commerce Drive, Suite 13, Stow OH 44224.

Discover for yourself why readers can't get enough of the multiple award-winning publisher Ellora's Cave. Whether you prefer e-books or paperbacks, be sure to visit EC on the web at www.ellorascave.com for an erotic reading experience that will leave you breathless.

www.ellorascave.com

Printed in the United States
31178LVS00004B/55-390

9 781419 950582